NATALIE

THE DAUGHTERS SERIES, BOOK TWO

LEANNE DAVIS

Raw. Real. Emotional
Romance

COPYRIGHT © 2016 by Leanne Davis

Natalie

Print ISBN: 978-1-941522-30-1

The Daughters Series, Book Two

Edited by Teri at The Editing Fairy

Cover Designer: Steven Novak

To Gracie
For making me smile all the time... even on days when I don't
want to!

No.

That is all that comes to my brain. That is all that I think to start shouting. Or whispering. Or crying. But I don't do any of that. I don't even utter the word out loud. I just stare and stare. I just stand there, frozen. I stand there destroyed. I stand there bleeding.

No.

Blood falls through my fingers where I clutch at my stomach. Blood. So much of it goes drip–drop, drip–drop down onto the ground under me. I glance down and my hand is gone. It's as if it's covered in a crimson cloth. So much blood.

Still, I stand there.

Is this me? Is this my blood? It's warm. The faint thought trickles from a weird spot in my brain. It's so warm. That surprises me.

I feel nothing. I don't feel it. I see it. I see it all. But I don't feel it. Is this what you feel like when you're dying? Am I watching myself die and my spirit is now floating out of my body and off away. To heaven? To hell? Surely not to hell. I was, or at least I tried in earnest, to be a good person. But now? Where will I go?

I see who shot me. She's right in front me. Not a bus length away from me. She stares at me as shocked as I am at her. She wronged me. She destroyed my life. How could she have shot me?

I don't know.

The world starts to shift. I fall to my knees. Shit. I feel that. Through it all I feel the thump of my knees to the concrete. The colors swirl and swirl, browns and greens and grays and blue, so much blue. Trees, leaves, concrete, buildings and sky. Sky everywhere now over me. Faces are all gone. She is gone. I am gone.

Sam.

Sam's face fills my mind's eye. Oh Sam. What would you do now? What would you do without me? What will you do with this? Oh Sam…

No. No, Sam is gone. He's gone. He's not here.

I'm sorry, Sam. I'm sorry. I'm so sorry I was wrong. I'm so sorry for myself most of all because it's too late for sorry. It's too late for forgiveness. It's too late for life.

I finally understand anything could have been fixed when I was alive. Anything. But this? Death? It's really the end. It's really forever. It's only now, this last moment of my life as the colors and the sky start to turn gray and are fading into black, do I fully understand all that I have wasted in my life. As the black pinpricks take over and my eyes start to close I understand that this is actually the end.

Like always, my need to be right cost me every chance to be happy.

CHAPTER 1

 AM

NO! GOD… JUST… NO. This can't be happening.

I close my eyes and then force them open and meet the gaze of my wife, who stands before me. She stands there frozen. Silent. In agony. I know this. I know in a second flat, what I've done to her. What this will do to her. I've emotionally done the equivalent of shooting or stabbing her in the heart. I know that I've ruined her life. I've ruined my life. I've ruined us. I just didn't understand it, not fully, until this exact second.

Physically everything stops. My body parts wither as my brain shies away from truth of what I've done. This isn't what was supposed to happen. This isn't supposed to be *me*. Sam Ford is not supposed to be the guy caught screwing some meaningless woman in my office.

I am not supposed to be the guy who cheats on my wife.

But I am. I am that guy. And I've just been caught. Literally. By my own wife. In this moment. This one endless moment. I am this terrible guy.

Natalie stands in the now open doorway, completely mute. A statue of shock. Her eyes are huge and wide. Her mouth just slightly parted. The only movement is the streaming of tears down her cheeks. There's no sound. She doesn't even seem to be aware they fall.

It makes them all that much more tragic.

We stare at each other. Directly into each other's eyes. Everything else is gone. The woman. The twenty feet of office that separate us. The furniture. Our future. Our past. All of it disappears as we stare in a hard, tragic eye lock with each other.

I only end it when I shut my eyes.

On my desk is a woman. A woman who is not my wife. A woman I don't even like. The only thing to keep this from being even worse for Natalie is that the woman's flouncy skirt is pushed up around her waist, sparing her the view of our genitals now connected.

With my eyes closed I clearly picture what Natalie has walked in on. It shreds my heart. I'm a lying, cheating sack of shit. I don't deserve to even spew excuses or beg my wife for forgiveness. I don't deserve anyone's forgiveness. Especially Natalie's.

But I wasn't always this guy.

I was once a loving, wonderful, adoring husband. I was upstanding. I worked hard. I was always honest and I never lied. Once I was the guy who despised guys who did this kind of thing. I used to quote that no real man cheated.

But I did.

Her name is Chantal Bailey. She is a secretary here at the firm I work for. Yeah, typical, right? I nearly groan at the clichés and ordinariness of what I am and what I've done. Chantal catches on that something is wrong and that I've stopped moving in her and my penis is shriveling up to a flaccid nothing. I need to cover up. I need to turn back time. But I can't seem to do either. I am too shocked and appalled to seem to gather my wits, and I can't change the laws of nature to make this not happen.

Chantal whips around and finally notices my wife. She sits on my desk, legs splayed and heels meeting around my waist. She has her weight held up by her arms.

Natalie still doesn't move.

It scares me more than if she came after me with a mail opener or even pulled her gun on me. That is what Natalie would normally do. That is who she is. She's a fighter. She takes shit from no one. Ever. She has a mouth on her that could stop a trucker in their tracks. Where is that now? Where is all her anger? Her rage? Her horror? She is not like this. Not the unmoving woman weeping in the doorway. Her heart is in her dark eyes. I have broken her heart. I have broken who we are. I have shattered every illusion and feeling she has for me.

Though all I can really do is withdraw from Chantal. The condom drops to the carpeted floor below my desk and I quickly cover my stupid, awful, shrunken dick. That's what I think of it now. It's contaminated. The shame burning in my heart heats up my chest and rises clean up into my cheeks. I am blushing in shame and violent regret. Oh God, I've never regretted anything in my life as I do this.

Still, Natalie isn't reacting. I wait for her to find her tongue. I imagine the slew of words she'll fling and hurl like weapons at me. I need her to do that. I deserve that. I'm ready and willing to take her verbal assault. It's just the beginning of what I'll deserve, but I need her to start.

Not stand there as if I've ruined her, ruined us, ruined *everything*, forever.

5

Then without a word or whimper or insult or even a sob she spins and disappears from the doorway.

I wilt. I literally fall over my desk, pressing my hands onto the surface to hold me up, not five inches away from where Chantal still perches, now trying to close her legs. She too is strangely silent. My chest hurts when I breathe. My heart is racing. My hands are clenched as is my jaw. I feel like my extremities are going numb. Shit. I'm going to die right here and now from a heart attack. I'd deserve it. My legs are shaking. It would be perfect divine justice.

There is no real noise. There is outside traffic that's kind of a muted constant, like a clock ticking in the background.

"That was your wife?" Chantal finally asks. Her tone is hesitant. I glance up at her. She's biting her lip. There seems only a bit of chagrin in her expression. Like oops. Like the face one might make when being caught cheating on your driving test or lying about how much you make for a living. It isn't the face of someone who just ruined another's life and family and marriage.

Oh wait, that's not Chantal's fault, is it? It's all mine. I did that. I did that to the only woman I have ever loved. Because despite how this looks… I love Natalie. I love her so much that what I've done makes bile climb up in my throat.

"Yes," I whisper. I stare down at my cluttered desk top. It's all blurry. Shit. Why? I realize then tears are coursing down my face. I haven't cried this hard since I was eighteen and my grandfather passed away. But I am crying now as I lean over my desk, unable to move. Unable to face what I've done. Unable to face the woman next to me. But most of all unable to face my wife.

"I see," Chantal says as she hops off my desk and smooths her skirt down. She bends over to grab her panties, which I'd ripped off her. She tucks them in her skirt pocket. "She doesn't seem like your type."

6

Not my type? How the hell does this blonde, girlie, ditz figure that? Natalie was in her uniform. Her hair slicked back in a tight knot at the nape of her neck, like how she always wears it for work. It's severe. She doesn't wear make-up to work either.

When she's at home, she lets the wild, softly curling hair of hers fly free and with just a little make-up she's so soft and sexy, the contrast drives me nuts. Or it used to. Until recently. Until...

Well, shit, already I start with the excuses. Why I was somehow justified to do this. When I know there is no good reason.

Still, how can this strange woman think my wife isn't my type?

She is all there is for me. But then if that were true, when Chantal came in here and started to come on to me, I would have thrown her out, any way it took now, wouldn't I? If I loved my wife like I proclaimed, that's what I would have done.

But the thing is, I do love her that much.

"Th-this should have never happened." I am whispering like a little scared girl caught cheating on a test by a teacher.

Chantal's mouth tightens. She knew I was married. There was no shock to her here. She had come after me for months. Explicitly made clear she was willing to do just this. Even though I had talked up my wife often and in excess just so she would stop.

"But it did happen, Mr. Ford. Not coming doesn't change the fact that you were having sex with me. She won't see the distinction either."

Mr. Ford. I want to sink to the carpet in shame and humiliation. She still uses my last name. She's nine years younger than I am. She's only twenty-two years old. She was also right. I don't see her suffering from too much of a guilty

7

conscious over this. Was it her age? Or did she just not care? Or did she think I was leaving Natalie now for her?

"I love her. This was a huge mistake. Chantal, I didn't mean…"

She has shoulder-length blonde hair and big cornflower blue eyes. She bats them at me. "You didn't mean to rip my panties off? That just happens to you?"

"No. I'm just… I'm sorry this happened. I'm sorry I did this. I can't—" I can't even believe I have sacrificed the best part of my life for this woman who means nothing to me. I don't mean that Chantal isn't a perfectly nice girl, making her way in the world. I honestly don't know. I don't know her at all. Not really anyways. I just know what she revealed while we were mildly flirting the past few months. That she's always smiling when she sees me. Her voice is a little breathless when she says hello and she's a decent secretary with good attendance. Until today. Until this evening that is about all I knew about her. I don't mean to imply she's a slut or anything. I get, clearly, this is all on me. I just can't believe I did this. It doesn't matter who I did this with.

I run my hands through my hair and start shaking my head. "I have to go. I have to—"

Fuck this. Why am I wasting time rationalizing this to Chantal? I don't care how she freaking feels about this. I care about how Natalie will be torn into pieces.

I'm crossing the office. My shirt is untucked. I am a mess. Everything about me. My appearance. My office. My marriage. My entire life. It's all a mess and I can't even picture how to start changing that.

"She won't forgive you." Chantal's voice echoes behind me. I stop in the doorway. The same one that Natalie had come to innocent enough. She was probably coming to see me and why I was again working late. Perhaps to surprise me. Or talk to me.

I turn and cock my eyebrow at Chantal. How the hell does she know what my wife will or won't do? "Pardon me?"

"She will start finding it all. And when she does she will never forgive you."

There is nothing to find. Natalie witnessed everything there was between Chantal and I. I stare at the woman I'd just been inside of. A chill runs down my spine. Her smile is soft and dewy and like one that might cross your face after realizing you're in love. Not having just got caught by a wife, fucking a married guy on his desk.

I don't know what she's about but I don't have time for this. I have to find Natalie. I have to...what? I don't know what I have to do. I just have to find her.

NATALIE

I said nothing. Never in my life have I been speechless. I'm usually the opposite. I am the girl who usually says what needs to be said to whoever it needs to be said to. I yell at bullies. I talk firmly to rule breakers. I cuss out criminals. I'm a good cop because I never take shit from anyone. I'm always ready and willing to say what I think of someone or a situation. I have a sharp tongue and sharp retorts. I have a filter, but I know how to rip it off and unfilter myself if the need arises. In other words? I perform well under duress and stress.

As it should right now. Yet the most critical situation of my life and I just stand there. Stupid. Silent. Crying in silent shock. I act like such a fucking girl.

I think I'm in physical shock. My stomach is jittery. My hands are shaking. I run through the empty hallway, past closed office doors and I hit at the elevator button a half dozen times while tears course down my cheeks and fall off my face. I rub at them and more come. I am now sobbing. I lean against the wall waiting, wanting to scream for the elevator to just *come*. I glance back, panicked that he'll come after me. I can't even look at him. I may never, ever be able to look at Sam's face again.

Sam...

The thought of him makes me lean over and clench my stomach with my hands. Oh God, it hurts so bad. So damn bad my stomach keeps cramping. My hands are fisting and unfisting. I am trembling everywhere.

Finally! The elevator door dings and opens. I jump inside and push at the close button in compulsive crazy swipes. I know it won't make it go faster, but I need it to close NOW! I cannot face Sam. I can't see Sam. Never again can I see Sam.

Even as his face swims and floats through my brain. Our entire marriage, hell, our entire life history floats through my brain and the pain the images cause make me have to stifle the moan of misery that escapes my lips.

I got off duty early. We have been having a hard time of late. I wanted to see Sam. I wanted... I don't even remember now. I think I wanted to talk. To work some things out. I think I was coming here to make some kind of peace. Find some neutral territory. My head feels so foggy. My reasons for being here feel like they belong to another person, maybe even to another life. In one second, the amount of time it takes to shove a door open and peek in a room is how long it took for my entire life to be changed. There will forever more be the moment before I opened the door and the moment after. The moment I was married, the moment I was not. That for me is what this has been.

Still, the shock hasn't totally even set in. I don't even fully comprehend what has happened to me. I can't process it.

Sam cheating on me.

There he was, standing between a blonde girl's legs. He was pushing into her. His face was intense, scowling, and hard. He was so mean looking. I don't recognize him, even before he realizes I stand there. I stand there for close to ten seconds before he senses me. Just seconds. They might as well have been ten bombs going off. Ten seconds that were forever.

The woman's back is to me. She is half reclining, holding herself up against my husband's deep thrusts. Her body shakes with his movements. She moans. Her legs are wrapped around him. I can't see his dick, thank God. That…. That might have ended me forever. But I saw him moving into her. I saw their bodies. I saw it all.

Then his face lifts just a fraction of an inch and his eyes dart towards the door. Towards where I stand. His eyes meet mine and in a second our entire history felt like it flashed through my head. And all I could do was stand there numb, because there was just no way to believe I was standing there witnessing this. No. Never. This can't be Sam.

But it was Sam.

I shut my brain down. No. Not now. I'll face this later. So much later. I am frantic now. I run across the parking garage after I exit the elevator. I scramble into my car and tear out of there. I get to our house and unlock the front entry. I stand there for a second. The silence permeates it. Sam permeates it. He decorated it. He made sure after we moved in to have the floors redone and kitchen updated and to get it all color-coded and upscale. It was supposed to match his up-and-coming career. The ideal and image he foresaw for himself.

I stand there now, knowing the only thing in Sam's life that never lived up to what he foresaw for himself and his life was me. I never fit into what he wanted. The power, the prestige, and the image he wanted to expel. He wanted perfection. He wanted to fit in with a class of people I don't even like. He wants to be *someone*. Someone important, influential and sought after. He wanted senators and judges and rich CEOs to call him their friends and peers. He wanted respect. The kind of respect that my adulation of him could not provide for him.

He had created this home to reflect those ideals. I had never really cared. It was a nice place to live. I don't get his perfectionist ways, but I let him have it. I thought I was letting him be who he needed to be. Turns out that just made it so nothing in there reflected me.

I'm what Sam could not turn into perfection. His working class wife, the cop. I wear a uniform and I'm not looking to ever change that. I don't have a bunch of kids at home to take care of or my own prestigious career that explains why I don't have kids at home. He wants kids. He wants that ideal in a wife. He never fully proclaimed it, but I know that's what Sam always envisioned for his life. I didn't fit into his life and perhaps we would have ended up here no matter what.

I feel cold now. All my tears have dried. I have no words. My tongue feels thick in my mouth, like I could not articulate anything if the need arises. I start moving through our house then. I don't feel an attachment to much. I grab the baseball mitt I had displayed on the mantle. It was my dad's. I grab some photos. I dig out my suitcase from the spare room closet. I start filling it with my bland undergarments and clothes. Jeans. Sweats. T-shirts. Sweatshirt. A few blouses and stylish shirts and jackets. I grab sneakers and flats and some coats. I don't know what I need. I quickly strip from my uniform and grab jeans to wear. I'm lowering a t-shirt over my head when I suddenly stop and stare around.

Where the fuck am I going?

I don't know. But staying here is not an option. It feels like Sam. All of it feels like nothing but Sam to me.

My parents aren't an option. Mom died eight years ago and Dad is in a nursing home now. He doesn't remember me anymore. He's got dementia. I visit him every week, but if I don't? He wouldn't know. And I can't run to him.

There are a few friends, but all of them know Sam. They are all our friends. Everyone knows Sam, who is connected to me. There is no one to go to.

There is no family for me. Just Sam's family. The Fords had made me their honorary daughter since the time I was five years old and first met them. First met Sam.

No. I clamp down on my thought. No reminiscing. No thinking about little Sam, or little me. No thinking about what I lost today. No thinking. Just going. Leaving. Running.

I sit on the bed and wrap my arms around my chest. I have to get out of here. Sam will come here. He'll beg and plead and be sorry. Or he'll tell me he's in love and didn't know how to tell me. I don't know which scenario will be worse for me. But I do know I can't handle either one. I can't hear either coming from Sam's lips.

I stand up and grab my suitcase and my purse. I haul it all to my car and roar down the street.

There is... family. There is distant family. I don't even know them. I just know that some girl came looking for me over a year and a half ago with the belief that she was my sister. I have no sisters. No brothers. I have no one. Now I really have no one. I have never felt this lonely or vulnerable in my life.

But there is some family who are complete strangers to me but might be biologically related to me.

Christina Hendricks. Her name. The girl, for she was all of eighteen when she came to find me. But I had to give it to her, it was a ballsy move coming after me on her own, without her mom, maybe my biological mother's permission.

Sister. I never allowed myself to wonder about it. Or even think about her. She said there were two more. Meaning I might have three sisters?

13

What could that possibly mean for me? I just don't know. I just need somewhere to go. And maybe something to do. Something to think about that isn't Sam. That isn't my husband and that woman screwing on top of his desk.

No. I won't think about it.

I turn my car around and start along Highway 101 across the Golden Gate Bridge north, towards Seattle to Washington State. I have no idea where in Washington State I'm headed. Ellensburg. I think that was the name of the city Christina mentioned. Is that right? I hope so. I hope that was the name Christina said it to me in a rush. Inviting me to come to her. That's all I have to go on. A place and a last name. I hope to God there's something to it. I have no idea what I'm going to do. Am I going there? I don't know. At least it's not here. It's far, far away from my heart. My wrecked life and my lost love. It's far away from Sam Ford.

I just know I can't be here. Maybe I can't ever be here again.

CHAPTER 2

$\mathcal{N}$ATALIE

AS I DRIVE NORTH, all alone, with no real destination and no real schedule, my fleeting thoughts nearly suffocate me. They twirl and dive all around my brain disjointedly. I hope I'm not losing it. Tomorrow I will call in sick at work and intend to leave it as such for at least a week. I can't even contemplate trying to put one foot in front of the other and going through a normal day as if my entire life hadn't just combusted in my personal equivalent of a nuclear bomb detonating in Area 51. I don't want to talk to anyone about Sam. It's too humiliating. It's too cliché. But really, it's too sickening for me to even try and envision talking about. I can't work right now. Besides, I'm not lying, what could constitute more of an emergency than knowing if I see Sam I might not be able to stop myself from hurting him? Which is, actually, far more comforting to think about than the strange, weak silence that came over me when I first reacted to him.

My phone is gone. I threw it out the window somewhere near the coast. Sam called it a dozen times or more. Texts, voicemails, emails even. I could not handle even seeing his name on my phone screen, so I cracked my car window and threw it out. I'm driving kind of aimlessly, taking only back roads and the highway beside the ocean. I have nowhere to be. No one waiting for me. I don't know what the hell I'm doing. I'm drifting. And now, I am no longer available. No one can find me. No one knows where I am. It's both terrifying and liberating.

Still, all I can do is think about how I got here, driving alone on a coastal highway, beside the vast ocean and trying to forget my life. All the while, my life keeps replaying in my head. The problem is, despite all my contemplation, I receive no profound revelation or even clarity.

THE FIRST TIME I ever saw Sam Ford was the day his family moved into the apartment next to mine. We lived in a four-story walk-up in San Francisco. Its brick exterior housed a small laundromat on the first floor and a small retail store, as well. My dad worked late afternoons into the evenings, throwing freight for a local wholesale corporation that sold everything under the sun, from diapers to tires. Mom worked as a cashier in a small corner convenience store. I was an only child, adopted when I was still a baby. My parents were in their forties before they met each other and got married. By then, having children of their own was biologically impossible.

So they adopted me.

I never really thought too hard about being adopted until I was five years old and Dustin pointed it out to me.

Sam and Dustin Ford. They are brothers, three years apart in age. Dustin is my age and Sam's older. He was eight to our five. The first time Dustin saw me after I walked past them while they were drawing with chalk on the sidewalk in front of our apartment building, Dustin asked me why I was brown, since my parents, whom I was holding hands with, were not.

Sam hit his little brother on the top of his head. "Shut up, twerp. That's mean. Sorry, don't listen to this bottom feeder."

He had my heart from that very first moment. I remember standing there staring up at him and my little five-year-old heart squeezed with desire. This is what having a brother would be like! I didn't have siblings, cousins, or much of any extended family. I longed for all three. I imagined it would have been amazing. You'd never be alone for long, or get lonely or bored while your parents had to work.

The Ford brothers became my playmates; or rather, Dustin did. Sam became my god. I followed him everywhere. I adored him. We all hung out at our apartment building and a small lot that was attached to some kind of youth center. It was a stretch to call the dirty lot a "park," but we used it as such. There was a baseball diamond, soccer goals and a small pad of concrete with a single basketball hoop. It was less than three blocks away. Back then, we were allowed to run around if we all stayed together. It was a working class neighborhood and most all of the parents both worked full time. The Ford brothers soon became my ticket to enjoy a lot of freedom. Sam would never let anything happen to me or Dustin, and my parents knew and relied on that. Tall for his age, Sam was also smart, focused, and responsible. Although he seemed a little too serious for his age, there was nothing I did not adore about him.

And so it went for years. Me chasing after the boys, and acting like one of them. I grew up with scabby knees and dirt on my elbows and under all my fingernails. I could kick a ball farther than any boy my age, and my pitching arm was fiercer than most any boy within a twenty–mile radius. Sam and I were eternal competitors. Dustin never cared. He just laughed and had a good time. Not like Sam and me, who were always in the death grips of some competition or another.

Sam loved sports and working out as I did. The only advantage he ever had against me was his maturity and size. As I got older, he stopped taking it easy on me and had to start trying to beat me. It was never easy for him. I was just that good. I played kickball, soccer, baseball, even football. The lot down from our apartment was mostly bare dirt and weeds; there was no real green grass field. The backstop had holes in the chain link fencing, and graffiti was sprayed all over the wooden boards of the dugouts. The owner of the property often tried to clean it up, but it just got tagged again days later. It was heaven for us, however.

Every evening, there I was with the Ford brothers. We played and as I grew, I simply played harder. I never trans-formed from an ugly duckling into the lovely swan. Nope. No way. High school found me on every team I could fill, and I kicked most of the girls' asses as well as any competi-tion. No weakness, no frills, no dresses. Nothing but sports and athletics for me.

When I became a freshman, Sam was in his senior year. The boy that was my best friend started to become a man. He went from being shy and awkward and always wanting to hang out at the field with me to ditching me. Suddenly, he was going to school dances and out on dates. The girls he chose to hang out with wore stylish jeans and short skirts. They simpered and preened and wore makeup all the time. Sam became charming and no longer had any time for me. He hung all over Kelsey, then Heather, then Megan, then Amy, and the list went on throughout his senior year. Never without a girlfriend, he held their hands or slung his arm over their shoulders.

I hated it. I sometimes even hated him.

He quit playing sports as often and hanging around the lot with me. I ran in and out of his apartment. Sure, I saw him, but it wasn't the same. Dustin and I still played ball at the park, but Dustin sucked; he was never nearly good enough. Sam would sometimes come out of his room with his hair all rumpled and lipstick on his neck or collar, even on his mouth! He was usually holding one of his idiot sycophants, who clung to him, and held his hand and laughed at his stupid, secret jokes. They'd come out only for drinks or food before returning to his room and making sure to shut and lock the door. Looking back now, I'm a little surprised my angry eyes didn't simply burn a hole through the wooden door.

I was so jealous.

But I didn't know it at first. I didn't know what this strange new feeling was. It made a lump in my throat and caused my stomach to knot up. I didn't understand how much I missed hanging around Sam. But Sam didn't miss me.

He went off to college, and I rarely saw him after that while I finished high school. I became the star of the school's volleyball and basketball teams. Being a jock was an honor I never concealed. I was also smart, but I didn't apply myself. My grades were lackluster. I was more into my teams' continued superiority than in studying.

Dustin and I stayed friends, although he and I never had

an ounce of chemistry. If anyone was more like a brother to me, it was he and I was practically his sister.

But Sam? I didn't felt that way about Sam.

College was not an option I wanted to pursue and I knew it early on. I drifted around after high school for a year, coaching one of the local youth organizations in soccer and baseball. I also waited on tables and took shifts at the convenience store where my mom once worked. It looked like that was where I might have stayed, just floating along, and playing sports in recreational leagues. I dated a bit, and had a lot of friends. Naturally, I partied some. This went on for a good few years until I was twenty years old. And then *it* happened.

I was directly involved in a hold–up one afternoon. It occurred when a young kid pulled out a gun while I was working the register at the small, local mini–mart and gas station. He was all of sixteen and planning to rob me. He waved the loaded gun right in my face. My hands were shaking as I tried to get the money out of the cash register. Sweat beaded down my cheeks and I almost hyperventilated. I was fully expecting my fumbling to heighten the scared kid's adrenaline and make him shoot me. And that one taste of feeling so helpless while someone held a gun on me revealed how much I wanted that gun. Not vice versa. Plus, it was wrong. So wrong. You don't pull a gun out on innocent people that are only stopping in to buy five–dollar snacks.

My mom had worked there for fifteen years. The owners were a little old Korean couple who had three more of the same stores, although they weren't rich by any stretch of the imagination. They were merely trying to make a living. People were in there buying snacks, or pop, or last minute grocery items... and almost all of them died for their efforts.

Just past my twentieth birthday, I decided my life's calling was to be a cop.

I didn't really grow up intending to become a police officer. I never had any real ambition about what I'd like to do. My parents never encouraged me to dream big. They also didn't sit me down and try to map out what my future could be. There was never any talk of college. I doubt they had any clue if I wanted to go or not. There certainly wasn't any money for it. My parents weren't too imaginative with their lives. There was no calling, or career path, or ambition for either of them. They were grateful for their menial jobs, and being able to pay their bills each month. They found quiet contentment with their lot in life. Sure, I often wished when I was young that they were a little more colorful. Or wanted a little more out of life. But in the overall scheme, those were minor complaints. My parents took good care of me. We always had enough to eat and decent clothes to wear. We never lacked any necessities. I know they loved each other in their quiet, solid, unspoken way. They also loved me. They accepted me as I was, and never once wished I were different. They came to all of my sport games, as long as their work schedules allowed them. They were at my high school graduation too, and took me out for ice cream afterwards to celebrate.

Just before my twentieth birthday, Mom was diagnosed with stage four colon cancer after ignoring all the warning signs. She didn't once tell Dad or me about them. Naturally, we were all devastated. It took a long six months for us to watch her die. The unhappy experience also took its toll on Dad and me. After another few years, I started to notice the signs of Dad's dementia coming on. By then, however, Dad was in his mid–sixties. It seemed like only a matter of months when he diminished from being slightly confused or "slow" in thinking to losing it all. He was gone. Letting him go turned out to be one of the hardest experiences of my life, especially since his body and his face were still right there

21

before me. We eventually found a small group home with twenty–four–hour care. I visit twice a week although he never knows it.

I started looking into the requirements for becoming a cop. The same day I turned twenty–one, I applied for the first job posting I found to start the process. I was ready for it all. I spent the previous year researching and preparing in every way I could. When I finally attained the minimum age requirement, I had the physical ability test down, thanks to all of my sports training. The verbal and written tests were a good fit for me. I am not shy. I speak well, and with a strong voice. I never flinch under pressure and think logically on my feet. I rarely have moments when I regret what I said or did after the situation. I usually find the appropriate words for any situation. I later learned, three fourths of my job is communication. From speaking to citizens or suspects, to writing reports, to testifying in court, they are all necessary skills required to be a good officer. It turned out I was highly qualified, and my choice to become a cop was a good fit.

While I was still researching and considering my ideal vocation, Sam Ford came home from college. He intended to earn his MBA. Dustin told me he planned to become some kind of high–powered business tycoon. No one we knew would have chosen such an ambitious path. I didn't even know what that meant. It seemed a strange direction for him to follow. Sam wasn't trying to nurture a certain talent or interest, he simply wanted to be rich. And busi- ness, *any business*, was the ticket to achieving his goal. Sam was so different than all the blue collar men who filled my world that it somehow fit him. He was so smooth and charming. He could talk the skin off a snake. He was already sophisticated, but became even more so in college. As a student of UCLA (University of California,–Los Angeles), he was introduced to many powerful people, the likes of which he would have never encountered in our small neighborhood.

Sam's family was working class like mine. His dad was the manager of housekeeping for one of the largest hotels on Fisherman's Wharf for thirty years, and his mom held several jobs over the time I knew her, from being a museum tour guide to an admission clerk at the zoo. They were a nice couple. They always treated me like their surrogate daughter. They also provided well for their kids. Sam never lacked the basics. Although there wasn't much left over, he had whatever he needed, and certainly had their love.

Still, Sam, even at age twenty-three, hungered for more. He refused to settle for middle class or to struggle. He didn't want *just enough*, he wanted it *all*.

But that didn't make Sam a bad guy. He was charming, sweet and he smiled all the time. No one really begrudged Sam for wanting more since he was so willing to do the work to get there. Even now, although his parents have long since moved from the old neighborhood and into the suburb of Dublin, about thirty-five miles from us, Sam still wants more for them and more for himself. They are retired now, and Sam and I provide them with a little extra income. We try to ensure they have a far better lifestyle than they ever did before. They now live in a gated community for residents fifty-five and older. But Sam wants so much more. He refuses to toil away his life for small rewards. He grew disillusioned after seeing how hard and long his parents worked and what little they received to show for it. His dad was laid off after thirty-two years with the hotel, when the franchise was sold. During its restructuring, he was forced to retire.

That is what Sam most wanted: the power to control his own life. He wanted to be his own boss, his own man, and earn his own money, so that no one could ever do that to him.

In order to accomplish his goal, he started cultivating the lifestyle he dreamed about during his freshman year at UCLA. He quickly ingratiated himself as part of a crowd that included many sons of powerful men. He found out who was who, and befriended them all.

Liking Sam was easy, and most people just naturally gravitated towards him. He joined a fraternity to increase his presence at parties, with girls and to nurture his fragile connections.

By the time he graduated, he was further up the social ladder than anyone else we knew.

Sam also had a particular type of girl he liked. I realized that back when I was freshman in high school after I started watching his parade of female company. He liked blondes: petite, white and blue-eyed. Those were his usual girls, and later on, co-eds.

I was never Sam's type, and as polar opposite from his preferences as a golfer trying to play football. I was tall, athletic and competitively fierce with everyone, including him. He liked girls who seemed shy, or extra giggly. He especially liked the girls who were in awe of him. The ones who adored anything he did and worshipped him. Okay, maybe none of them actually worshipped him that was just my impression. I also assumed Sam would never again be close to me. I thought he'd never visit me again. I finally started to accept the fact that Sam was no longer in my life, when he showed up after his college graduation.

He stayed home that whole summer, and I got to see him once again.

Having all but ignored me for the last four years, I seemed to have become the pesky, neighbor girl he used to play with. I often saw Dustin while secretly seeking to catch a glimpse, or even hear news about Sam when he journeyed home every once in a while. But I tried to make sure neither of them realized it. Dustin and I had an enduring friendship where we hung out all the time without any kind of planning or pre-thought. We just hung together. Whatever. Doing nothing. We ran the streets together or just enjoyed each other's company. I came and went from the Fords' apartment just as often as Dustin did mine.

That is, until the summer I turned twenty and figured out Sam was home.

I found out when I came in one afternoon and Sam was making out with another typical blonde of his. She and I had attended high school together. She was actually kind of nice, which didn't help my cause, since I really wanted to hate her. They lay together on the family couch, their legs entangled, with Sam on top. They both kind of gasped when I came bursting through the front door to see Dustin, as I often did. Their parents were rarely home, and Dustin usually lost himself in his music, failing to hear a door bell ringing or a knock. So I just let myself in during the day.

Well, the oops! was on me. I pushed the door open and stopped dead when I saw Sam's long legs, perfect butt, and tapered back. Upon seeing the back of his head, I easily gathered that his hands were rubbing a breast, and his mouth and tongue were inside the girl's mouth. Or had been, until I slammed the door and they both jumped and turned towards me. Sam's gaze could have melted me if I were made of ice. He was so mad! He kind of tilted his head as if silently communicating for me to go! Git! Get the hell out of there! He was shirtless and his torso was smooth and gleaming. He was so pretty that I was a little surprised he didn't abandon his corporate plan and just take up modeling. He could probably have made a fortune.

I quickly shuffled off into Dustin's room, my face warm with obvious humiliation. The girl muttered something like *What was she doing there?* Sam quieted her by sucking her face some more. I noticed, of course, when I sneaked one last look. Her name was Jennifer and she was as bland, pretty, nice and boring as all the bimbos Sam sought out. She smiled sweetly when he said things. She was also polite and ladylike and invariably well-groomed. I leaned against Dustin's door once I was safely out of the make–out zone. Clueless, Dustin didn't even look up. He had headphones on and was staring at his computer. I knocked my head back on the door. Damn. I don't know why, but Sam was the one who did it for me. I couldn't believe the way my heart started hammering when I simply saw his face or heard his voice. I got all hot and cold and something weird and achy churned my stomach. Not something I felt very often. I was not boy crazy. In fact, I tended to be their friends, confidantes, and sports partners. Rarely was I ever considered the kind of girl a boy wants to date. Sam included.

Still, it's always been Sam for me.

But he liked the blondes. The girlie, cute, sweet, shy, flirty blondes.

I stayed hidden in Dustin's room, talking intermittently until he finally noticed me. By the time I heard voices, I thought their parents were home and I could come out of the bedroom. The girl was gone and Sam was leaning on the kitchen table, his arms folded over his torso. He was talking with his mom. His gaze shifted to me when I came out of Dustin's room before he scowled hard. I straightened my shoulders and raised my eyebrows, responding to his dare. *Screw him!* I shouldn't feel weird for walking through a living room. Maybe he should have made better use of his bedroom door while she was there.

"Did you want to stay for dinner, Natalie?"

I looked past Sam to his mom. A tall, handsome woman, and the source of Sam's tall, dark and handsome looks, I smiled at her. She was warm and welcoming. She rarely wore makeup, but usually looked a little run down. She seemed more so that night than usual. "Yes, if you don't mind."

I often stayed. No biggie there. Sam scowled again at me. I rolled my eyes. For God's sake! He was more of an inter-loper there than I. While he was gone at his big shot college and meeting important people, I was here, hanging with his brother and spending long evenings with his parents. They were several decades younger than my own parents. Mine were very quiet. Having been retired for several years by then, they often went to bed by eight. So I'd go hang at the Fords never tiring of all the razzing and boisterousness that accompanied two brothers and their big, burly dad.

But Sam spent the last four years mostly away from there. I could count on my hand the number of times he came home. Despite having the greatest, all-around nicest family in the world, he was off at UCLA, playing the big man on campus, and was far too busy to visit them. I didn't see what more he needed, other than what was at the kitchen table that night. There was a father who worked his hands to the bone for thirty-plus years to support his family, as well as a mother who worked and came home to do endless, tedious chores and raise her two boys. There was fun, warmth, and most of all, love. There was an overabundance of love, although half the time, Sam was completely blind to it. He seemed oblivious when his mother entered his room carrying his pile of folded, fresh clean-smelling clothes. Or the heaps of food he and Dustin would devour each night without so much as asking for it. I didn't get it. What could all his ambition get for him that wasn't right here already? I didn't totally believe his drive to succeed could take him anywhere better than our small, tightly knit neighborhood and the families that shared our lives. There were friends and relationships everywhere. There wasn't a lot of money around all the time, but we were never lacking. Sometimes, looking back, all I can see now is how much we had. In more ways than today, we had *everything.*

That summer... oh, that summer was the summer of change for me. It was also the summer I got held up. It was the summer I determined what path I wanted my life to go on. It was the summer when Sam finally looked at me like I wasn't Dustin, or his equivalent. It was the summer I last had with my mom. It was a profound summer that changed everything after it. And it all started with a kiss.

But now, that summer only makes my heart clench and ache, over and over again, until the pressure feels like it might explode inside me. *No.* I refuse to think about that summer. Or love. Or hope. Or youth. Or trust.

All the things that I once felt sure I found with Sam.

Now? Now I have nothing. No one. I've never had any blood relatives, now I don't even have one *relative* alive that knows me still. Not one relative that remembers me, anyway. And the surrogate family I adopted to substitute for mine would have to side with Sam. *I have no one.* Literally, no one in the entire world anymore.

I had no idea how alone I feel until today.

So I lie down on the anonymous, generic bed, in a strange town, in a forgotten motel and watch the night ticking away on the clock.

CHAPTER 3

AM

I HAVE NO IDEA what to do. The elevator already came and went with Natalie. While trying to get decent, she escaped. I hit the metal door with my fist, but all it accomplished was making my hand ring. I shake out the pain while swearing under my breath. I finally lean into the wall and flip over. What should I do? Race after her? I should. Yes. But what do I say? How do I explain... *this?* I don't think she'll listen to me if I say I didn't mean to do it. It just happened. I got carried away. I was angry at her. At us. I was... there is nothing more I can possibly say.

I might want to go after her, but how could I explain myself to her at this moment? After she found another woman on top of me? *Literally.* I shake off the urge to throw up and stomp into my office. Chantal has cleared out thankfully. I start picking up the miscellaneous items that got scattered and shifted. Papers that were crinkled by Chantal's ass.

I flinch as I pick up a file containing the new ad campaign we were considering. I try to flatten the crinkled sheets, cringing as my hands smooth it. It feels contaminated, so I stop and fall into a slump, dropping onto my office chair. I lean my elbows on the desktop and sigh as I stare down with unseeing eyes at the desk I dreamed of having for most of my life. It became the physical representation of all my ambitions and goals.

This is all I hoped for and dreamed about: the big office, the big desk, covered in actual work, correspondences, reports, budgets, and figures; in short, the lifeblood of a functioning corporation. One I had recently been promoted in. It meant I was someone, I was going somewhere, and I had power. I had control. I had money. Yes, it represented every desire I ever wanted. I was hungry for it. Every decision I'd made in the last decade was based on it. It pushed me past being tired or exhausted. It made the sixty–to–eighty–hour work weeks doable, tolerable and expected. I managed it. I managed it all. Or so I told myself. Until today. Tonight.

My shirt is buttoned, but the collar is loose. My tie? Where is it? I glance around and find it shoved off in the corner on the floor. My suit jacket still hangs respectfully at the door. I stare at it, somehow stunned by how normal it looks, hanging where I meticulously placed it when I walked in this morning. At what time? Seven–thirty, wasn't it? I glance at the clock. It's going on midnight. I worked fourteen hours. Well, at least thirteen by the time Chantal showed up. Blurry–eyed and exhausted, I wasn't my usual, careful self. Did I even think of Natalie once in that time? I can't say for sure. I can come into this office and forget about everything except what is directly in front of me. I can compartmentalize better than most, or at least, that's what I've been told. Chantal was a total surprise to me. I believed I was all alone here tonight. During the quiet hours of late evening was often when I got the most work done... despite it being one of Natalie's biggest complaints. Work early, or late; but not both. She had a shift, didn't she? Late, I think. I shake my head. Unsure when she worked today. I'm sure she mentioned it to me, maybe last night. Yes, I remember talking about it, but I can't recall when.

And isn't that part of the crux of why my marriage was crumbling around me before tonight. *This night.* I worked too long and paid too little attention to her. I was too ambitious. I was too... everything. Natalie pointed it out to me in many of our arguments over the last year. *A year?* Was it that long? Yeah, close to. For a whole year we'd been arguing, fighting, and generally not getting along. It was strained, awkward and seemed endless.

It ended just now. That dismal thought weaves through my brain and I suddenly spring to my feet before slamming my fist on the desk. *No! Just fucking no!* I refuse to allow this to be the end. I refuse to believe that all of our years together, eight to be exact, could come down to this. Tonight.

I can fix it. I can fix this. Somehow, someway, I can fix this. I have to. That is what I do. I fix things. I think outside the box. I solve things that others can't. It's why I'm so valuable in business. It's also why, as my heart sinks down into my stomach, I realize I might not be able to fix my personal life.

Seizing my office phone, I start calling her. I know she won't answer. I text her. Several times. I plead for her to just talk to me.

I know she won't respond. I know she won't want to see me. Why should she?

I grab my paperwork and start stuffing it into my brief-case. I won't be in tomorrow. Of that I'm sure. I can't imagine how I'll come back in, period. Screw me. I had sex with my secretary. She'll be right here. Tomorrow. The next day. The next. The realization makes me collapse in defeat. I don't know why I did that. I may as well have imploded both my personal and my professional life. And to be honest? Until this moment, they vied for priority in my life. Or at least, I thought they did. But the bottomless pit lodging in my stomach while thinking about Natalie now makes me realize I was wrong. She is the most important person or concept in my life. She is the only woman who ever got to know me, and loved me still.

What am I going to do? I scan the area around me. The office is big for this company's perspective. It's not a corner office, but it has big windows and a postage stamp view of the bay. It is pristinely furnished with contemporary décor. It's the mark of a respected and distinguished office executive. It is the representation of everything I ever wanted to be. Here it is. But if I come back, I'll be working with Chantal. Or she'll turn me in for sexual harassment. That could be next. I deserve it. Maybe that's what she meant by her cryptic remark. She set me up for this.

More importantly, how could I even try to reconcile with Natalie if I'm coming here every day and seeing the very woman I cheated on her with? It's simple, I could not do that. In this one act, I've lost my marriage, my self-respect and my job.

It shouldn't have hit me so hard, but it feels like I got punched in my gut. I worked for years to get where I am today. *Years.* So many long hours. I simply wilt at the thought that all my hard work was for naught. *I am done here.* I glance around and stand up a little taller. I am sure of that one decision. And strangely enough, in that exact moment when I make my choice, my spine stiffens. I made a decision. I took control. I chose a course of action. I am good at that. I am good at having a plan, and executing it. The only person I could never persuade to follow my plans or meet my expectations was Natalie. That's the reason she drives me nuts, and the reason I love her.

So. Damn. Much. My knees almost collapse under the weight of my revelation. It feels like my shoulders are being crushed by a giant tidal wave that is both pushing me under and drowning me. It sucks my breath from me. In that moment of stark clarity, all the things we argued about and got petty about with each other cease to matter. They are all gone in a flash. In losing her, I finally have the clarity to see her, something that had been fuzzy during the last year.

I still love Natalie.

That should not be a great revelation to have about my wife. I get that. But there, in that moment, faced with the actions that decimated her and us, I realize the full extent of my feelings for her.

That epiphany made shoving my work back on my desk, donning my coat, and walking out the door without another glance as easy as walking out of a grocery store. I am so done here. It is over. Whatever happens to me from here on out, it won't be here.

IT IS the middle of the night now. I pull onto our street and my stomach twists. There are no lights on. Natalie is a careful person. Especially when it comes to outdoor lighting. Nothing. I knew before I walked through the open front door, which was not locked, that she is gone. I walk through the house, finding evidence of only a few things missing. Her dad's baseball mitt, a beloved possession. A few photos. I open her drawers. I'm pretty sure they were messed up. I don't know exactly. She rarely keeps things folded. She doesn't believe in an iron. But I know she's gone.

The real pisser is, as I sit down on our rumpled bed, I

33

have no idea where she's gone. Dustin? Maybe. But since he's my brother, I think she'll try to keep my family out of it. Shame makes my skin heat up as I think of them finding out. My parents... Dustin... shit! They will never speak to me again. Maybe no one will.

She has friends at work. Her entire life, like mine, is her career. But somehow, I can only see her fierce pride. And her humiliation. I don't picture her going there with that. It would hurt and embarrass her, and I can't imagine her letting anyone she works with see her as either of those things. She always keeps a cool, professional exterior at all times with her coworkers. As a woman cop, she works too long and hard to be judged just for being a woman. She works harder than anyone I know, and dutifully hones the necessary skills. She can be calm, cool, rational and analytical. She keeps her emotions under guard. Didn't she keep all her emotions tucked far away from everyone, even me? I clench my fist as my anger starts to percolate. She keeps a lot from me too, not just those whom she works with.

So much so, I haven't the faintest idea whom she'd run to about this.

NATALIE

Town. Ellensburg to be exact, or so my GPS says. It feels like a stretch to call the place where I've pulled into a town. I'm just off the highway in the parking lot of a Super 8 motel. I can see far off into the distance. The land is flat, like one would expect to find the ocean, but it's all land; and the sky seems like an endless dome of blue over me. I tap my fingers on my steering wheel, feeling completely aimless. My car idles. I glance around. McDonalds. Dairy King. A Starbucks. A truck stop with gas and a café. They all surround me, but it's completely underwhelming. After traveling across three states in a numbing, catatonic stupor, all I keep thinking is, *This is it?* An abundant display of all things American and cheap? Cheap food. Cheap lodging. I notice some mountains with purple smudges and trees mixed in here and there. Farms dot the horizon. The sign ahead of me indicates Central Washington University is up ahead. I have no idea what to do now. I'm here. So what? So the hell what if I'm here? No one knows I came here. No one knows I was coming here. No one knows where I am, or what I'm doing, including me. It's tempting to swing a U–turn and head back down the interstate, going further down the same road I've been traveling for the last three days. I'm anonymous. Completely and utterly anonymous to those I pass and all I pass through.

The anonymity makes me feel numb and invisible. And silent. My entire insides feel frozen. I don't want to think about Sam or our past, and definitely not what just happened. Thoughts of Sam, however, stubbornly stab through my numbness with the laser precision of a scalpel. I can't deal with the sharp, sucker–punch–in–the–gut sensations. So I'm not thinking or feeling. I'm just numb. Teflon. Rubber. I'm trying to convince myself I'm anything but who and what I really am.

I finally park and grab my keys and purse before heading towards the café. I enter a large room, brightly lit, which looks out towards the parking lot. It is half full of semi-trucks, and beyond that, all I can see is farm land, which acts as a backdrop. Big red booths with yellow Formica tables fill the space. It's mid–morning and the pleasant buzz of voices combined with the clatter of dishes cheer up the atmosphere. It has the familiarity of any small–town diner/café/truck stop. I think every town must have one. This place with its worn, ripped booths from all the years and all the patrons probably attracts most of its customers from town to eat there. Although it's unhealthy, it most likely is melt–in–your–mouth good.

I slide into a booth and pick up the large, rectangular menu, coated in plastic and smeared by greasy fingerprints. I browse it, but nothing appeals to me. My stomach is queasy. Now that I'm here in Ellensburg, the town I believe my birth mother lives in, I feel totally conspicuous. It seems like any person passing by me should stop by my table and recognize me, which is ridiculous. My first clue that isn't true, however, is my supposed half–sister. She is as lily–white as a snowflake. I'm sure my birth mother is also white, and I'm Latino. Somehow, I don't expect my birth mother to be white.

Still, I feel as if I should have scarlet letter on my back somehow indicating what I'm doing here. Even though I don't have the foggiest idea why.

"Hey, hon, you want to start with a coffee?"

I jerk to attention as the terse waitress comes beside me with an empty tray in her hands. I nod. "Yes, thanks."

"Unless you already know what you want?" The waitress nods at my menu, which has dropped flat on the table while my thoughts drift off into space. I nod again. "Uh, sure. How about just the oatmeal?"

"Okay. Easy enough. Be right back."

In not even three minutes, the fast-moving woman wearing the red–and–white uniform of the establishment returns with a half-full pot of coffee. She deftly flips over the white cup that is already set. "You visiting a student there at the college?"

I glance up. An opening! A perfect, clear, easy opening to ask about the name Hendricks. It's all I have. I wasn't sure I would even stick around here long enough to inquire, but a casual inquiry is the perfect opener.

"Uh, yes. I think. She's a local. A friend I met recently. She told me to look her up if I was ever in town. Do you know a Christina Hendricks?"

The woman was only half listening as she filled the cup. "Hmm. Christina? No. But I had a Hendricks who installed central heating in my old, drafty house a few years back. Will Hendricks. Any relation?"

How should I know? But any Hendricks seemed a good place to start. Thank God their name wasn't Smith, or Brown, or something even more generic than Hendricks. "Uh, yes. Sure. You wouldn't happen to remember their number?"

"Nah. Look it up. He advertises under Hendricks Heating and Cooling Systems."

And there it was! I smiled my thanks and stared into the black depths of my coffee. I had a name. A resource. A place to start. I can't believe this. Too bad I threw my phone out or I would've just looked it up. Stupid, careless and short-sighted move on my part. And I'm so freaking stubborn I won't just ask someone for help.

I eat the oatmeal she serves ten minutes later. Lead burdens my legs as I get up and take my meager bill to the front cash register. A young kid stands there who quickly handles my transaction. As I turn to leave, on a whim I ask, "May I see your telephone book?"

The kid smiles. "Phone book? I don't even know if we have one. Hold up." He leans down behind the counter and starts ruffling all around it. He comes back up a minute later blowing dust off of one whose date shows it being several years old. I step to the side and take the book with a curt *Thanks.* I'm still numb. Out of body. I find it. A small adver-tisement for Hendricks Heating and Cooling Systems with a number. I write it down on the back of a gum wrapper I dig out of my purse. I push the book away and turn to leave.

What do I do with this now? I have no idea. Again in

my car, I stare at the gum wrapper. Is this just some stranger's phone number? Or is it *the* number? I wish now I'd taken Christina's number when she came to me. I intended at the time to never, ever see her again, much less investigate her claims and *her* family. But now? I have a business number. What do I do? Call it and ask for Christina?

There's a relic of a phone booth tucked off behind the front office of the motel in front of me. I groan. Really? A pay phone? Weren't those all scrapped by metal recyclers by now? But no, right there, as if waiting for me, is a phone. They are nowhere else, and yet in middle of nowhere, I find one? I'm not a believer in fate, and I don't usually think that signs can guide us to places where we should be, but this coincidence is too much to deny.

I face criminals. I face situations where I don't always know what the outcome will be before going into it. Some things like domestic abuse calls, I handle without much hesitation. But this? An innocuous phone booth? I wish now for the confidence of my chosen profession. I feel devoid of it in ways I've never known before, but I finally cross the parking lot. There is a phonebook there too. I haven't looked at one in a few decades, and I find two in one day now? I reach down and glance through the white pages that list the local residences. There are three Hendricks and one is W. Hendricks. It's a different number. *Their home residence?* Sighing, I copy it down too. Now I have two leads. And two other Hendricks residences to try.

Taking in a slow breath, I dig the change out of my purse. I put the change in the slot and dial before my nerves motivate me to cease and desist my efforts. It starts to ring and my heart lodges right up into my throat. Not really, but my nerves soon have my fingers tapping the wall near me. The rings sound loud and insistent. *Hang up!* My brain can hear me screaming in a secret corner to hang up. Two. Three. Four—

Shit. There's an answer. A woman's voice says simply, "Hello?"

I'm shocked that anyone answered and pull the receiver off my ear and stare at it as if expecting it to morph into a writhing snake before striking me in the face. But no. Just a black, typical phone receiver. I jerk it back to my ear and hear the tail end of the woman's next *Hello?* Her tone reveals her annoyance at my lack of response. She's going to hang up. I should let her. Let this be done and over with. Don't do this. Just move on. Go back to the disaster I already have going on. But then...

"Hi."

There's a pause after my rushed greeting. "Can I help you?"

I blow out a breath but it doesn't do much to soothe my nerves. "Yes, I, uh was looking for Christina."

There. That would determine if I called the right number. It is probably the wrong number. Just some woman I'll never meet. Just—

"Oh, she's still at school. She won't be home until next week. You can reach her on her cell phone. Who is this?" The woman's voice warms slightly, believing me a friend of her daughter's. Her daughter who must be at college. Christina would be about that age. This woman... and it socks me in the gut this time... this woman could be my birth mother!

"That's all right; I'll just call... some other time."

Maybe. Never. No. I'll be gone. Most likely back to San Francisco. Right? I mean how long can I stay hidden and running? How much longer can I avoid this? I can't. I know that somewhere in my heart, but something else inside me wants to keep running.

Is it my tentative pause? The woman is silent. I feel a shift in something. Her breathing perhaps? I don't know how, but I swear, I can physically feel the woman's energy changing.

"Are you a friend of hers?" The tone is soft and crisp. Like she's trying to keep herself steady.

I squeeze my eyelids shut. *Hang up. Hang the fucking phone up!* I scream inside my head. But I remain... silent. It goes on and on. Her breathing changes again and she seems to take in a sharp gasp. Is this one of Christina's sisters? I want to think so, but somehow, I know it's a middle–aged woman I'm talking to. I know for sure, I just know deep down, in the sinking of my stomach, this voice belongs to *my mother*.

Finally, she says, "Please call back. She'll want you to."

With that surety, I suspect she somehow figured out who I am. Is it the mysterious way I answer?

"Um... how do you know who I am?"

She is quiet. "I wondered if you'd ever try to find her. She never thought you would. But she's black–and–white about things like that. She's very young. She doesn't understand sometimes how complicated things can be."

"Things like us?"

"Yes, Natalie, things like this us." *Natalie.* My name crosses her lips. Her voice shakes something deep inside me. I've never heard my biological mother speak my name. Assuming of course, this is she.

"Are you... I mean, is this..." I can't get the words *my mother* past my throat, which feels swollen shut. I finally almost whisper, "Christina's mother?"

Pause. Shuffling. I wonder what the woman is doing. I must be blowing her day to hell, just as Christina did mine that day. "Yes." Her tone is heavy with reserve. *Regret? Regret I've called? Or regret I exist? Or regret she now knows my name?* "My name is Jessie. Jessie Hendricks."

"Married to Will Hendricks, the Heating and Cooling Systems provider?"

She lets out a soft snort. "The one and only. You found us through an advertisement of the business?"

"Yes. Christina told me your last name and the town. Nothing else. I didn't give her a chance."

There's another long pause. No idle chit–chat. We're strangers. We don't even know what the other looks like. Yet we can't be totally casual or whatever to each other; because there is something. We do have some kind of connection. Wanted or not. It's biological. And I'm still trying to grasp the name of my true mother: *Jessie Hendricks*. Her voice is nice. Feminine, clear, and kind of soft. She talks with confidence about Christina. From a quick glance, it seems she's very much in Christina's life like any normal mother would be.

"Would you like her cell phone number?"

"I don't know."

"The area code you're calling from tells me you're already here. In this area. I can't believe it is only a coincidence you're traveling through. I think... you came specifically to see her."

"Well, I sure as shit didn't come to meet you!" I snap, biting down on my tongue, and causing sharp pains to resonate in deep tugs throughout my body. I didn't mean to say that. But typical me, I said it anyway. I never thought the phone booth would show the local number. I wasn't prepared for this woman to know where I actually was. I thought I could hide longer, safe in my anonymity.

"Fair enough. But don't let me stop you from knowing her. She isn't me. She hasn't hurt you. She never would."

"What did she say about me?"

"That you were tall with dark hair. Half Latino. Which I knew, of course. She said you seemed confident, successful, happily married with a nice house and that your husband, Sam, seemed pretty cool. Her words, not mine. She was upset you wanted nothing to do with her. But she understood why too."

Sam. Damn. There was that name again. Everywhere and in everything. Happily married. Who was ever happily married? Who knew if anyone really was? It had been a long while since I could classify myself as happily married.

"If I call her, she'll come home and be here in two hours. She'd do it without blinking. Would you consider coming here?"

She knows her daughter. I feel it by the way she so easily speaks about and predicts her daughter's behavior. I squeeze the phone in my fingers. My real mom used to know everything about me. Before she died. I miss that connection. A relationship so close that people can speak for others. I suck in tears as a sharp jab of longing fills me and makes the back of my eyes sting. *I want my mother back.* The real one; the one who died. I want her now, here, to help me deal with what I witnessed Sam doing. I miss *my* mother. I don't want this stranger.

Have I come here on this strange odyssey simply to search for someone to fill a dead woman's shoes? I wilt and sag in the small phone booth. I don't want a stranger, I want my real mom.

"Please, Natalie. If you've come this far, don't let me stand in the way. I'll even leave if you prefer. I'll tell her where to meet you. Something. Give her some kind of chance here. She goes to college, which is just over two hours from here. You met Max too, right? Her boyfriend?"

I remember the kid, short and quiet. He was nice enough, and respectful too. He was Latino like me. I suppose that is something. They aren't racists. Good to know. "Yeah. I remember him."

"He lives in town here. Would you meet with him? At his house? He lives with my sister…" She trails off. "That sounds a little odd. Max and Christina... are cousins by adoption, so it can get awkward to explain. Anyway, you'd be welcome there. They... neither of them is responsible. I did it to you."

Wow, I didn't picture the first conversation... No. Scratch that. I never pictured we'd have *any* kind of conversation, ever, but here we were and already she admits she did something to me? I turn my shoulder and stare out with unseeing eyes at the parking lot. The few cars parked randomly before me blur. I don't care what I'm looking at, yet it all seems to suddenly sharpen in my eyesight. I twist the old fashioned, metal phone cord that connects the receiver to the phone booth with my finger. I am tempted to forever end this conversation; not because of my anger over her abandoning me, but because the desperation I hear in this woman's voice isn't owing to any desire or need to meet me, but rather, because she is acting on her daughter's behalf. Her daughter, my sister, who harbors an urgent desire and need to meet me. And, good mother that Jessie is, she wants to make sure that happens. I can hear the guilt in her voice, not towards me, but towards Christina.

Fucking bitch.

The uncharitable thought hammers my brain and I shut my eyes as I lean my head against the edge of the booth. My silence is rather lengthy. Jessie's breathing takes a sharp incline. She's worried I'll hang up. Not answer. Disappear forever again. I want to. I can still. I think hard about it. I take the receiver off my ear and hold it over the box, thinking and almost slamming it down to cut off the call. But... I don't. My curiosity is too powerful. And this sudden prick of feeling, interest, even wonder is new. It's the first sensation that managed to forge through the thick numbness I feel cloaked beneath.

I put the phone back to my ear. "Max? Fine. I'd be willing to hang out and meet with him."

"I've been texting him. He'll be there in an hour. He's just getting out of class and will get there as soon as he can. Where are you?"

"The diner by the highway and the Super 8."

"I know it." Her tone is crisp. Then she adds softly, "Natalie... Please—"

I wait, wondering what Jessie is begging of me. Don't leave? Don't go? Don't come? Don't hate me? Don't come near me? What? What will this woman ask of me? Her long lost, unwanted daughter whom her other daughter found, not she. That irrefutable fact is not lost on me.

"Please just give me a chance to contact Christina."

I hang up. That's my eloquent answer. That's the answer I see her deserving. All about her precious Christina! The daughter she raised, loved, nurtured, nourished and *wanted*. Yes, there is that undeniable fact, but contrary to my bitterness, I don't think it extends to Christina. She was very sweet when I met her. Almost tongue–tied in my presence. At the time, I came off as cold and callous, totally uninterested in her, and I felt bad later. It took a lot of guts to come to me as she did, and totally without any warning or notice. I had no notion my biological family was interested in me; not to mention, this innocent, sweet, unsure, young girl. Eighteen. I think she was barely eighteen or nineteen. I don't really know. I know nothing about these people. Or what could possibly benefit or injure me by meeting them.

CHAPTER 4

$\mathcal{N}$ATALIE

I CROSS THE PARKING lot again and nab the same table with the same waitress. "Hey, hon, back already?"

"Connected up with the friend."

"Well, that's nice. Beauty of small towns. Can I get you more coffee?"

"Sure."

I stare out the windows, watching traffic that stops and goes at the one, lone signal. Some cars merge onto the highway while others keep moving forward in a lazy speed, gliding under the overpass. Things feel slow and easy here this afternoon. The sun is slanted now over the sky.

I first have trouble picturing Max, but the minute I see a young, rather short, but handsome Latino kid getting out of a sedan and crossing the lot with fast, purposeful strides, I instantly remember him.

Max Salazar. He enters the establishment and glances

around. He obviously remembers me. His facial expression loosens into relief: he was obviously quite prepared for me to have already left. Honestly? So was I, but here I am. I stare at him, my best neutral, kind of cold cop face. I'm purposely using my intimidation skills. No simpering from me. No making him feel at ease.

He stops in front of my table and says nothing. Glancing down at me when I don't stand up, he observes me sweeping my hand over the table, indicating for him to sit down. He slides into the booth and leans back, his gaze fastened on me.

He looks like a baby with his face almost completely scrubbed free of hair. His youthful eyes don't even have a single wrinkle. His smile is genuine, however. And hard. There is no innocence in this kid's stare. I realize it now, although I think I missed it before when he was with Christina. She had innocence. That was so obvious. But not this kid. "You don't talk much, do you?"

His smile is small. "No, not much. Christina always makes up for my conversational deficiencies."

I smile back. "Yes, except when meeting me. She was quite tongue–tied."

He raises his eyebrows. "You were also trying to intimidate her. As you are trying to do to me now. You should know, however, that nothing about you intimidates me. I don't worry or even care if you like me, like Christina, or would leave on account of me, like Jessie. So, Natalie what are you doing here?"

I lean back, and my smile becomes secretive. I don't expect his suspicion of me. It's kind of ironic. Funny. Interesting. And as I said before, not much else interests me now. "You're worried about my motives? You all were the ones who came and found *me*."

"Yes, but a year and nine months later, out of absolutely

nowhere, you don't even call first and just show up in town, looking for her?"

I shrug. "It was a spur–of–the–moment decision." Which was totally honest. No plans to seek out long-lost family until I happened to stumble upon my husband when he was screwing someone else. "I had some unexpected time off, and I started thinking and wondering… so I guess I'm here finally to face it all. You have to admit, you couldn't have expected a good reaction that day you two came to my house. I was in complete shock. Unprecedented. I had no idea how to react."

Max inclined his head. "True enough. I'll give you that. So now you're interested?"

Am I? Really? I don't know if that's too strong of a word. I just literally have nothing else to do, and nowhere else to go. "I want to know more."

Max kind of straightens up and leans his elbows on the table. His gaze is boring into my face. "Don't mess with Christina. If you really want to do this, and meet her, then make sure it's genuine. She doesn't deserve whatever this really is. Your attitude is totally apathetic. You don't care if you meet her, or any of them. Yet you're here. The two don't match at all. It's a long trip, one, I venture to say, that should have been made by someone who was actually serious about meeting another person, like Christina was. Yet, here you are; and I get the feeling that is not really why you're here."

"Aren't you like her cousin or something?" I raise my eyebrows, taunting him, trying to deflect his grilling of my true motives. I'm a little impressed that some kid, a guy especially, could manage to read me so easily and clearly.

He smiles. "I was adopted when I was fifteen. I didn't even meet Christina until I was thirteen."

"And now? You're her boyfriend?"

His smile is cocky this time. "Yes, I am. And she's far nicer than I am."

I squint my eyes at him, and reply, "And more naïve I'm guessing too."

He nods. "I didn't grow up here. I didn't grow up in a family like hers."

She grew up in my life. I don't say it though. I'm confused as to whether I resent her or not. Max is watching my face intently, trying to figure out if I am too. I know he said it on purpose to gauge my reaction. "You want to know if hate her, or want to be her sister? I have no idea. I wish I could tell you where my motives lie. I just… kind of came. That's as deep as it gets and as deep as I feel about my motives right now."

He stares at me and nods. "I might believe that."

I nod too. "So back to the cousin and boyfriend thing. That's really kind of gross, you know."

He shrugs and leans back while stretching his arm along the back of the booth. "Nothing cousinly between us."

"And the whole family is okay with that?"

"They didn't love it at first, but I think everyone's used to it now."

"What about her sisters?"

"Melissa and Emily? They're your sisters too. Why not just ask me instead of this passive/aggressive questioning? What do you want to know, Natalie?"

This kid is good. "Okay, I'm asking. What is the family like?"

"Kind, caring, supportive. Jessie and Will are good parents. The three girls are fine people. Are you disappointed or glad?"

"Confused about where I could possibly fit into the scheme of things."

Max shrugs. "Who fits in anywhere? They do have the capacity to accept the, shall we say, unexpected?"

"Like cousins who start dating."

"I was brought here by my brother who was a drug

dealer. He got caught dating one of their friends' daughters. We came here at first to hide from our other brother. He was the drug runner and looking for both of us. As in, he would most likely have killed us if he found us. They took us in. The Hendrickses, and now my parents, Noah and Lindsey."

"Who are they?"

"Your aunt, Jessie's sister."

I lean back, studying Max, and cross my arms over my chest. "A whole damn family is here?"

"Yes. They are a whole damn family."

"Yet, they took you in. For no other reason than…"

"I'm sure if you ask them, they will say 'because it was the right thing to do.'"

"And Jessie? What do you think of her?"

"She is my aunt. I love and respect her. But I can't speak for you, or what you should feel for her."

"Do you know the circumstances of my birth?"

"Yes." His tone seems crisp and confident. "But only in the capacity of Christina's boyfriend. Otherwise, as her cousin, I would not know."

I consider him. "Will you tell me?"

"No. You want to know? You need to ask Jessie. Not me. Not Christina. It's her story to tell you… or not, if she so chooses."

I think many things about my birth. I work as patrol officer. I've seen a lot of bad domestic situations over the course of my job. I've met the dregs of our society and the black sheep of some families; and it sounds to me that Max has too. That accounts for the edge he has, which Christina lacks. I'm thinking, from first glance and first proof, that maybe Jessie was a decent mother. So now I'm guessing she was too young when she had me, or got raped by my biological father. Do I care? Do I feel sympathy? Yes. Of course. Something tightens in my heart. I have considered every possible scenario

LEANNE DAVIS

throughout my lifetime as to why I was given away as a newborn infant. But now I'm sitting here, staring at someone who knows *her*, and I realize in an almost suffocating moment that I have talked to *her*, this same woman who gave birth to me and then let me go. It seems to hit me finally for real. This did happen. I can have the answers I seek. Maybe. If I want to know them. Do I? Am I brave enough to accept the worst rejection possible? Either way, this woman who gave birth to me did not want me. My life, for whatever reason, was a mistake. And no matter how healthy anyone is now, no one wants to admit, much less feel that.

Max is staring at me as I take it all in. "Look, Natalie, you came all the way here. You're close now and I have to believe if someone came this far, curiosity is at least part of their motivation. Why not put off all this bullshit and just go meet her? Go meet Jessie for yourself. I suspect you're just pretending to want to see Christina. It's a first move, and you're ready to pussyfoot around, but what you really want is to meet Jessie. So why don't you let me just take you there?"

"You really try to protect her, don't you?"

"Who? Christina? Yeah, I do. The whole naïve, nice thing she has going on? It's real and I don't ever want to see it get ruined or lost."

I appreciate the sweet sentiment. Max has been around real life and real situations; or at least, his attitude and essence convey that. I get it. Honestly? I was never all that naïve or innocent. I grew up a lot differently, none of this small town stuff, but probably nowhere near the way, I'm gathering, Max grew up. I was spared the drug–dealing brothers and death threats and all. Plus... Sam always looked out for me. No matter how tough I pretended to be, I could always rely on knowing no one in the neighborhood dared to pick on me, or bully me, or insult me, or even look at me the wrong way. Sam Ford had my back then. God, not a day in

50

twenty–plus years has gone by without him having my back. Almost instinctively, I glance over my shoulder when a shiver goes down my spine. For the first time in two decades, there is no one who has my back. Not like this kid before me has for my naïve, stupid–sweet little sister. A sister I don't know. I don't even know if I want to know her.

But the kid is right. I'm here to meet my mother.

The rest is all bullshit.

Perhaps only because I respect him calling me on it, I nod. "All right. Yeah. Let's just get on with it."

Max nods, his expression neutral. He approves.

I follow him in my car. I'm finally on my way to meet my mother. Someone named Jessie Hendricks.

CHAPTER 5

 AM

I LAY ON OUR BED, sprawled out with only a t–shirt and my tightie–whities on. I've been drinking for three days straight. I might have eaten something... sometime. I don't remember. I'm drunk. I've dialed Natalie's number so many times, I'm starting to believe she really isn't going to talk to me. Worse yet, I really don't know where in the hell in the entire world my wife could be.

The third day, I finally get around to calling the office. I ineloquently tell whichever secretary—it might have even been the one I had sex with— that I, Sam Ford, am quitting BorderLine Solutions; effective immediately. Now. Pronto. Forever. Goodbye. The female voice rises in alarm as she starts calling louder into the receiver, "Mr. Ford! Mr. Ford! Please let me put you through to—" but I cut her off. No more job.

I'm aware enough, despite my stupor, to realize that probably wasn't the best way to handle things.

The need to piss enters my comatose brain. Heaving myself up to a straight posture, I stumble to my feet and weave my way to the luxury bathroom adjoining our bedroom. I often don't bother to lift the seat rim. I dribble on it. Natalie hates that. Always cusses me out over it, explaining how she doesn't need to sit on my piss. How would I like it if she peed on my underwear? Yeah, Nat was never too subtle. Never too shy. Never did she avoid me. Or back down from any fight. Until now. Telling, isn't it? She has more to say about my piss than she does about our marriage.

The phone rings and rings. It's done that on and off for the last few days. Work mostly. Dustin. My mother. Never Natalie. I ignore it all. Texts. Calls. Even the few times when the front doorbell peals.

I don't look in the mirror. I'm having trouble doing that. Shame stares back at me. I am too ashamed to even catch a glimpse of my own reflection.

I stumble out and back onto the bed, lifting one of many bottles off the nightstand. We have a pretty decent stock when it comes to liquor. Mine mostly, usually reserved for entertaining clients and associates and friends. Now, it's all the shitty things I filled my life with in my effort to ignore the crumbling façade that used to be my marriage. Was I doing it more often of late in order to avoid my loneliness? Or just to piss Natalie off? I honestly don't know. Neither scenario makes me feel proud.

I sleep some more, or pass out, which is more descriptive, and try to ignore my thoughts and feelings. All of it hurts. All of it makes me want to shut my eyes forever.

Knocking. So much knocking and doorbell–ringing, it keeps waking me up. I roll over, pushing two pillows over my head, trying to muffle the sound from my ears as well as the way each pound of the door and ring of the bell split my head like a cleaver. Not to mention the echo! We have one of those bells that sounds like a bullhorn when announcing visitors.

It won't stop. Knock. Ring. Scream. I finally throw the pillows off and stumble to my feet. I ineptly weave and slide to the front door. My coordination is gone. Gripping the doorknob desperately, I use it to steady my balance. Just as the knocks rap again.

"Open up, Sam!"

Groaning, I lean my head against the wooden door. It's Jayden. Of course. My cryptic "I quit" no doubt got passed on with some alarm to the higher–ups.

I finally find the strength to open the door. Jayden stops moving or speaking and his mouth falls open. His astonished gaze roams down to my feet and back up again. Yup, still in my underwear and t–shirt. I don't even care. The stubble is rather long on my face and I'm sure my eyes are bloodshot.

Jayden's jaw clenches with alarm. "What is going on?" He pushes me backwards before moving past me. I don't have the strength to stop him. A sudden wave of nausea is too strong as it sweeps over me.

"What is this shit? You quit? What the hell? You look like a mental patient. No, you look more like a heroin addict in need of a fix. Are you on drugs? Oh shit, Sam, did you start using?"

I get Jayden's elaborate connection, from me looking a little under the weather to a jonesing heroin addict. I once came to work with a hundred–and–two degree temperature and a raging case of strep throat. I refused to admit I was sick until my throat almost closed off and I could not swallow. So here I was, out of nowhere, looking like this in middle of a workday. And, oh yeah, I spastically quit.

"I'm not on drugs," I mumble, sounding defeated as I stumble to the couch. I let myself fall onto it, grateful for the reprieve from swaying on my feet. "I've been drunk for a few days."

Jayden follows me, and stands in the room, his hands on his lean hips, dressed in an impeccable black suit over a purple silk shirt. His elbows poke out. The bright sunlight falls through the downstairs windows, blinding me. The dazzling white soon has me blinking and rubbing my eyelids to try and soothe the aching. "Is this about Chantal?"

I go still. The fuzzy vertigo of too much drink instantly seems to fall out of my head. I stiffen as I lift my gaze to his. "What about Chantal? How do you know about her?"

He nods and slowly lowers himself gently onto the opposite couch. The couches face each other like a quaint little conversation ensemble. I am beginning to see what Natalie meant; this place does look like a formal, personality–less, furniture showroom. And how perfectly the backdrop fits Jayden's smooth elegance. He almost perches like a formal society dame might have back in the Victorian era.

"So it *is* about her. Look, guilt is a normal thing to feel. But don't take it so hard. You're only a guy. You work harder than anyone I know. Maybe you were tired. Maybe your judgment was off. But a beautiful woman like her? How could you resist her?"

My head whips back. "She told you?"

He shakes his head, and his mouth twists as he gives a little half shrug. "Well, no. I hired her."

Speechless can't begin to cover what my drink–addled mind spins into. I don't comprehend what he just said. "Hired who?" I mean, what the hell is he talking about?

"Chantal. I asked her to help you alleviate some of your stress. I know how hard we've worked you on the Steckler account. After we had that talk about you and Natalie, I figured you needed to blow off a little steam. You deserved a reward for all your late nights and hard work. That's why she showed up so late. Didn't that ever occur to you? What other secretary would stay there so late? It wasn't a set-up. It was just... a gift. She's known for helping some of us with over-exhaustion and stress. For a fee, of course. Pretty mind-blowing, huh? That thing she does with her tongue—"

I'm on him before I realize I've even moved. Underwear and all, I attack Jayden on my couch. I shove him, my torso knocking hard into his before pinning him onto the couch and slamming my fist in his face. Completely taken off guard, he doesn't react for a few seconds until his mind registers what his body is feeling. He raises up his arms, blocking my next hit, and shoves hard at my head, pushing me while he tries to rise. If I were one hundred percent myself, or even sober, he'd never have gotten me off him. But drunk and in my present sloth-like condition, he easily gains the upper hand. I land on my ass, sprawled out. "What the hell is your problem, Sam? I was helping you. You didn't have to do it. All you had to do was say no if you didn't want to."

All I had to do was say no. The truth of his offending statement fills my ears and singes my brain. I hunch forward, totally defeated, cradling my pounding head in my hands, and pressing hard against my temples. Damn. He's right. I wasn't forced. It seems incomprehensible that Jayden would hire a woman for me, but even worse that I'd have taken him up on it.

In my peripheral vision, I see Jayden smoothing out his suit. I didn't hit him hard enough to hurt him by any stretch of the imagination. His disdain for me now is evident. "Don't you think your guilt here is a bit over the top? Quitting? She's not going to sue you, or expose you. She's as safe as it gets. You think I'd risk damaging any of our reputations with bad publicity?

Chantal is the best and the most discreet. Plus, she has just as much to lose as we do! Her discretion is as real for her as it is for us. Relax, Sam. It'll remain our little secret. The dramatic resignation? A little much. I don't appreciate that. Not any of it. "

"Natalie walked in. She—she saw me. She saw us."

Silence. "Ah. That's what this is all about? Well, I can't say I planned for that possibility, although it's kind of perfect. Look at this for real, Sam. It's your chance to get ahead and really focus on your career. She never wanted that for you. You can't deny that. She held you back. No, *us* back. Come on, shower, and get yourself together. Let's go talk. We can work this out. I'm sorry, really, I didn't intend for that to occur. But is it really the worst news?"

"Get out!" I finally whisper through gritted teeth. My anger, shock, and rage simply overflow from me. I hunch over on the floor of my expensive, pointless company housing, banishing the very man who gave me all of it, and suddenly see the transparency of all the mistaken illusions I ever harbored about what was important in life. I don't even have the energy to passionately say it. The urge to beat my fists against my chest and scream at Jayden for what he did and for no good reason is pointless. He refuses to see or admit he did anything wrong.

"Sam? You don't mean that. You're just in a bit of shock. Stress. I know… Take a few days off. Let the dust settle. Take as long as you need. We'll talk when you're sober and have had some time to analyze everything."

"I quit, Jayden. *Forever.*" I look up, my speech no longer slurred. Slowly rising with as much dignity as I can muster in my underwear during the middle of the day, I stare right into his eyes. "Just leave."

"Don't do this. You need me. This is your chance to pursue your dream. We can make this work. We can—"

"Get out!" I command one last time as I pass around him and disappear. I plan to hibernate in my bed some more.

~

"WHAT'S GOING ON, SAM?" I nearly drop the bottle I'm tipping to my mouth when my brother's voice startles me. Grabbing it just before it falls, the sticky liquid covers me and the bed.

Oh, hell no. I don't want to tell my brother about it. My brother stands there in his work uniform, all shaved and properly put together. My brother, the most decent damn person I've ever known. His job is installing media for private homes. He works for a ginormous conglomerate, nine–to–five, five days a week. He's never missed a single day. Nor worked an hour longer than his daily schedule. He has humble ambitions, and is perfectly content with his well–paying job and solid hours. He's amiable, kind, and decent. He does not have an ounce of resentment or jealousy for my financial success in comparison to him. Nothing but good will from Dustin. And Dustin's best friend is Natalie. I can't tell him what I've done. He'll think I'm a total scumbag. He'll think I'm horrible, awful, nasty, and a complete prick… and worst of all, he'll tell my mother.

I cringe and drink more liberally, picturing my parents when they discover what I've done. What kind of man I truly am. And not the son they raised and made sacrifices for.

I lift my blurry gaze to my brother. He is staring at me in his quiet, patient way, waiting for me to answer him. He must've used a key to let himself in. His uniform is still ironed and neat. His service van is parked in my driveway.

At first glance, I appear by far to be the successful brother. My house is huge and in a neighborhood that we should not have been able to touch. In all honesty? We can't.

The house I live in belongs to the company; and we rent it at low cost; it's one of my employee perks. It's their way of projecting a more positive image. My car is a high-end sports car, and my brother drives a nice, reliable, mid–grade sedan. Some of the suits I wear cost as much as he pays to finance his car for a month or two. Yet, never once could I say that I am the better man. I've always known that. Dustin is content with the man he is and what he has managed to attain. He's always been that way. Even worse still? He's happy for me whenever he observes me getting something I want. No resentment, envy or jealousy.

I glance down at the underwear I've been wearing for the past three days. Look at me now.

How do you tell a guy who would rather sell his last possession than tarnish his integrity what I've done? He's the one who works every Sunday at a soup kitchen, actually believing he can make a difference in the community we grew up in. Our old neighborhood is now mostly gangs; the working class has, no doubt, fled. With rampant poverty, the field we once played and roamed in has been tagged and graffitied countless times. Except no one even tries to maintain it now. No one with a brain goes there unless it is to score or sell some dope. Nonetheless, Dustin faithfully appears there, serving soup at the shelter closest to our old neighborhood and spending the day helping and encouraging others less fortunate than he. In short, Dustin is always decent.

How do I tell someone like that what I did?

How can I not tell him? It's not like I can lie. One can't lie to someone who's as good and decent and kind and just plain nice as Dustin. Especially not when he's staring right at me, quietly waiting for me to answer. *Whenever you're ready*, his casual slouch tacitly conveys to me. He'll stand there, waiting until he's gray. Never in a hurry, he doesn't expect anyone else to be either.

I lean forward, feeling miserable, and rest my elbows on my knees. I'm too ashamed to look up at him as I rub my hands through my hair. "I screwed up. Everything," I mumble.

"What's happening, Sam? Where's Natalie?"

"I don't know," I whisper shamefacedly. I am so horrified. Who loses their wife?

"What do you mean, *you don't know?*"

"I mean, I literally don't know where on Earth she is right now."

The ensuing silence is heavy and somehow passes judgment. Dustin's silence is always telling. "What did you do?" Dustin asks in a strangled voice. An upset voice.

I look up at my brother. He is shaking his head. His eyes grow bigger. He knows. He can tell. He knows me well enough to see when I've screwed up. I've done that so often in the past, when my greed and ambition go too far. Or while trying to reach for something far beyond what I deserve. Or when I am selfish. I recall when we were only eleven and nine. There on the street was some homeless guy, lying around our stoop, asking for money. I stepped over him and ignored his request, snickering at him mercilessly with my friends. While he tried to sleep, I would often play pranks on him. Sometimes, I'd place raw eggs in his hands, hoping he would squeeze and crack them open all over his palms. My friends and I derived great amusement in our torture of the poor guy. At the very least, I always bullied him. I never once thought I was wrong until I witnessed my little brother, who once followed me, gently removing the egg I put in his hand and replacing it with the few dollars he'd taken from his piggy bank. He never said a word of rebuke to me. I can still remember the snickers of my friends, and even more, the heat of my embarrassment. Sure, I knew what I was doing was wrong. I wouldn't have done it on my own, but under the power of mob mentality, peer pressure and being eleven, becoming such a bully got easier. Dustin? Never. Never once could anyone convince Dustin to do anything he knew deep down was wrong.

"I cheated on her."

The words come out in a strangled whisper. My voice sounds like sandpaper and nearly abrades my vocal chords. The words alone fill my head with dizziness.

"Sam..." Dustin's voice cannot conceal his shock.

"She saw me. She saw me having sex with another woman. So you see, Dustin? She's gone. Forever. There is no more Natalie in my life. Go ahead, tell me what a piece of shit I am. A selfish, awful piece of shit. Just tell me. Go ahead."

Silence. More of his awful silence. I finally raise my eyes to observe his reaction. His eyebrows are drawn down in what? Shock? Horror? Hatred? Disdain? Sympathy? I don't know. Then, he finally shakes his head gently and asks, "Why? Why did you?"

I shrug as I stand up, the sudden movement making me wobble. I want to storm around, stomping my feet, raising my fists, and railing about what she failed to contribute to our marriage, defensively claiming I wasn't all to blame. The silence endures. So much judgment. So much loneliness. But that's all a cop-out. Dustin won't buy it anyway. "I don't know," I finally mumble, and the sad, pathetic, worse truth is that I sincerely don't know why I did it.

"Is it an on-going thing?"

"No. It was a one–time mistake. Never again."

Dustin nods and says calmly, "Tell me about it. What happened?"

Staring at my brother, his caring words make a lump in

my throat, which threatens to suffocate me. I blink my burning eyes. "We can't have kids. It started... it started then. Everything that happened, well, it all started with that."

Dustin nods as he sits on the edge of the bed. "You never told me that."

"We never told anyone. She didn't want anyone to know."

"And you? What did you want?"

I stare at my brother, my face and mind blank. I have no idea what I wanted. We hadn't talked about it for many months now. I tried to ignore any feelings I had concerning it. Due to Natalie's history, she didn't want to adopt. She interpreted her inability to conceive a child of her own as an ironic sign that she wasn't supposed to have kids. Therefore, I was also not going to have kids.

I wanted kids. Badly. That's what first made us start trying. It was all because of me. And after we figured out it wouldn't be as easy or as natural as it was for most couples, I tried to be as kind and considerate as I could. She took the news pretty well and never seemed to dwell on it. But now? My mouth is hanging open as I realize I was never okay with it. I really wanted to discuss other options, any options with Natalie. But how could I insist when I didn't want to hurt her or make her feel any blame for it? She was okay about it, and let the matter go. But I'm realizing now, I was not okay, and I didn't let it go. Instead of facing it with her, I tried to pretend things were okay, when everything was actually all wrong after that.

I pretended we were focusing on enriching the lives we did have. We loved our jobs and the business of our lives. We loved being able to do what we wanted when we wanted to. The trouble is, I'm realizing now, it wasn't enough for me and yet I didn't tell her and I resented her deciding it for me. My anger built from that resentment until we stopped doing anything with each other after that. "I don't know what I want. Even if I knew, I'm not sure how I'd tell her."

He shakes his head and sighs. "You were always the smartest, savviest student and businessman in the room, but you never had a goddamned clue about your feelings."

He's right. I've never had a goddamned clue, and I have less of one now than before. I've completely demolished my life. I was never prone to self-destruction before. I don't have hidden addictions, or kinky fetishes. I don't secretly go off and gamble and have sex outside of my marriage has never been something I even considered. Yet, I did that. Clearly, with no real thought, I did that. And Dustin is right, I'm almost clueless about my reasons for doing so, more so than anyone. How can I figure out the best way to fix something when I can't even figure out what the problem is? And now that I've clearly divulged the huge disparity between us, how can I even begin to fix it?

CHAPTER 6

 AM

THE SUMMER I CAME home from college, before I started earning my MBA, she was there. With Dustin, of course. Those two hung out like dudes. Never once, to my knowledge, did anything romantic ever occur between them. Friends 'til the end. Not even a flicker of looks at each other, or flirting. Dustin was always kind of methodical, and easy to be with, and he let me and Natalie occupy the forefront. We both had dominant personalities that took front stage to Dustin's quiet steadiness.

The summer I went back home, I was coming down off the high of college life. College went well for me. I earned excellent grades, and made even better connections. The freedom of being away from our street on one end of Mission District was heady and intoxicating. I didn't often reveal my upbringing, or mention where I came from. I could play the part of a preppy guy with no worries, monetary or otherwise. I got pretty good at pretending I had more money and higher social status than I actually did. After befriending the guys in a popular fraternity, I made the kinds of connections that would lead to my future success. One guy in particular stands out.

And that of course was Jayden Hall. He was the typical president of the fraternity, earned straight As, and his dad ran a huge firm. Those were all the buzz words I needed. The firm was named BorderLine Solutions, which managed the investment portfolios for dozens of highly visible millionaires and billionaires. They handled the fortunes for individuals, families and corporations whose fortunes were made off of anything from inherited riches, international banking to large retail stores. When I graduated, Jayden recruited me to start working for his dad's company. At that point, I said no. I intended to move to Los Angeles and finish my MBA at UCLA, after which I planned to get a job there. I also had a few other job prospects in mind from an internship I did a few summers back.

But when Natalie's mom died, she had a mini-emotional breakdown, and I ended up in San Francisco, eventually taking Jayden up on his offer. Jayden was already one of the executives, but having his endorsement, along with my natural intelligence, hard work, and charisma, I managed to go pretty far. Starting as an investor and paper pusher at the age of twenty-three, I was fresh out of college. Sure, I had visions of dollar signs hanging in front of my eyeballs. I was motivated and unabashedly ambitious. I had so many things I wanted to do, and buy, and status I wanted to obtain. It wasn't just about material possessions and greed. I wanted to do something significant with my life. I wanted my work and my life to matter. I wanted to achieve the status that went with being an executive. I longed for the lifestyle as much as I wanted the salary.

Jayden became my mentor, colleague and friend. I trusted his advice. Jayden taught me how to dress, where to shop, and what shoes to buy. I knew nothing at the time. I had to study and learn about all the things that Jayden was weaned on. Things like how to behave and entertain others with polite, innocuous conversation. And the country club? That was a foreign language to me. I studied men's magazines just to try and remember all the hot brands and designer names and stupid, uppity shit like that. It was all new for me. Jayden knew his stuff and didn't steer me wrong. I spent a lot of my time learning how to be a member of the elite class that Jayden inherited at birth.

It worked. I soon started to garner attention and interest. I worked harder than anyone. I was the most detailed-oriented, and also an out-of-the-box thinker. Some of my ideas earned the company big money. Always an attention-getter, my clients trusted me. Perhaps my greatest asset was that women liked to flirt with me. Their mild attraction toward me and coy flirtation often landed me clients I might not have otherwise appealed to. Even the men seemed drawn to me. They were mostly older, corporate types who saw me as a younger version of themselves. I was "mentored" by about half a dozen different clients. Of course, they never knew the others were also "mentoring" me, and they seemed to find that role flattering. Again, my desire to become their case manager was owing to my gift for schmooze. Maybe I'm downright manipulative, but I prefer to call it charismatic.

All the while, I started what I call my crash-course in behaving as if I were born to wealth and privilege. I tried to smooth out all my rough edges.

I became brilliant at it. Except for one thing: I was soon married to the roughest, least smooth and anti-privileged woman I knew. When Jayden met Natalie, he told me quite pointedly I needed to ditch the foul-talking, crass wife, and I quote him: "destined to become a spokeswoman for blue-collar workers everywhere." And yeah, Natalie was kind of like that. She supported unions and fought for the people who worked in manufacturing jobs. She couldn't have cared less about hanging around the upper executives who ran them. She never met one she wanted to impress. Me included. But she especially didn't care to impress my boss, and my friend, Jayden Hall.

Jayden was equally opposed to her. From the very first dinner we all shared together, those two hated each other, like rabid dogs fighting over the same piece of meat. The meat, of course, was me in that scenario. Natalie wanted me to remain humble, caring about people in general, not just for profit. Jayden, meanwhile, wanted me to drop the hindrance he called "Natalie." She was, too. She *was* a total hindrance.

But I swear, I never cared. I think that's why I loved her so much and what attracted me to her. Her moral compass points true north, no matter what, all the time, regardless of the situation, or the people she is with. Whether addressing the local garbage man, or the President of the United States, Natalie would act the same with either person. Status, money, and all the other symbols of success to which I measured myself and my life meant nothing to her. They were just silly little *symbols.* The house we shared? She always resisted it, hating it from the start. Nothing and no one could sway Natalie from being who she was and doing what she thought was right. Me? Not so much. I often tend to waffle. I conform. I can be the good, old, white boy at those snobby country clubs one evening, and hanging with my brother, old friends, and Natalie at some little hole-in-the-wall dive bar the next. I enjoy both worlds.

Jayden spent a lot of time trying to discourage me from pursuing Natalie. I finally put my fist in his gut, and thought he'd fire me on the spot. Instead, to my surprise, he slapped me on the back of my shoulder in a good-natured *man-bump.* "Fine. Fine, you win. Natalie it is."

And so it was. It was always Natalie. I was deeply in love with her and I think it might have happened when we were still kids. There was never anyone else, no other girl, teenager, and later woman could have ever touched my heart, my soul and my brain like Natalie. The others were all fun, but no more than easy distractions from the school work I took too seriously, or later, my job, where I worked too many hours. But Natalie? She fully engaged me. Always did. My heart, mind, soul and body. She had me captivated from the very beginning.

What happened then?

Life happened. Now as I sit staring down at the wood floors of my too expensive house, I realize I let life happen more than I let *us* happen.

I'm thirsty now. Food makes my stomach queasy. My eyes feel full of sand. I'm sure my breath is as sour and foul as it tastes. Dustin says to me, "Tell me from the beginning, how did you come to do this?"

As I begin to tell Dustin what I did, all the while, my mind is far away. I am remembering different times, better times, especially the first time Natalie and I ever knew there was something more between us. It's as if I can't stay focused on what my mouth is saying because it means I have to admit in my heart what I actually did.

THE SUMMER we first got together was when I came home from college. Before I even arrived however, I ran into a girl I vaguely remembered. Her name was Jennifer something. I can't recall it now. She batted her big eyes, and giggled a lot.

When I asked her to come over and *catch-up,* it quickly became a kissing scene on the couch. She was blonde and pert, my favorite type of girlie-girl, and she smelled good. My parents weren't expected home until dinner. I had no idea where Dustin was. But the damn front door burst open and there she was.

That annoying, pesky, tomboy, neighbor girl. There was Natalie, scowling at me and nearly snarling at the girl. Jennifer kind of cowered and backed down in embarrassment. Natalie's look was so mean. I glared at her and she swiftly retreated into my brother's room. I was a little surprised she left without much more of a fuss.

Well, imagine how quickly that threw a huge wrench of *unsexy* into our catch-up session! Jennifer only stayed a few more minutes, which were filled with awkwardness. I shut the door after her, running my hands through my hair and seething at my little brother's stupid tag-a-long.

I came out eventually when my parents get home. Full of smiles and hugs, Mom cried how happy she was to see me. The last time I was home, I only spent three days there at Christmas. I was too busy. I had friends, parties, and dates to escort.

But now I had the summer off before returning for my MBA. A summer to take a break, party, and relax before my real life began. Even though I really didn't want to hang around the old, broken, rundown neighborhood, at that point, I didn't have any money. I did have a shit-brick of college loans and ambitions, and that's all I had.

When my brother's door opened, Natalie came out. She felt more comfortable in my apartment and being around my parents than I did. I felt awkward, and out of place. Sort of like I touched the sun and now was relegated to living back on the dark side of the moon as some kind of punishment.

Natalie, meanwhile, was invited to dinner the very night I

was back. I held in the groan. As long as I was there, I wanted to enjoy my family. Without her. I did not want to share my time with my old kickball and jogging partner.

I glared at her again. Now twenty, and out of high school, she hadn't changed much. Always with the thick ponytail of dark hair, she was just lucky to be so naturally pretty. She never wore a speck of makeup or hair products. I'd have been shocked to see her put a comb near that thick, frizzy mat of hair she had. Her huge, dark eyes and smooth, brown skin enhanced her tall, thin, muscled body. Her biceps were more cut than mine.

I didn't see her last Christmas. She had changed somehow since last I saw her. I didn't know if it was just female maturity or what, but there was definitely something more startling about her face. That evening, we all stayed up late. My parents listened to me talk about school with rapt attention. Dustin too. Natalie stayed, and I remember thinking how badly I wanted her to go home so I could relax and just be with my family. After all, it didn't happen very often.

My parents soon grew tired and went off to bed. It was just the three of us and we soon became quiet. Dustin started to doze and shuffled off to his room sometime around midnight, leaving only Natalie and me. We were watching the late night comedy show, but hardly a laugh did either of us utter at the comedian's monologue. She finally glanced over at me and said, "They really miss you."

"That's why I'm here." I replied, my tone laced with grumpy guilt. I knew that. I was too busy to bother to come home before. True. They understood that and forgave me. Now this rug-rat neighbor girl thought she could give me crap over it?

"Why didn't you come home?"

"I was busy. College isn't exactly like high school. Not that you'd know."

She didn't get offended. "No, God willing. They talk about you all the time. They are so proud of you. And yet, you're too busy to come home and appreciate that? Must be nice."

"Why do you care how often I see my parents?"

"Because it's just so stupid. What happened to coming home for a weekend here or there? You couldn't spare them that?"

I shifted around. Her criticism might have struck a little close to home. "No, I couldn't."

She turned her head and her eyes were filled with hate as she pinned me with her glare. "You are so selfish. You take them so much for granted."

"Yeah?" I remember fisting my hands. "And who, at age twenty–three, doesn't?"

"Those of us who are about to lose them, I guess!" she snapped.

I remember the rush of air escaping my mouth, almost like she had shoved her fist into my gut. She turned and bent at her waist before burying her face in her hands. She didn't make another sound. Her hair was in a ponytail that fell to the side over her shoulder, totally obscuring her face from me. I sat there, stunned, and eventually moved closer.

"Nat? Natalie? What is it? What's happening?"

She shook her head. She was staring down at her feet. I leaned forward so my hands could clasp her shoulders. For such a fit girl, she had narrow shoulders. She refused to lift her face and tried to push my hands away. She was so damn stubborn even then. She never shared her feelings. She was worse than any guy I knew. Especially if it were sad news. When she felt hurt, she always reacted with anger. It was the first time I truly understood that about her.

"Come on. I know you're crying. What the hell is going on? You have to tell me."

71

"Why do you even care? You leave without a backward glance towards those of us who might tarnish the new, shiny Sam Ford."

She always had me so damned pegged. And being like I was didn't live up to her ideals. "That's not true," I lied. Even if it shamed me to hear it stated so blatantly out in the open.

"You used to be my friend," she muttered.

"I'm still your friend. I've just been away at college. You're overreacting way too much over that fact." But nothing. Finally, I realized I had to goad her. I sighed. "Come on, why are you crying like such a girl on my couch? Are you on the rag? Did your boyfriend break up with you?"

She was too quick to respond. Turning in a flash, this time, she really socked me in the stomach before I could defend myself. I let out a surprised *oof!* Damn, the girl had some strength, no denying that.

"I do not cry like a girl!" she protested through gritted teeth.

She moved and was no longer in the protective position. I could tell her face was damp with tears. I was stunned. I'd never once seen her cry. Sure, I'd seen her turn three shades of red and go after more than one dude, and once even after a girl with her fists when she got upset or mad. But crying? Never. I sat back almost as if we'd exchanged an electric shock. Natalie crying like a girl? For real? I was almost speechless. She ducked her head down again and started shaking it.

"Come on, Natalie. What is it? What's wrong? I was just teasing you. What's going on?"

"You really don't talk to anyone, do you?" Her voice was muffled by her sweatshirt sleeve, which she tucked her face into.

"I—I have no idea." I guess I thought I did. But I knew of

no reason why that could make Natalie cry. Had anyone mentioned her to me in a year? I didn't think so.

"Did you know I'm going to be a cop?"

"No." I didn't know why that would make her cry either. It fit though. I could picture her long legs running through the field, or down the street with swift speed and accuracy along with all her other efficient skills. I could picture her smart mouth and attitude, going up against any number of opponents over the years. She could trash talk any NFL football player into shame. So yeah, it fit. "That's the perfect career for you."

"You didn't hear about the hold–up, then?"

"Like, a for real hold–up?"

"For real. It happened a few weeks ago. Gun and all. I hated feeling helpless, and knowing the criminal had us all at his mercy. There I was, unarmed, and without any training. It frustrated me that I was unable to do anything."

Knowing Natalie since her youth, I was well enough acquainted to realize that would've been the catalyst that pushed her forward. I could totally see her devoting an entire career to making her feel stronger and more powerful. Sure, helping people and all that too. I swiftly realized this was the essence of my tomboy friend. She was cursed with being female, which she considered physically weaker than males and something she constantly railed against. She couldn't tolerate feeling helpless, vulnerable or weak. So yeah, I clearly saw it. A cop. She would have the gun, training, authority and power. She wouldn't be the victim anymore, or the weak link. She would be part of the solution. That all made sense to me. What didn't make sense was why Natalie started crying about it that night.

"No more losing again to some guy 'cause he's bigger, right?" She lifted her face to catch my eye. There was something in it. An understanding seemed to ripple between us. She nodded.

"You remember that about me."

"I remember." Her eyes shone with tears, changing everything all at once between us. I stared at her. My heart suddenly beat faster and harder in my chest. My hand reached forward to touch her thick knot of hair and push it back. The gesture was an old one. When she was eleven, twelve, and thirteen, I'd often tug her ponytail just to annoy her. As she got older, it became a tug of brotherly affection. Her head turned a fraction of an inch toward my hand. Natalie was acquiescing to me. Remembering.

Tears started tracking lines down her cheeks. Her nose flared as she took in a breath, still holding my gaze captive. "Mom—"

She swallowed. I knew then by her hesitation it was bad. Like, death kind of bad. Natalie was a flaming firecracker. She didn't stall or hesitate, even when she was wrong, she always charged full steam ahead with it.

"I didn't know," I whispered. I instantly lost the ability to be cavalier, or share our normal banter. The thing with her was, we always interacted like two dudes in a locker room, throwing shit and trash at each other to show our affection; but also to convince each other that we weren't too crazy about the other.

"I haven't told anyone."

I didn't point out since no one else knew, they could not have told me. Therefore, my lack of interest in my own family couldn't have been the source of her anger now. But now I see clearly, this was the only way Natalie could allow herself to be vulnerable long enough to let something be wrong, when she shared it with another. This was Natalie having a heart–to–heart with me. And I starkly understood the weight of that gesture: *she chose me*. It meant something huge. It even suggested she had feelings for me. Finally, something beyond the locker-room dude smack we shared.

I leaned forward then and took her hand in mine. She jerked up and started to withdraw it. I tugged her forward so she was next to me and leaning into my chest. I had to wrap both of my arms around her to hold her there. She resisted. She even pushed against me. The only thing I had on her was brute strength. A fact she still refuses to accept. "Stop. Just stop fighting me, Natalie." I finally kind of shook her by holding her biceps in my hands as I pushed her back to stare into her face. "Please quit always fighting me. You don't always have to push everyone away. You especially don't have to be so tough with me."

She stared at me. The naked pain in her eyes was visible as her tears fell. She wiped her hand across her nose. No simpering. No gasping. She stared at me before offering a small, infinitesimal nod. I pulled her against me again. Minutes passed until she finally relaxed the rigidity of her body muscles. I was sure I'd never been this close to her for so long. Her hair sprouted up off her scalp and kept sticking to my lips. It smelled like shampoo. She was skinny and muscular and yet, there was something so feminine and lithe about her body pressed against mine. There was something so womanly. She most definitely wasn't another dude on me.

"What's wrong with her?" I asked after almost fifteen minutes of us sitting there in the quiet of my parents' apartment.

"Stage four colon cancer." Her voice was crisp and clear, but very quiet.

I squeezed her closer. My heart froze. I pictured her mom: a small woman with dark hair going gray at the roots. Her parents retired when she was still in high school. They were already in their mid-sixties by then. Both of her parents were reserved in their expressions and thoughts.

Natalie was like a huge boulder, gaining momentum and running over everything, while her parents were more like little pebbles that you walk past without ever seeing. They never seemed to question or regret how strong Natalie's personality was. She was loved and she loved them. I knew that. As clearly as I knew my parents loved me. We didn't all run around saying it every day, but it was just there. You know? Like breathing. You don't have to think about it, you just do it. It plays a huge part of your life. That's what my family did for me, anyway, and for Natalie too. But I see now that the concepts of immortality and happiness forever were meant for young idiots like me.

I can't believe Natalie was crying about her dying mother. We seemed too young to face such a possibility. Even as I know her parents are older than mine, it sends a sharp pang of fear down my back.

"Is there any…"

"No. Months at the most."

Silence. There was no need for platitudes with Natalie. My presence was all she wanted. Somehow I got that. As it was what I'd have wanted. We were often, to be honest, more alike than not in how we handle emotions, which was a little disconcerting during our adolescent years. She was a girl and I was a boy; and it never seemed normal to find so much kinship and understanding with the opposite sex. But we always remained friends. The best of friends. Dustin and she hung out together, but she and I were the two who completely understood each other. The endless races and games until long after dark not only proved who was faster, stronger, smarter, and better; but also that neither of us could admit defeat. Or give up. We got that about each other. When I did grow taller, stronger, and faster, I refused to let her win. I knew she'd have kicked in my balls if I ever treated her like a "girl." She, at least, demanded the respect of a fair game/run/contest no matter what we were doing. That never changed about her. Or me.

And then? What changed? Over the years, as we did things together, we sometimes had conversations that came to resemble two people sharing their honest feelings and real thoughts about each other. We often jogged together, or played catch, or kicked a soccer ball back and forth. During those private times we discussed things, *real things*, subjects that might have surprised anyone else. It was not often, but often enough that I shared some of my most intimate thoughts with her over the years. And she didn't fail to reciprocate in her own cryptic way.

I nudged her back a little so I could stare into her eyes. I needed her to be honest. Something felt different about it. Something felt more intense in a way I'd never noticed. Like, opposite sex kind of intense.

"Why didn't you tell Dustin?" I finally asked. It took a long while. The TV provided background noise. My voice was still a whisper. It was a small apartment. My room, Dustin's and my parents' bedrooms all opened into a little, tiny alcove. Only three steps away from it, and you found yourself in the kitchen, and further still, a dining room where a table was set up.

Her shoulders shrugged up and down in exaggerated motion like she was thinking hard about that, or perhaps avoiding the real reason altogether. "He's my friend. We don't talk about personal stuff."

Did she mean we weren't friends? It was ridiculous she'd even say that. It made far more sense for her to talk to Dustin because I was not around during the last four years. I remembered the last night we spent together before I left for my freshman year. We shot hoops until two in the morning. We didn't talk much, but got hot and sweaty as we tried to annihilate each other. She seemed especially aggressive that night until we fell to the pavement of the court and stared at each other. We made passing comments for another two hours and eventually hobbled home. Nothing profound was said or discussed. I didn't even mention I was leaving for college, yet there we sat together. I'd always been confused by our relationship; and unsure if our association should even be considered a relationship. She was just unlike the typical girl. She never talked like one, flirted like one, or even seemed to acknowledge she was one with me.

"You haven't talked to me for real in four years," I finally said. It was rare for me to share my thoughts with her now. Even rarer when I showed her my doubts.

"You haven't wanted me to."

"That's not true. You were…"

"What? What was I ever to you, Sam? Because you left all of us like we were dirt under your fingernails; you even seemed relieved to get rid of us."

"That's a load of bullshit, Natalie. I went off to college, sure, but I never treated my family or you like that. You have chip on your shoulder about me and you have for a long time. What is it? Because I got bigger? Stronger? It's human biology. I can't help it if you're a girl, whether you want to be or not. But you'll punish me for it, won't you? Friends? How do you figure?" She fidgeted next to me, and I knew I was agitating her. It stunned me when I finally figured it out. "Holy shit. It's because I left, isn't it? It's simply because I left here, and you perceived it as me leaving you?"

Her face was turning warm with blush and she shoved me off. "You don't know anything!"

All at once, I knew something. Something so far from what I ever considered: *Natalie liked me.* Her mother was dying and I was the one she told. This was Natalie, my diffi-cult, obstinate, rude, funny, brave neighbor girl. This was

Natalie telling me how she felt *about* me. Not just her mother. This was her way of reaching out to me.

"Don't I?" I said finally to the silence that grew taut between us. She hid her face from me, but it was due to her embarrassment this time, not grief. I'd never seen her hide, or cower, or avoid people or situations. Nothing. Never. She faced any bully with both fists clenched and her shoulders back, even if they were a foot taller and a hundred pounds heavier in muscle than she. But this? She was hiding her true emotions.

"Natalie?" My tone was soft, but clearly taunting her. "Can't you look at me?" She could never resist a dare. Not even an emotional one.

She raised her head and scoffed. "Duh. As if looking at your ugly face is hard."

I smiled. That was better than the tragic, embarrassed, suddenly girlie–acting Natalie. This Natalie, who was emotional, yet so valiantly tried not to be. This Natalie, who, for perhaps the first time ever, I noticed was a girl... a woman, warm and near me. I moved my hand almost by rote to her face. My palm cupped her cheek even as she stiffened at my touch and her gaze skittered off in a different direction. Wow! It was so weird for me to touch her like I would another girl. Like I was with Jennifer a few hours ago. But that was casual, easy, and almost flirting. So what if we kissed and cuddled? It didn't mean a damn thing beyond the confines of this afternoon, and a casual afternoon make–out session. But Natalie? It felt like my heart grew heavier in my chest. That was strange. And huge to me.

"I'm sorry," I said lamely after an almost embarrassed pause. We weren't good at this. We didn't know how to be caring or emotional or intimate with one another. Yet here we were, almost out of nowhere, trying to be. She told me something devastating, tragic, and truly horrific that she hadn't told anyone else. That meant something. I knew it clearly, as clearly as I knew her dark eyes and how she swung a baseball bat. I knew telling me was tantamount to another girl offering me her virginity, or her love. She was trying, albeit awkwardly, to connect with me, to let me know for some reason she needed *me*. It had been years since we'd done more than say *hello*, or pass through the same room together, always with my parents and brother close by. But here she was needing me, now. I never considered what moving beyond this might mean because until this moment, Natalie was just a girl I grew up with. Or at least, I pretended to think she was just a girl I grew up with, even though there was always something more between us. Whatever that was, it was eternally fierce. We were fierce rivals, fierce competitors, fierce friends, fierce teammates; whatever we were to each other was never casual.

I leaned forward and my lips touched her temple, half on her hairline and half on her skin. It was just a soft kiss of my lips to her head. I held her there and she kept her head tilted towards me. We paused that way for a long, sustained moment. Her face was looking down. This wasn't the fierce Natalie I knew and remembered. This was a timid, embarrassed, almost holding her breath Natalie. Perhaps more than anything she could say or do, that showed me there was something there I never dreamed of, or caught on to, or even wanted. But there it was. And here we were.

I just barely lifted my mouth off hers and brushed my lips towards her ear as I whispered, "I'm sorry." This time, I apologized because I never knew what was happening between us. This time, it was because I couldn't imagine losing my mom, much less fathom Natalie enduring the loss of her mom.

Tears once more gathered in her eyes and streamed down her cheeks. "I don't know how to let go of her."

Pain filled her voice. No long rants, or cries, or telling me how she felt. I knew that about Natalie. This was just as telling as most girls who break down. Somehow, seeing someone who was usually so strong and tough now crying and showing her soft side was much harder than observing it in anyone else. It clearly showed how big this was for her, and how far-reaching her grief extended.

There were no words for us. I knew that, and Natalie knew that. She lifted her eyes and we stared at each other. Her lips pressed together as she shook her head. Her eyes swimming in tears, this was Natalie talking to me; but mostly, *needing* me. The feeling of being needed by the strongest, most obstinate personality I'd ever encountered, male or female, was heady stuff. Like the President of the United States asking you for advice kind of heady. I think now, although I couldn't articulate it at the time, knowing that she needed me then might have been the biggest compliment of my life.

People like me. They think I'm fun and smart and want to hang out with me. But have any one of them ever needed me? Or sought me out, or my comfort, or maybe even my opinion or advice, as Natalie seemed to? Had I ever felt like my existence mattered to someone else's survival; let alone, to the extent they couldn't survive without my support? Until that moment, I never felt that sensation. I had no idea I even *wanted* to feel it. I had no clue how powerful the feelings it unleashed in my chest would be.

Her lips parted slightly as if she'd taken in a gasping breath. Her tongue came out and she touched her lips with barely the tip. I stared and she saw me staring. I lifted my hands and buried them under her hair, just behind her ears, pulling her face to mine and our lips touched for the very first time.

It was shocking. Pressing our lips together was like

offering newly planted seeds a glimpse of the sun, or pouring water on dry dirt. Everything seemed to bloom from that moment on. We were soft and easy at first, something Natalie and I never were before; but right then, we separated and stared at each other. I have no words for the way my breath caught in my chest. Our kiss seemed to hypnotize me. I'd never been kissed like that before. She leaned in and her hands cupped my face as she pressed her lips against mine, slipping her tongue inside my mouth. I closed my eyes and felt like I was falling into a deep, swirling hole. My stomach started pitching this way and that. My reaction to her kiss was like I'd never been kissed before.

Pressing my fingers into her scalp, I tried to make her mouth immobile under mine as the passion between us seemed to grow more intense. It soon became a fierce kiss of lips and tongue and teeth and most of all, us. So much of us. We did everything physically the same, so why not that too? We were all in, no matter what activity it might be. We were hard and demanding on each other without pause. This was how a kiss that mattered was supposed to feel like. It consumes and engages every part of you, from a physical plane to a mental and emotional dimension. I had never felt so engaged from a single kiss.

She moved up and straddled me. We were holding each other's heads. I linked one of my hands with hers and she gripped mine with the familiar strength and desperation I knew she was capable of. But instead of competing with me, now she was gripping me in an almost desperate grasp. What was she trying to hold on to? Her sanity? Her emotions? I didn't know exactly; I just knew how tightly and critically she was reaching out to me for whatever she sought.

We turned eventually and she lay on top of me. We kissed and kissed and kissed. It might have been an hour until somehow, it all kind of slowly ended. She lay on my body, warm, silent and content. Natalie was so rarely warm, silent or content. We fell asleep that night on my parents' couch. I was already long past the age of parental rules or concern. The next morning when I woke up with a kink in my neck, she was gone.

That kiss... never again has any kiss felt that good. Never again has any other woman kissed me like that. That kiss was the start of the rest of it... the rest of what I thought would be the relationship that lasted all of my life.

EXCEPT NOW, as my brother sits staring at me in reproach. All these years later. After something as innocent as a kiss was long buried in our history. I slogged through my pathetic story of how Natalie caught me at the office and the woman I was with. He didn't once interrupt me or try to chastise me. His facial expression didn't even change.

At the end, while I humbly sit in my underwear, he asks, "Well, what are you going to do about it? Give up?"

I glance up at Dustin. "What can I do? I don't even know where she is. And when I find out... what can I do?"

"Anything more than you are now. First, you find her, Sam. You know her better than anyone else. Figure it out. Figure her out like you used to. And what do you say? Whatever it takes. You say and do whatever it takes."

"What if it's still not enough?"

"For once, you'll have to make it enough, Sam."

"What do you mean, 'for once'?"

He shrugged before leaning against the wall, then came over and sat next to me. "I know you always worked hard and were ambitious, but it all came pretty easily to you. School. Friends. Girls. Even your job. But Natalie? She's never been easy for you. I always thought that was the draw, and half your problem with her. You need to figure out why you did this and tell her why you did it, then tell her what you intend to do to change it, or fix it, or what you should do together. But it's going to take all you've got. You owe each other more than calling yourselves names, or being holed up drunk without even an apology to her. Find out why you did it and fix it, Sam."

"I hear you. More than just an apology. But first, do you have any idea where she is?"

"None. She didn't answer my texts or calls and neither did you; that's why I came here."

I stare at my hairy legs. "Every person I think she might have gone to, I have to discard because they are connected to me, or our family, or her job. I doubt she'd go to any of them. It makes her too vulnerable. Too weak–looking. No tears with Natalie, and especially not with outside people."

"Anything change of late? Could she just be driving somewhere? She'd run. I think she'd run fast and hard from something like this. Imagine what she's got to be feeling; she can't handle that. You know it, and I know it. What else would she do, but try to ignore her thoughts, or else run from them?"

"Run from them. You're right," I agree, and my heart squeezes again, because my actions sent her off into the night, literally alone and running.

So she must be driving somewhere. She probably threw her phone out the window after I bugged her once too often. She would try not to think about me, or what she saw, or what it signified to her and her life. She would definitely never want to just stop and think about how it made her *feel*. Dustin was right, she had to be running.

Okay, so my wife is driving aimlessly around the state somewhere. And worse, she isn't one to do that. Natalie Ford always has a goal, a plan, a starting point and an ending point. She doesn't do anything without a reason for doing it.

I find it hardest of all to accept there's no way to predict where she'd run to.

Changes? Of late? No. But I might not know. Of course, there were all kinds of subtle changes. The kind that build on each other like the nacre in a pearl, layer upon layer, until what started as a small change becomes buried and frozen underneath all the layers. It finally obliterates the original source of irritation. What used to be good and true fast becomes false and negative; somewhere we got lost in it all.

The only two times I ever saw Natalie lose her composure was when her mom died and when we put her dad into the home. Those were the only times that iron will of hers slipped beyond her control. But this? This is way different because she has someone to blame. Me. The anger she harbors for me right now must be eating her alive.

Her mom... As my thoughts review Natalie's life, I am looking for any clue as to where she might be. I suddenly remember the other chip on Natalie's shoulder: someone abandoned her.

Someone with whom we'd recently connected.

Christina Hendricks in Ellensburg, Washington! I rise with confidence as if a lightning bolt just flew up my spine. *I know! I know where she is.* There is no doubt. That's where a running, scared, hurt, but unwilling–to–face–or–admit–it Natalie would flee to. I have something, an end point, a destination. My mission.

I forget my hangover, as well as my pathetic life and my guilt and shame. With renewed energy, I start hauling everything I need from the drawers and our closet. Dustin gapes at me before asking, "What? What did you realize?"

"I know where she is!"

"Where?"

"At her long-lost sister's. She's there. I know it."

I go to the bathroom, and stop. The mirror shows my

unshaven, unkempt reflection, and I stink. I have to clean up first. Frustrated, I start the shower.

"Are you sure about that? That you should go there?"

"Never more sure of anything in my life," I reply. Finally, I have a plan. I do well with plans. Something else Natalie and I share. We need a goal, a mission, and an endpoint. I just hope that this endpoint isn't the end of us.

CHAPTER 7

*N*ATALIE

FOLLOWING MAX SALAZAR'S CAR, we drive exactly twenty–three minutes. We start along the highway before passing the college and turning off onto increasingly rural streets the farther we go. Finally, we're on a two–lane road, traversing acres of empty land. Barns. Houses. Fields. Livestock. This is for real. We are truly in the middle of nowhere. We turn onto a single lane road that takes us through the woods before ending at a one–story house with outbuildings and fields of wildflowers beyond. Trees dot the land here and there, but the vast, open spaces keep it from being heavily forested. The house has an impressive entry that welcomes and almost beckons visitors inside. With great care and hesitation, I turn the car ignition off before opening my car door and stepping out. After all these miles, and years of questions, this is where it ends? My head feels overburdened and muddled. It's all too much. Sensory and emotional overload.

Here I am, on an ordinary Thursday afternoon, pulling into the home of the woman who gave birth to me? It feels completely unreal.

I often face situations with strangers as a police officer that are very much out of my comfort zone. Even everyday traffic tickets can place me in awkward or weird situations. Human behavior can be odd, scary, weird, crazy, gross, annoying, and often violent. Yes, some humans are genuinely good. Some are so respectful of my authority, they appear intimidated and can hardly look me in the eye. I also witness acts of strangers helping strangers, and those make me glad I'm human. Unfortunately, however, my job often makes me question what has become of the goodness that used to identify the human race?

None of that, however, could prepare me for this moment. I had no intention of meeting this woman only an hour ago. My "Sure, let's meet her," was merely a retort to Max's taunt. I did not give it enough thought or consideration. And now I was here. Doing something I just didn't know how to. What should I do? Just knock on the door, and say, "Oh, hey, long-lost mother... here I am?"

My attention returns to the presence of my mother's nephew/daughter's boyfriend. He parks and gets out of his car. There is no doubt how comfortable he feels here. He has no qualms about stopping by like this. I cannot believe I allowed myself to come *here*.

I assume he probably called her from the car. That would make sense. The front door clicks and starts to open. My heart nearly explodes with anticipation. I swear to God, my heart feels like it is detonating in my chest. My ears roar, my breathing increases rapidly, and my palms grow clammy. I can't focus, although my gaze is riveted, and I stare hard at the opening door.

And then... there she is. *My mother.*

No, *not* my mother. *My mother*, the mother I loved and the woman who raised me, is dead. The woman who stands before me is no more than blood and tissue. The source of my life, yes, but not the person who took responsibility for it. Before me stands just a woman. A woman with no real significance in my life. I must cling to that thought. I have to cling to it.

I'm fine. I'm fine, I mentally chant. I finally command my racing thoughts and heart to slow down. Shut the fuck up! *I am fine.*

I'm simply meeting a woman named Jessie Hendricks.

She shuts the door behind her and leans back onto it. She is wearing ordinary clothes. I mean, what did I expect? A ball gown, or fancy suit, out here in middle of nowhere, on a Thursday? It's not like we planned this encounter. No getting all spiffed up for a proper introduction. I glance down at myself, feeling road weary. My jeans are crumpled, torn and frayed on my thighs and under the knees, as well as faded and old. I wear a dark gray jacket over several t–shirts and tanks that I've layered. My hair is a heavy hunk that I hastily wrapped up on top of my head.

Jessie wears slacks, the kind of dressy–for–work black pants I would not be caught dead in. She is average weight, with large breasts. Her blouse is muted in color. She wears a loose scarf, which she knots elaborately around her neck. It's splashed in a rainbow of colors. She has shiny, black, straight hair that ends at her shoulders. She's pretty. Even from a distance the length of my car and ten feet of pavement, I can tell that. I don't know what I expect. A series of distorted, grotesque images fill my mind. *Fat. Slothy. Pristine.* I don't know, but I don't expect her to look the way she does. I don't know if I'm disappointed or glad.

Christina is breathtakingly similar. That fact becomes clearly evident after only thirty seconds of scrutiny between us. Jessie's face is solemn, serious and strained. Locking her jaw, she rivets her eyes on mine.

I step back, still holding her gaze, just as unfriendly and serious as she appears, and push my car door closed. It echoes with a "clonk" that all of us hear. Max walks towards Jessie, thankfully coming between us.

When he reaches her side, he leans in with a quick hug, and says something into her ear. She nods, breaking eye contact with me to respond to him. I think she takes some small comfort in Max's reassuring and familiar presence. Then, he goes around her, entering the front door and shutting it.

We are alone.

I step forward. Standing there, frozen in place, is a sure way to convey how scared I am. Not acceptable. She ditched me! She abandoned me! She should be miserable! Not I. She should be ashamed and nervous and horrified. Not I. My righteousness boosts my courage. I suck in a breath and force myself to walk the symbolic distance it takes to reach her.

What does a woman feel upon seeing the baby she once gave birth to and subsequently abandoned? Is Jessie overwhelmed with regret? Longing? Relief? Hatred? Is she glad I am alive and well? Or does she wish she aborted me to avoid this critical moment almost thirty years later?

There is no feeling of instant connection. As I look into her eyes, no sudden, overwhelming sensations of love or daughterly affection fill me. I don't really feel anything. She's just a woman. I'm a woman and we are looking at each other. That's all I feel.

But still, it's so awkward that it's painful. Jessie finally approaches me, away from the safety of the front door. She's shorter than I am. She tilts her head back just enough, and a chill runs down my spine. I can't believe I'm here. Doing this. Today.

"Hello, Natalie."

So, so simple, isn't it? After all these years, the most simple of greetings. Yet, it's also kind of epic. As far as I know, she never heard my name until about a year and nine months ago. I sort of put together that Christina found out about me, and insisted on hunting me down. Not Jessie. Not this woman. So really, it's rather epic that after several decades, she now knows my name. She is standing before me, offering the most ordinary greeting one can say to any stranger. *Hello.*

"Hello..." I almost blurt out *Mrs. Hendricks.* Or should I call her Jessie? I have no idea what to call this woman. "What shall we do now? Introduce ourselves?" I try to ignore the banal greetings. I'm tired of pretending like this is all normal and shit. It's so not normal. I can't bear to pretend it is for another second.

A small, barely-there smile lifts the corners of Jessie's mouth. Okay, she might get sarcasm. Maybe there is some humor inside her.

"Or did you want to pretend to welcome me here?"

Her eyebrows rise. "You're not unwelcome here."

"Let me guess? For Christina's sake?"

She nods. "Yes as well as... *yours.*" She adds the "yours" softly. Like she just barely dropped it in there.

I search her face. Yes, naturally I'm looking for any indication of similarity to mine. Our eyes are similar. Same shape, same shade of brown. Our hair too, same color, texture and thickness. Like Christina's. I noted that when we met. But Christina's was brown, not black. And Jessie's? My exact shade of black. "She found me all on her own, didn't she? You never looked for me, did you?"

Silence as she considers me. Perhaps she's trying to

decide how honest to be. Finally, she gives a small nod. "No. I never did. I didn't know your name until after Christina went looking for you."

I want to ask so many things… Like, didn't her heart twist? Or did she ever long or want to know me? Especially after hearing that her daughter, whom she seems to have legitimate feelings for, was looking for me, didn't this woman want to know what happened to her firstborn? In many ways, it might have helped if she were a strung–out drug addict or mental patient, drooling in a dark corner, or even a nasty, mean drunk, spouting obscenities at me, and yelling at me to *Get out!* Then I'd know it was because of her, and not me that she decided to give me up.

But this? She seems so normal. Nice. I know nothing, of course; and being a cop, I'm fully aware of what nice exteriors can hide. All kinds of nasty. But this time, I think I was expecting some of the nasty to be more apparent.

It means, she chose not to keep *me.*

"She showed up at my house out of absolutely nowhere. You didn't send her there. She admitted that much."

"She was mad at me for hiding your existence. She believed you two could forge some kind of relationship. She is smart and resourceful. But she surprised even me in how she actually found you. She had a family friend hack into old records of the place where I gave birth to you. She deduced which one was you, and managed to track you down through that small piece of information."

A weird shudder travels over my body. I never expected her allusion to the circumstances of my birth only minutes after meeting me.

"Did Max tell you I was coming?"

"Yes, but I asked Max to try and convince you to come here."

"Why?"

"For all of us, I think. You exist. You are here. Christina knows about you, and my other two daughters will find out soon enough. I expect you have a lot of questions. Why don't you come inside, and I'll try to answer them?"

I stay rooted to the spot. *Is this woman for real?* She intends to answer everything I've wanted to know? After all these years of knowing nothing, can it all be revealed in a single afternoon? I can't believe it could be so freaking easy.

Except there is not one easy thing about any of it.

Compliantly, I follow Jessie inside. The interior is spacious and homey, appearing comfortable and well cared for. It's four times as large as the apartment I grew up in. Does that mean anything? Not really. I don't feel bitter about having just enough while growing up. We were working–class poor. We always had just enough, and not a bit more. But I was *loved,* and wanted, dearly. I was cared for and was shown by example how to work hard. I loved the neighborhood that became as much a part of my personality as my IQ, or my skin color, or my hatred of onions.

I don't bother with idle comments. Max isn't inside there. I guess I thought he'd be waiting for me. Jessie walks forward and invites me to sit down. I choose the breakfast bar where she's gone to the kitchen counter, to what? Get coffee? Make this all nice and civilized? I sit on the rotating bar stool and watch her. I refuse to be relegated to the living room like a formal guest. I'm definitely not that, nor am I a casual friend stopping by. So what am I?

She serves me a cup of coffee, and I wonder why she assumes I drink it. It's still warm from the coffee maker. I grip it in my hands, glad to have something to do, and idly play with the handle before taking a breath. Jessie turns and leans back against the counter. She hooks her hair behind her ear, then presses her hands flat on her thighs. "I don't

93

know what to say to you. Do you want to ask me something? We could start there?"

I also don't expect her to let me ask questions. I shrug listlessly as if it's never occurred to me until now that I'm in the presence of my birth mother to ask why the hell she gave me away when I was only days old.

"Were you young when you had me?"

"Twenty–one. Matter of opinion if that's young or not. I wasn't sixteen, or anything like that."

"Married?"

She hesitates. "Yes."

"To my… father?"

"No. Will."

"Will Hendricks?" *As in, the guy she's married to now?* This isn't a scenario I ever considered. Could it be as simple as she cheated on Will? And to save her marriage, she gave me up? I shudder in disgust. It's so close to why I'm here. My head immediately bounces back to now. *To Sam. To Sam and that strange woman. On the desk. He's moving… he's inside her. He's—*

No. I have enough trauma to deal with.

"You cheated on him?"

"No. I was pregnant when we got married."

Oh. Okay. So… what? Will just couldn't handle it? I instantly hate the smug SOB who wouldn't have me because he came into the picture after I was conceived.

"Do you know who my real father is?" I ask, cutting to the chase. I guess there are any number of reasons why a mother would give away her baby, and maybe they're valid. Maybe not so valid. Right now, I need a fact. I need something concrete I can grab on to.

She shakes her head in denial and my heart sinks. "I'm sorry, Natalie, but I'm afraid I don't know the true identity of your father."

I stare at her in disbelief. A one–nighter? After all this

time, I'm simply the unwanted by-product of the oldest story there is? A one-night-stand that turned into a life-changing mistake?

I try not to judge. I fully support the idea of women sleeping around just as often and with as many partners as society approves of men having. I just didn't expect it was the most ordinary reason of how I got here and why she didn't want me.

"I see."

She shrugs, and her lips compress into a tight line. "It's not easy to hear the truth."

"Is that why you never told your kids? You were embarrassed?"

She stares right in my eyes. "Yes."

"Your husband was with you when you gave me up?"

She sighs. "No, we separated and divorced for a while afterwards. We didn't remarry until later."

"So... I was just the result of a hook-up gone wrong?"

Silence stretches between us. I sense she must be working very hard to keep her facial muscles from twitching. She is visibly concentrating on retaining her composure and remaining unfazed and neutral. I don't know why, or what it might possibly mean. "Yes."

She is terse and succinct. To the point. There are no ugly details, but she seems honest enough.

"You don't even have a remote idea of who my father is? It's a small town, I mean..."

I'm desperate. And surprised at how badly I want to get a name.

She shakes her head. "It wasn't here. We lived on an Army base in North Carolina."

That only spawns a million more questions to ask. How did you end up *here*? Why did she live on an Army base? Who was she? What was her life like then? What is it like now?

How did she feel when she found out she was pregnant with me? How did she feel when Christina found out about me? I shake my head, physically ordering myself to *stop*. There is no reason for this sudden hunger for more details. She is a woman I know nothing about. And should or will never know. "A soldier?"

"No. Not a soldier, Natalie." Her tone of voice is freakishly calm. *She must be struggling,* I think, *to remain so stoic.* She holds my gaze, but offers no smiles to me.

"So… just some guy? You met him at a bar or something?"

"I really don't know who fathered you. I'm genuinely sorry I can't give you anything more."

I suppose it must be hard. Being middle–aged and seemingly respectable now, having to relive a past she obviously wasn't proud of and which ultimately resulted in me; sure, I see her discomfort.

"You didn't tell Christina that story, did you?"

"No. I didn't tell her."

"I imagine that would have been awkward."

"What's not awkward about this?"

"Nothing," I finally concede. She might have done the deed, but I was suffering for it too. I wished she would feel physical discomfort, if only because it was that way for me too. I stare at my fingers clasped on the counter before me, my best effort to stop fidgeting. No surer way to betray me than expressing my nervous anxiety and true feelings by fidgeting.

She glances at the clock over my head. "My daughters will be home from school in half an hour. Would you like to meet them?"

I shrug. *Do I?* I could walk out the front door immediately and drive away from here. I could take along the mental picture of who and what my mother is. I know her name, her house, her voice. I know something about myself now. It fulfills some of my longing and lifelong questions. My bio-dad, however, seems like a dead end. I know that for sure now. At least, I have more information than I did this morning, and more answers than I've had in a lifetime of questions. I could let this be done. And let this lifelong fiasco rest. I could go back to Sam and try to face what I should be dealing with.

Thinking of Sam, I reply, "How do we do that? They don't know about me."

"I can simply introduce you as a friend of Christina's. They are fourteen and fifteen. They won't overthink it too much."

"Do you want me to? It seems rather odd to me that you'd even offer."

"I've hidden your existence from everyone for a lot of years. Decades, really. It was almost a relief for me when Christina finally discovered you. Now? I know the answer isn't to continue hiding it. I will tell them, eventually, but only after they can process what I did and hid from them. You saw how far it wigged Christina out."

She doesn't seem such a terrible mother, and I really don't know how I feel about that. I mean, it's not like I want her kids to be miserable, or for her to be a bitch, or obviously flawed right off, but it also doesn't fit with some of my long-held fantasies about her identity. Do I want to pursue this by meeting more of them? *More sisters?* It feels surreal. I was raised as an only child. I was lonely until I met the Ford brothers. And then? They became my family more than any real siblings could be.

Before I can answer, Max strolls out from the hallway. He stops at the end of the bar and casually leans on it, studying each of us. "So Christina will be here in about an hour. Tell me you'll stay that long, at least?"

"I... guess so." They both nod their heads, and I can see

my reply pleases Max, but Jessie? She isn't rude, but she isn't especially nice either. She doesn't really want me here. I think she's paying penance by suggesting she tell her other kids, and only because her back is against the wall. I see the strain in the tiny muscles around her mouth as she listens to Max. *She has to do this,* if only for her other kids.

Sisters? I try to formulate what that is like, and what it means. *Are we sisters?* Would it change anything? Especially finding out so late in my life. It's not so late in the younger ones' lives. But Christina definitely thinks it matters. I can't believe she's dropping everything to drive over here.

Max nods. "Good, cuz I think she skipped out on her last final."

Jessie groans. "She can't do that!"

"You think you could talk her out of it?" Max raises his brows at Jessie as if she just suggested they take a quick shuttle trip to the moon. Jessie sighs and nods. I watch them. There is a visible comfort and ease between them, even though the kid dates her daughter. *Interesting.*

I have to admit, if not for Max, I really doubt I'd be sitting in my mother's kitchen. I actually once considered they were racists who didn't want me because of my ethnicity. But Jessie seems to embrace Max, and approves of him dating her pristine, lily-white daughter; while Max acts so blasé and like it's normal for him to be so readily accepted. And I haven't forgotten that Max dared me to come there. I don't back down to a direct challenge. Probably a not-so-attractive quirk of mine.

"Natalie?" I shift my gaze back to Jessie, who is wiping off the counter. "I know this must be hard for you, being one against us all, but why don't you stay for dinner? I think with all that's going on now between us, and the girls, please, just stay for dinner. You're already here. You found us, and I think for making that effort, the least that needs to happen is for all of us to spend a few hours together. Perhaps then, we could all relax and let things unfold a little more naturally."

She's right. I nod and agree. It will be awkward. I feel very alone amidst all of them, but I'm here. And I'm doing it, so why not do it full on?

Max grins. "I agree, but only if Will cooks. Something tells me there is no way Natalie could be a vegetarian." Rolling his eyes, his smile is teasing as he says, "Jessie and Melissa, she's the middle girl, you'll meet her, are total vegetarians. The rest of us insist that Will always cooks when we come over. He sure can grill a mean steak."

Jessie's unexpected smile is like a beam of sunlight after a showery, dark day. I see the relief as the lines of her face relax. Max is familiar and obviously makes her feel grounded. I think he's doing it on purpose too. I get it, but kind of resent it. I'm the awkward outsider, and that's solely because of Jessie. I don't belong here. I have never met my own blood relations because of her, and now she's beginning to feel more at ease.

"How did you know?" I ask the kid.

He shrugs with a cocky grin. "You strike me as a girl who appreciates a good steak. You look like you work out and lift weights. I bet the last girlie thing you did was probably wear a wedding dress. I get it. I like it. I'm into that stuff too."

"You're more than into it," Jessie scoffs as she turns.

Max ducks his head as if embarrassed and gives me a little, helpless smile. "I used to fight a lot."

"He used to be a regular in a fight club. And if you ever do that again, you'll wish one of those losers you went up against got to you before Christina or I do."

He rolls his eyes with a good-natured shrug. She pretends to be kidding, but her warning is serious. I sit back, content to witness the microcosm of their lives. I know nothing about them, or what makes them tick. I probably should, biologically speaking. But I don't. I don't know how to feel around them. Max's presence and light humor take some of the pressure off. Otherwise, this momentous occasion would overwhelm me for sure. A sense of panic enters my head and the need to ask as many questions as I can think of. My mission is to gather information, but I almost don't know where to start.

I'm wound too tightly. I feel out–of–body weird.

Jessie is busy washing the vegetables she just pulled from the fridge and Max says, "Jessie? The steaks?"

Over her shoulder, she rolls her eyes and replies with mock–exasperation, "Fine. Will can grill them. But we will have some vegetables and rice as side dishes. I hope you like that?" The question is directed to me over her shoulder. Naturally, she wouldn't know because she never fed me. *Not once.* For a second, a weird flash of déjà vu fills my brain and I have to lower my eyes and stare at the countertop. I so easily recall seeing my own mother years ago, turning to listen to my day at school as she washed vegetables for my dinner. My mother, who knew I would never touch the onions Jessie is now so busily setting out on a cutting board. My real mother knew I couldn't even stand the smell of them, and consequently never allowed them in the house.

But Jessie isn't my real mom. I mutter, "That's fine."

The sound of thumping causes Max to straighten up. "Cousins are home."

"*Your* cousins?" I ask, an edgy tone to my voice.

Max grins and shrugs. "Yup. *My* cousins."

"But Christina isn't? How does that work?"

"Very strangely," Jessie interjects as she dries her hands on a dishtowel. She skirts around the bar and I wait for her to reprimand me with some kind of warning that I should not upset her younger daughters. Or tell me to behave myself. Or forbid me from telling them the truth of my identity… just something. But instead, she presses her lips together and says, "I hope this is okay? If we are deluging you with too much too soon, please tell me."

"No, I'm here. I guess…"

"You'd like to see?"

"Yes, I'd like to see." Jessie holds my gaze and we share a long look for the first time I almost think some kind of understanding could exist between us. She finally shakes her head, as if reminding herself to stay in the moment. She turns when the entry is suddenly filled with loud voices and shuffling.

In walk two young girls, both slim and adolescent. One has dark hair, the other blonde. They eagerly deposit their backpacks and coats, while kicking off their shoes carelessly. Without even glancing around, neither seems to notice the three of us adults sitting there.

"I can't believe you said that in front of him! I mean, he's going to think I like him or something. You're so dumb."

"No, I'm the smart one; everyone knows that. He doesn't like you anyway. He's—"

"Girls?"

One word and both teens whip around to face Jessie. She stands there quietly, her hands on her hips, her mouth pursed and both eyebrows raised. Only a low, quiet *Girls* could end their adolescent bickering. They immediately straighten up and look around, finally taking in Max and me.

"Mom! What are you doing home so soon?" the blonde replies. Now her voice sounds polite and sweet, despite insulting her sister over how smart she was only a half second before. She smiles and so does the brunette.

So soon? I guess I assumed Jessie's always here. I glance at her and she shakes her head.

"Something came up. I was home for lunch when I got a call from Christina's friend, Natalie. I didn't go back in to

101

work. Girls, I'd like you to meet someone if you can quit being rude and horrible to each other. Do I miss this pleasure every afternoon?"

They glance at each other and their guilt is clearly on their faces. Our cars are parked out front, so I'm a little surprised how unaware they seem to our presence. I suppose they are just teens who don't think beyond what they're doing. I remember Sam, Dustin and me, coming and going from each other's apartments after school. My heart squeezes with nostalgia. We were always talking that way to each other. Usually, Sam would try to get me going by saying what I could not do. He was always implying, and quite convincingly at times, that it was because I was a girl. I reacted by spending the next few hours proving him wrong. I was hell-bent to demonstrate I could do anything he could. Screw boys! My heart aches now as I slide to my feet. All the fond memories I have of Sam are flooding my brain. What upsets me more? Meeting my long-lost sister and mother? Or surviving the betrayal of the boy I once adored, trusted and loved?

"This is Melissa and Emily. Girls, this is Natalie. Natalie is the friend Christina went to see in San Francisco the summer she graduated." I glance up, startled at Jessie's comment, and she widens her eyes, squeezing her shoulders together as if to convey she is trying not to lie.

"Hi," both girls chorus. Their gazes settle on me for only a moment, but I instantly sense there is nothing all that compelling about me to them. Unlike my interest in them, theirs is only casual disregard. I stare at each one in turn, searching again for any recognition, or feeling of connection. Or resemblance. But I don't see it. They don't even look like Jessie. Not like Christina does.

"Hey. Nice to meet you." I try to keep my voice casual, easy, the same way a teen might respond. I often deal with adolescents, and I know sounding proper, mannerly and old immediately disqualifies me from being at all interesting.

Passing by me, they start talking with Max, who easily engages both of them. They eventually start foraging for snacks and drinks, talking over each other with their mom or Max, and even me. All about the dramas of high school. One girl's a freshman and the other is a sophomore. I listen to them, trying to believe they are my *sisters.*

Emily asks, "So are you staying for a while? I mean, that's a long way to drive, isn't it?"

"Yes, it is. I have no plans. Just, uh, you know, taking a short vacation."

"Yeah? From what?"

"I'm a cop." All eyes turn towards me with unmasked, avid attention.

Emily exclaims, "Really? That's so cool."

Melissa watches me a little closer. "Like for real?"

And Max grins. "Lucky you didn't know me way back when."

Melissa thumps the back of his head. "What? Like two summers ago? Didn't you fight your last one just before school started?"

He laughs and shrugs. There is an easy affinity here. I can feel the positive energy in the house, and so far, it's natural and real. The only person who seems uptight and to be acting strangely is Jessie.

"You ever shoot anyone?" Emily asks.

I swear, that's every teenager's first question for me. I shake my head. "No."

"Taser?" Melissa asks in rapid succession.

I smile with indulgence. "Yes, I actually have done that."

"So cool!" Emily hops off the bar stool. She's suddenly more animated and talks with her hands. "Like this?" She pretends to convulse on the kitchen floor and soon has Max laughing with her. Melissa and Jessie roll their eyes. I start to answer when the front door swings open with an audible creak and Christina rushes in. Her sisters are still laughing while pretending to tase each other. Of course, I see Christina and she immediately finds me. We stare at each other from across the room. Christina isn't smiling. She is pale and her eyes are wide and huge. God, she's an incredibly beautiful girl. She might be one of the prettiest teens I've ever met. No wonder Max started dating his cousin!

She stares at me and a weird silence descends over everyone when the girls notice their older sister is home unexpectedly and acting so strange. She's like a glacier, crawling between us, and freezing the air all around her. She steps in further, shutting the door behind her without looking at it.

"I can't believe you're here." Her gaze is riveted on me as if she thinks I might disappear.

I lift my hands, palms up, as if to say *Who knew?* "I'm here."

We stare at each other a bit longer and then, Christina shakes her head. "I hoped, no, I prayed I'd see you again. But I never dreamed that it would be in my own living room."

Or on a random afternoon, almost evening, on a Thursday. I know. I almost echo her sentiments. I feel the same way.

"What made you come?"

She does not spare a glance to anyone else. Not her mother. Not her boyfriend. Not her sisters. Just me. I am very important to her for some reason. I start to realize this as her gaze stays fastened on me. I can't tell the truth of why I came, but she is visibly waiting for an explanation. I lie. "Curiosity."

Melissa's eyes alternate between us. She steps forward, her interest now focused on her older sister. "Who is this, Tiny? Why are you acting so weird about her coming here? Isn't she your friend?"

Christina glances over Melissa's head to Jessie. I can see them sharing a deep, intense look, a mental discussion, a total understanding. They are that in sync. That close. My heart thumps. Screw this! I don't need to witness that, do I? But then again, what do I care if they are so close? What are they saying? Whatever the girls picked up on, I'm something much more serious than a friend.

"She's not my friend," Christina finally answers before riveting her gaze back on me. No. No way could we claim friendship. I doubt I'd let her say more than four sentences to me when we first met before I threw her out. We don't know a damn thing about each other, except that we co-exist.

"Christina." It's Max's voice behind me, low, deep and full of warning. He walks around me to her side and gently touches her lower back with his hand. "Not like this." She doesn't spare him a glance. All her attention remains on me. *Whatever.* Christina seems more hostile than I expected. I thought she'd be practically throwing her arms around me in gratitude for coming there and having us all together. My first impression of her was that she appeared pretty innocent, naive and almost bubbly in her eagerness to know me. Not so today.

She doesn't trust me. Something must've tipped her off about me. I think she's feeling protective of Jessie from me. I'm shocked; she was the one who tracked me down. Now I return the favor and she worries I'm suspiciously after them?

"You came after me," I finally say gently. She's just a girl. I mean, she's maybe all of twenty and although she lives away from home, and has a boyfriend, she's kind of a kid still. I can see her confusion and general distrust of me. I hurt her once, and she isn't glad to see me now.

"I shouldn't have," she says, her tone crisp. "It wasn't the right thing to do."

"It wasn't the wrong thing, either," Jessie interjects. We

105

both turn towards her. I'm surprised she's participating at all. She steps forward. Her face is pale too. Christina comes over to her. Her sincere concern shines brightly in her eyes.

She touches her mom's cheek with her fingertips. "I'm sorry."

Jessie nods and covers her hand with her own. "I know. It's okay. We should just do this. It's time, Christina."

She shakes her head back and forth. "Not without Dad. You need Dad here."

I step back, feeling like a complete interloper. I don't belong here. They are a happy family and my presence here can do no one any good. I don't get Christina's odd reaction to her mother. She's obviously hyper–worried and extra sensitive to Jessie's reaction to me, far more than her own. And needing the dad there? I'm beginning to think she isn't a very strong woman.

"I don't need Dad." This time, Jessie's voice is firm. She steps back and her gaze finds mine. "Why don't you come in and sit down? All of you?"

I let the others file ahead of me into the large open room with plenty of seating. They all sit, and it's obvious they each have their own usual spot. Jessie sits on the edge of a couch. I walk around and choose a side armchair. I keep my legs uncrossed and my hands firmly planted beneath them to avoid the temptation to fidget.

All eyes are on Jessie. I observe them looking towards her with perceptible apprehension, need and daughterly concern. Under all her daughters' scrutiny, Jessie changes. Her spine straightens, her head tilts up, and her smile grows firmer and more confident. When they need her she comes through for them.

I wait. What is she going to say? How can she spin my odd arrival? Judging by Christina's reaction, I'm so obviously not a welcome surprise. "You want an explanation first, or after I tell you who Natalie is?"

I'm shocked when Jessie explicitly says that, to which Melissa replies, "After."

Jessie nods. Her eyes search mine out and she presses her lips together. "She's your half sister. I gave birth to Natalie twenty-eight years ago."

Her stark, unanticipated, scandalous statement plops down like a giant elephant and instantly overwhelms all of our minds.

CHAPTER 8

$\mathcal{N}$ATALIE

MY MOUTH POPS OPEN as both of the younger teens'
heads whip towards mine, their own mouths agape. "No
way," Emily says, her eyes huge. I'm thinking the same thing.
She just told them! I never expected so much honesty and for
the whole story to come out this afternoon, the first and
maybe only afternoon we spent together. Christina gets up
and sits closer to her mom, taking her hand in her own and
separating her fingers, since Jessie keeps kneading her hands
together. Her nerves are quite evident. Man, those two are
close.

"You're our sister? But how? When? Oh my God! Does
Dad know?"

Jessie's smile is slight. "Dad knows. Dad's always known."

"Then how the crap did that happen?" Melissa asks.

Christina and Jessie exchange a glance. It's a small nod,
but I don't miss it as Jessie again communicates something

big with her oldest mini–me. "I was young and I made a lot of mistakes back then. I met someone, and we, well, things happened and I got pregnant. I met your dad after that and we decided not to keep the baby. That baby was Natalie. Christina found her last year and introduced herself." Jessie lifts her gaze to me finally. "And Natalie's decided to meet us now."

"Holy shit," Melissa mutters.

"Missy!" Jessie automatically admonishes.

Melissa glances around. "You're worried about my swearing? Can you think of better words to describe this? That's some screwed–up stuff, Mom. All these years and we never knew?"

"It wasn't an open adoption. There was really nothing to tell."

Christina speaks up. "She did the best she could. You two certainly can't pass judgment."

"This is hard. I understand that. But Natalie didn't come here to feel weird about being in our home. She just wants answers."

"That I started," Christina mutters. I'm still clueless why Christina so adamantly seems to have almost turned against me.

"That Christina opened up for us. It's good she did that. I'm glad, Natalie, that you came here. So, yes, this is a very awkward and unique occasion, I still hope you girls will give each other a chance. It was my mistake. Not yours."

"I have about a trillion q's," Emily finally says. Her expression is stunned shock. Narrowing her gaze, she tilts her mouth up to the side as if she's chewing on her lip.

"I get that. Could we discuss those questions later?" Jessie says softly. I see through the subtle context. She means, when they are alone and Jessie can be fully honest. Not in front of me, the stranger.

The teen nods and finally glances at me. I have only a weary smile to offer her. I have no idea how to handle this situation. Nothing in my life prepared me for what to do with this occasion. I'm the interloper, the monkey wrench in their perfect family, and the living embodiment of their shocking family skeleton.

But I did nothing wrong. Somehow, we share bloodlines. Somehow, we are connected.

"There are four of us?" Melissa finally says. Her gaze is frankly on me now, studying me with renewed and more heightened interest than before.

Jessie sighs. They aren't processing this. "Yes. I have four children. Four daughters."

"And you just gave Natalie up?"

I watch Jessie, and the words on my tongue are nearly as simple as the fourteen–year–old. *Why did you just give me up?* It wasn't my fault that she got knocked up during a one–night–stand. But as one adult to another, I can appreciate how awkward this must be. How best to discuss such a sensitive topic with this woman's adolescent girls? Neither teen seems all that street smart, or sophisticated, or fast for their ages. So the idea of their mom having premarital sex, and later an unplanned and unwanted pregnancy, seems to blow their minds.

"Yes. Two days after she was born. I didn't know her name until Christina found her."

"Maybe I should just go now," I suggest as I get on my feet. This is a colossal disaster, along with the rest of my life right now. But watching the reactions of these teens… well, I realize they don't deserve this dark shadow in their lives. After all these years, I should never have come here.

"Wait. Please. Don't just leave like that. I mean… I mean, we're, well… don't go." Melissa stands up and a strange, disjointed plea comes from her mouth. She stares at me with hopeful eyes. Seeing her confusion softens something inside me. I remember being that age. So much angst and confusion while trying to figure out who you are. It can't be easy for her, having the perfect family and suddenly discovering they're not so perfect. I'm actually surprised to feel a little ashamed and embarrassed, since I am the "something" tainting their perfection, or what they would like to believe.

"This is too... forced. Hard. This is way too hard on everyone."

"So?" Jessie suddenly stands up. "So what? It is hard. But you're here. They finally know, and you can't just leave after all these years. How anticlimactic would that be? I agree, it's a bit too forced like this. What about dinner? Remember? You are staying for dinner? Why can't you do that? Just stay for dinner. No more huge pronouncements or questions. Can't we just... see what happens?"

Her eyes are hopeful; but I know she isn't inviting me there for her benefit. There is still something about Jessie that refuses to connect with me. This last "Hail Mary" pass is only designed to keep me here, once again, *for her daughters.* But I finally acquiesce with a simple nod.

She nods back and offers me a small smile. *Thank you,* she mouths.

Then, the front door opens *again*, and in walks a man. He is older, and my instant assumption is he must be Will Hendricks, her husband. He's a few inches taller than me, and handsome. His blond hair is speckled with gray around his temples. He is in good physical shape, better than a man in his late fifties would typically appear. He comes in wearing casual clothes and sets down some kind of notebook thing and a bag. He glances around the room, nodding at me with a small smile, but his eyes search out Jessie, his sole focus and goal. The others keep talking as they greet him, and he answers them, but his entire interest is monopolized by Jessie. She retains his steady gaze, and her brown eyes are full of conflicting emotions. Her shoulders seem to sag slightly as if she can finally relax because he is home. He comes close to her and I swear I can almost hear their silent conversation, as evident by their eyes and facial expressions. It's intense, whatever else it is. Jessie nods just barely, indicating the positive. Telling him… what? I am her first daughter? That she is fine? Or miserable? Or she wishes I'd disappear? He nods back very slightly. You'd have to be watching them pretty closely to see it. And, yes, I was watching both of them, like a sniper through a scope. I'm trying to find some common ground with my biological mother.

He turns then, and finds me. Stepping forward, he seems ready to approach me. I assume he has to check in with Jessie before he feels free to meet me. "Hello, Natalie, I'm Will."

He's simple, direct and to the point. His frank introduction is a small relief to me. I sense his genuine interest, along with his respect. Whatever the man does, he seems pretty good at defusing any anger I might have felt about him. I don't know his role in my adoption process, but obviously whatever complication haunted their past, they seem to be on solid ground now. I put my hand out to shake his. "Hello, Will."

Giving him a firm handshake, I stare solidly into his eyes. No waffling. I got this. Or at least, I feel like I can handle him. A lot better than I can deal with Jessie. He seems frank and open, almost like he's glad I'm there. That is kind of strange to me. How could he be glad that I showed up there? I obviously am affecting his wife, whom he loves very much, judging by the silent exchange I just witnessed. Despite his emotional attachment to his wife and daughters, he's still nice to me. Now I am very unsure about everyone's reaction to my presence.

Glancing around the room, he seems to take in the shocked, strained and upset faces of his three daughters. He puts his hands on his hips and nods. "So... you all had a discussion, I see."

The girls nod back in the affirmative, their faces staring at him for more answers. I can feel the urgency in their need for him to take control, to help them understand, and make it all better. This can't be faked. He must be a decent dad for them to garner so much faith in him. I wait for him to weigh in, further substantiating this great, big, gigantic revelation; but instead, he says, "Missy, why don't you guys take Natalie down to the barn? I'm sure a city girl like her could never even begin to imagine the zoo we have."

No one moves at first. So Will nods, holding Melissa and Emily's attention as he smiles tenderly and leans over to gently touch Emily's shoulder. "It's okay. Go ahead. Your mom and I will start dinner, okay?" He glances at me. "I hope you're staying, Natalie?"

I nod, even believing he actually *wants* me to stay. But why? His precious wife doesn't want me there, and I know that. She wants to teach her daughters something. But he really seems to hope I'll stay? *Interesting.*

I am startled, never having anticipated any of this, much less Will's benign suggestion. I expect more discussion. Maybe even some tears. Maybe I should leave. Instead, he proposes I take a simple tour of their ranch? Weird, but brilliant. I realize that the same second the girls grasp onto his suggestion in a talisman. They jump to their feet, instantly agreeing and racing off to find their shoes. It's something for us to do. I know that. It's something tangible to remedy an afternoon that left them feeling shell–shocked, hurt, confused, and totally unsure of their mother. Something, I'm quickly gathering, that none of them are used to feeling.

Great. I've dropped in like a bomb, disturbing what

appears from first glance to be a very happy family. Shit. I never considered this scenario in all the wild scenarios I imagined over the years. Oh, yes! I imagined them all. Except that she'd be a good mother. No. Nope. Not once in all my musings, wonderings, and daydreams was there ever a time when I considered my birth mother to be a relatively attractive, pleasant, polite woman, raising a family who appeared to adore, love, need and look to her for all of their emotional support. She is clearly the center of her family.

I feel twitchy. I don't want to sit there. I too spring to my feet, latching on to Will's escape plan. Yeah, he's right. Christina stares up at me, but her gaze is dark. She doesn't like any of this, yet she slowly gets to her feet too, locking her gaze on mine in some kind of dare. The stupid part is, I refuse to accept her dare. I simply offer her a neutral expression.

Melissa and Emily go out first through the back sliding door that leads to a huge deck. The view overlooks more of their yard, along with distant mountains and trees and empty land. There are rural outbuildings too, but they're far enough away that they do not affect the view, but rather add an idyllic, country sweetness to the scene. Yeah, not one thing about this family is what I could ever have predicted.

The crisp, clean scents fill my nostrils with the refreshing air. The smell of freshly turned dirt is nice, too. I have to admit, although it's not my scene, or anything I'd ever choose to live in, I can certainly appreciate the place. The silence thickens between us all. Max doesn't follow us, and I'm surprised he doesn't. I wish he did. Somehow, that kid seems easier for me to be around than anyone else. I have a strange kinship with him that I don't feel with anyone else here. Pretty weird, considering Will and he are the only ones here that I'm not actually related to.

Christina follows, crossing her arms over her chest, and

making her message clear. She is under visible duress. Her sisters notice and follow her cue. They act very suspicious of me. Melissa takes the lead, Emily walks off to the left and slightly behind me. She often glances at me, however, and I can feel her checking me out. I'm wishing I thought this out better. Or taken the time to try to look my best. I wish the phone call I made could have led me somewhere more satisfying. But it didn't and here I am. There is no whitewashing my experience. We are here, and we are all (supposedly) sisters, yet we don't know a blessed thing about each other.

Emily is a slim girl, and small–boned like Christina. But now that I've met Will, I can see that she is the only one who got his looks. She's all him, but in a feminine, gentle, beautiful version. She keeps peeking up at me, then quickly looks away as if she's embarrassed to even be walking near me. I hold my tongue. I know how to handle awkward silences. Lots of experience on the job with that one. I can hold in my feelings and appear unaffected, calm, cool and totally neutral to any and all situations. Even this one. Despite how I am freaking the fuck out inside. Yes, it's a bit of a gift for me in this situation.

It's also a complete curse in other instances, like my marriage.

But that's another story for another day.

Melissa enters their barn. It smells faintly of farm odors. Hay, I think. And dirt. It gets a bit stronger in some spots where the actual animals reside. A horse wanders inside from the outer corral. Although it is fenced outside, the horse has ready access to the barn. Entering its stall with a neigh and nudge of its nose, it stomps one of its hooves. The animal seems huge to me. I'm sure I've never been this close to a horse. I visited the San Diego Zoo a few times. It's a vast, gigantic world confined within San Diego city limits. It houses a variety of exotic, interesting, and gorgeous animals behind displays of natural and tropical, lush vegetation. But a horse? I don't recall every seeing one there, and there was nowhere else for me to see one up close.

On my left, a few lambs are baa-ing as a dog runs up to us from the outside. He is very excited and happy as he wiggles all around our legs.

"Do you like animals?" Melissa asks me. Her eyes stay on my face a few seconds before they skitter off toward the horse she's compulsively stroking.

"I don't hate them. I honestly haven't been around many. We never had pets. And no one I knew did. There were never any horses or sheep, of that you can be certain."

"Where did you grow up?"

"San Francisco."

"Oh. In the city?"

"Yes."

Silence. I can see Melissa tapping her finger against her leg. Nerves? Definitely. I sense her discomfort. She seems to want to ask more, but doesn't. "We have three horses. Several dogs and cats, some sheep, chickens, a pig, two cows, and a goat."

"Wow. Farmyard fun, huh? You eat them too?"

"Never." Melissa's face scrunches up as if she feels pain at such a thought.

Emily giggles. "Missy's like Mom. She refuses to eat any meat. She goes even further and almost won't eat anything that comes from animals."

So Mom is an animal freak, I'm gathering. Their mom. Not mine.

"So, you have cows you don't butcher?" I'm a little puzzled, never having heard of people keeping them as pets.

Christina snorts behind me. "Yes. What's it to you?"

"Mom's a veterinarian. She prefers to foster animals than ever to harm them," Emily adds softly. Her tone is almost muffled as she stares down at the barn floor with her hair covering both sides of her face.

I don't expect that either. These little tidbits keep coming to me. They mean nothing; and they mean everything. Nothing is like what I pictured. But then again, I had nothing for reference but my own imagination.

I glance up at Christina. So do her little sisters. Emily looks unsure, her gaze alternating from Christina to me to her again. She's interested in me. She's also intimidated by me. I can tell she wants to talk to me, but she obviously picked up on how her big sister feels, and doesn't want to go against her. Or perhaps she trusts her sister's judgment. *Whatever.* Both little sisters are confused about what to do with me. Turning my back on the proverbial burr in my ass, Christina, I ask Melissa about the animals. I inquire as to their care, what it takes to keep them healthy, and she warms up to my questions. She's almost eager to answer, just to talk to me. Emily stays close and listens, interjecting her own questions sometimes, but her gaze still skitters off whenever I try to make eye contact with her. Shy. She is painfully shy and self–conscious with me. Silence falls again, and Christina stands behind us, her arms crossed, scowling. Her blatant frigidity feels like a brick wall. And is just as noticeable.

"This is stupid. She doesn't care about our farm animals. Or what Mom does," Christina finally states, ending the quiet between us.

"I don't think that's accurate. I don't know, but I want to know."

"I think Dad wanted us to, you know, maybe talk. 'Cause it's so weird. I mean… this…" Melissa tries to explain after a lengthy silence.

"It is a shock to you both. I'm sorry for that. I didn't really think it out beforehand."

"How do you not think it out? It takes hours to drive here. I should know! I did it when I came to see you. But how could you not know you intended to come here and confront us? I told you about them. So that's just bullshit."

I turn my full attention to Christina, who stands off to the side, still scowling at me. "Yeah, you did. You came to me. You opened that door, Christina. Not I."

"You slammed it shut in my face."

"I was shocked! Can't you, for a second, try to understand how shocking it was to meet you? Out of nowhere. Absolutely *nowhere.* That stupid Saturday, after working out at the gym, I came home, and was getting ready to shower when I heard a knock at my door. And it was you. With this story. About this woman. And this relationship. I didn't handle it well, I admit that, but why don't you take a look in the mirror on that one?"

Christina shakes her head. "Max and Mom called me within minutes of each other. I was in the middle of class, and neither would ever call me during class like that. I left to call them back, and was fully prepared for some unforeseen tragedy, only to find out *you* are in town, and going to meet Mom. They mistook my shock as unfounded jubilation. I might have searched you out once, but that doesn't mean I want you here now. I honestly don't trust you."

"Why should you? But then again, why wouldn't you?"

"Why didn't you tell us?" Melissa interrupts, glaring now at Christina. "You knew, and you didn't tell us? All you ever do is treat us like fucking babies."

Christina doesn't admonish her. Melissa, at fifteen, seems like a baby to me too, but I guess she really isn't. Her swearing actually annoys me. "Because I was trying to spare you! I never dreamed she'd show up like this. I'm sorry. I came, didn't I? As soon as I could."

Melissa scoffs. "To protect us? That's so stupid. From

what? An awful truth that was kept from us? Mom had another baby? No small thing. But as usual, you think it's something special between you and Mom. Somehow, it's only about you. Well, Christina, it's about us too! We're also her daughters, and we're Natalie's sisters too!"

Melissa is hot–faced. Emily steps back, her eyes widening with fright. Christina stares at Melissa and her shock is evident. I step in. Christ! Only an hour here, and I already have two innocent sisters, who had nothing to do with the chip on my shoulder, crying and fighting in girlish sister-hood drama. Maybe I dodged a bullet. I'm not really cut out for the typical drama queen stuff. I preferred having Sam while growing up. He simply would have tried to kick my ass at soccer, or baseball, or in a foot race.

"Okay, okay. This is all life changing. Maybe I should have told you, but I didn't because I wanted to protect you from the confusion I felt over it. I met her and she wanted nothing to do with me. I didn't think she'd ever come here, so there-fore, I never expected her to have any more to do with any of us."

"If that were so, then why were you so affected by the discovery you obviously made about her? You ran away to find her. Not a small thing, Christina."

"No. It wasn't a small thing," I interrupt before Christina can answer Melissa. "I don't think I appreciated that. She was embarrassed to tell you about my existence. I'm sure, after meeting me, it wasn't a careless, easy thing Christina did by coming to find me. Your own mother couldn't have done it."

Christina snapped. "No, it wasn't. But who are you to comment on our mother?"

I throw my hands up as if I'm under arrest and surrender-ing. "I'm just commenting. I'm not trying to claim her as anything to me. My point is, they are upset, just the same as you were. The same as I am. It's a stressful, hard situation.

We can all agree on that. But fighting about it isn't resolving anything either."

"I suppose you want to judge Mom. But you have no right. You don't know a damn thing about what it was like for her."

"No? And you have no idea what it was and is like for *me*. So back off, Christina. You now regret opening this door? Too bad, because you did. I didn't. And here we are. So are you going to make it miserable for everyone? Or can you understand that everyone here is in an unprecedented situation? And we all have as much right as you to express our feelings over it all? Very deep, confusing emotions at that."

Christina's mouth tightens in obvious disdain, but she nods finally. "It is unprecedented. I'm sorry. I guess I just panicked when I heard you were here. I know how confusing it is to find out. I didn't want Emily or Melissa to suffer through that. I guess I hoped they wouldn't find out until they were old enough to handle it. And Mom... well, I was worried too for her. But you're right. I opened up this can of worms. I found you so you could find us. I overreacted today."

I shrug. Understanding it is a hard situation. All of our emotions are stressful and on edge. Seeing the confusion in Emily and Melissa's eyes, I totally respect Christina's worry and concern for them. However, her protectiveness toward Jessie seems a little excessive and misplaced. She is the woman who started all this, and Christina feels the need to protect her from it? "I understand. It is very hard. And I could see worrying so much about your sisters."

"Sister..." Christina mumbles as she shakes her head. "How do we do this? We're strangers, yet our biology says we're sisters. Do we ignore that? Or deal with it? I have no idea what to do."

"I don't either." We all four stare at each other. Our faces express the strain and confusion that clearly pervades all of our thoughts. I'm older and an adult and all that, so I imagine this has to be doubly hard on the younger two. Christina isn't handling it all that well either.

"We deal with it," Melissa says finally, seeming to take control for us.

Christina and I are kind of eyeing each other up, trying to figure out who is more dominant. It's obvious neither of us are shrinking violets. It seems like such an anomaly when I think of Christina at the time she first found me. She didn't know what to say to me and was hopelessly tongue-tied. The girl I'm seeing now is nothing like the girl I first met; she isn't Christina at all. This Christina knows exactly what she thinks and feels and, I'm guessing, usually speaks with polished articulation and confidence.

"I think we deal with it. I think we don't ignore it. We don't fight. We talk. We get to know each other, and see what happens." Melissa's gaze meets all of ours as she speaks.

"I agree," Emily utters for the first time. She has a low, almost soothing voice. When she finally chooses to speak, she reminds me of someone that people naturally follow and listen to easily. Perhaps she only speaks when she feels sure and ready, and has something important to say. Christina's eyebrows are raised in obvious surprise. I doubt if Melissa is usually the leader. Christina is. That much is far beyond obvious. She's the mother hen here. Not only to the sisters, but also to Jessie.

"I think we need to. You can't just leave now, Natalie. We just met you and learned about each other! We can't go back to how we were three hours ago, like it never happened. You two might have tried to do it, but here we are. There's too much curiosity on both sides. There's too much still unknown. If we don't try now than when? After I'm eighteen and decide to find you? Because that's what I'll do. If we don't do this now, I'll come after you later. Or Emily will… or just… shit! We're sisters! What the hell does that mean? Don't we owe it to ourselves to find out?"

Melissa swears a lot; but I'm a little surprised and impressed by the teen's logic. It's pretty mature for one of so few years. Then Emily nods, and Christina finally follows before they all three look at me. The decision rests on my shoulders now. They are a unit. Used to each other. They share an entire childhood and history together. There is no room for me. Is it me against them? Or me with them? I don't know.

"I guess the curiosity *would* drive me nuts. So yeah, I guess. But how do we do that?"

"You stay longer than just for dinner," Christina says. "I'm all done with school. Formerly scheduled to come home for the summer in three days. I'm home now. You stay through next weekend. That's just over a week. Can we give this a chance? Can you spare the time of a normal vacation so we can try and make up for a lifetime of separation?"

"What? You mean stay *here*?" Oh hell no! I am NOT trapping myself here with strangers who are now seeking something from me. I don't need their judgment. Or their answers. There is absolutely no way I'm staying at their house.

"How else will you ever do this? You're old. You live far away from here. If we don't spend time together now, nothing will come of this encounter! You know that as well as I do." Christina's eyebrows are raised and furrowed. Is she challenging me?

"I'm pretty confused. I thought you didn't want me coming here."

"I don't know what I want. But I think Melissa's right. I can't decide for them. And I guess, yeah, I want to find out too if sharing the same mother means anything? Or are we forever destined to just be strangers? Whatever. Obviously, we can't make you stay; but it seems like the most logical thing to do. You must have earned vacation time or you wouldn't have come all this way. Not without Sam. Where is he, anyway?" Her gaze returns to my face. I am careful to make all the muscles in my face stay lax. I don't scrunch it up, or shut my eyes for even a split second of recoil from thinking about why Sam isn't with me. Keeping my voice casual, I say, "He had to travel for work, so it seemed like a good time for me to do this."

"This? As in, come and find us? So you found us... now stay."

She is a dynamic force; I'll give Christina that. From scowling and angry to pressuring me now to stay here? I'm surprised by her rapid flip around. Sighing, she seems to deflate as she leans back against the barn wall. "I'm the oldest. Until you entered our lives, I was always the oldest sister. I guess I resent knowing that my sisters met you before I could be here to introduce you to them. I'm protective. Of them. Of Mom. But, yes, I did want to know you. When I first found out about you, that's all I wanted. To meet you. And talk to you. To see if there was this instant 'Oh, my God! We're sisters!' connection. Obviously, life doesn't work that way. You were nothing like I pictured, yet so much more. And now, here we are. All together. And all unsure about what it means. Even separate from each other, we all seem to agree it means something. So stay. Let's see if it does."

Emily discreetly and very shyly keeps lifting her eyes to mine. She was nodding upon hearing Christina's impassioned speech and still glancing at me with a hopeful, but weary expression. She has no idea what to think, or feel, or say about my presence and my unforeseen existence. I bet she is not only intrigued, but also totally freaked out. I represent her mother's huge, lifelong secret. A shocking secret that is far reaching. A horrible secret that involves sex; and what kid could ever stomach imagining such things about her own mother? I get that. I really do. I also see their point. There was something compelling me to find them. And now that I'm here, they feel the same way about me. Even Christina's rather psychotic switch from being desperate to know me to distrusting me to what she is now, I see why she feels that way. She doesn't want her sisters getting hurt.

"I can stay through next weekend," I answer simply.

"Here? You'll stay here?"

Here? As in their house? No. That's too much. And their mother isn't inviting me, the kids are.

"No. At a motel close by."

"Nothing is that close to us. There is a small guest apartment over Dad's shop. It would be private, but at least, we'd all be here together."

"You need to ask your mother first."

Christina shakes her head. "No, I don't need to. She'll do whatever I believe is best."

There is no waffling for Christina. She seems pretty confident that she knows exactly what her mother thinks, feels and would do for her. No doubt in her mind at all. The other two girls nod. Same self-assurance. I'm a little thrown off by the sudden invite and their visible confidence.

"Maybe."

"Why don't we go back for dinner?"

We stand there another moment, all of us sizing each other up. When I finally nod, so do they. These three strangers who are my sisters.

DINNER IS difficult and strange because I feel clumsy and

124

awkward. They all have defined roles here. They all know each other so well and play off each other. There is mutual respect, caring, humor, sarcasm, and annoyance. Max acts like a big brother to the girls; and he is fully at ease with Jessie and Will. Christina knows her place. Jessie is quiet, but respectful, and Will keeps glancing her way. I also notice him touching her arm, her shoulder, or her leg in silent support as he passes her, or while sitting beside her. He's probably the easiest one to be with. His questions are sincere and they convey his interest without grilling me, or sounding inappropriate.

I soon learn that he served in the Army Special Forces; Jessie has a sister living in the area, Max's adoptive parents; and she was once mayor of the town. I discover where Christina and Max go to school and learn that Emily is a good writer, while Melissa likes to draw.

I learn personal facts. Quirks. All the niceties. I find out most about them, however, by watching them interact. I notice the subtleties that define and nurture people's relationships. The real stuff. I don't miss that Christina and Will are both worried about how Jessie is handling my presence. And it seems a little more than just typical concern. It seems like they are watching out for her physical well-being. The younger two girls, of course, don't sense any of these intricacies. They talk around and over their mom with total teenage, clueless apathy. They don't worry about her. I also believe Will and Jessie are authentic in their feelings toward each other.

I tell them where I live and work and answer their generic questions about how I grew up. I don't elaborate in detail. I don't see any reason to. Dinner ends and I offer to help, but Jessie waves me off.

I finally step outside for a breather. Fresh country air and stars that go on forever overwhelm my already overburdened senses. After a few minutes, Jessie steps outside and comes over to me. She breathes in deeply as she leans against the deck railing.

"The girls told me they invited you to stay. For a week."

"Yes, but don't worry; I won't."

She is quiet for a long, intense moment. The air between us feels cooler than the air around us. "I think maybe you should."

"You're just saying that for them."

"Yes." She nods as she raises her shoulders in a half shrug, and her gaze drifts upwards to the myriad stars. "I am saying it for them. They want to explore and try to define whatever this is. I think you need to do that too."

"You don't really care what I need. They don't see it, but I do. There is a distinct coolness coming from you. A hands–off feeling that you will merely tolerate all of this for the three daughters that you do love."

She sighs and shakes her head. "No, it's a shame actually. It's not that I don't want you staying here, or don't want to know you. Imagine the most shameful thing you've ever done. Well, imagine that baby as an adult, now with thoughts, opinions and feelings. I gave up my rights to all of that long ago. It was a shameful thing I did."

"You didn't regret it though. I don't think you regretted it for even a second."

She briefly holds my gaze, then turns to survey the empty land beyond the deck. "You're perceptive. Smart. And you want honesty. I get that from you. No bullshit. I don't know what I feel. I did something that I believed I had no other choice but to do at the time. I banished it from my mind although it never ceased to hurt my heart. But as time passed, things eventually get released and forgotten as life moves on. And, Natalie, that doesn't mean I don't want you here. It means, quite frankly, I'm scared."

"Of what?"

"I don't know." Her tone is direct and simple.

"Did you ever wonder about me?"

"No. Yes. Always."

"What does that mean?"

"It means a day didn't pass without me thinking about what I did. But I firmly believed, no matter what, that you were better off than you'd be with me and what little I could have given to you."

"You don't seem like an awful mother," I grumble. I'm unwilling to explain or elaborate my shock over the quality mother she seems to be.

"I was by the time I had Christina. But not when I had you. I changed a lot. In ways you can't comprehend."

"But you never felt the urge to look for me?"

She stands up to her full height, turns to me, clasping her hands in front of her stomach and says simply, "No. I never felt the urge to find you."

It feels a bit like she punched me in the lungs. My stomach churns, and my heart lodges in my throat. Now I feel like she smacked me in both places. That is so mean! My mother is standing here before me, the woman who donated half my DNA, and gave birth to me, yet she didn't even wonder about me. She didn't care if my life turned out all right. Or if I were safe. Perhaps that's what happens in typical adoptions, but she seems like such a good mother to her three other daughters. It doesn't make sense to me.

"But I think you should stay. Please. I think it's important to all of you girls. Barring me. You don't have to associate with me. You don't have to even talk to me. I get why you'd prefer not to. But I think the girls and you need to figure out what this revelation means to you four, collectively and also individually."

"You mean, please don't start seeking you out for a heart–

to–heart or any kind of bonding." I raise my eyebrows in a serious dare. I hate knowing she doesn't want something more from me. No matter how tough I pretend to act, I really can't believe she has absolutely no interest in *me*.

"I don't know what propelled you to come here. But since you have… stay. It's only a week. It's not forever. You'll have plenty of privacy. And you'll also have an opportunity to explore and understand your collective kinship."

I stare past her and cross my arms over my chest. I tower over her by about five inches. "I don't have a blessed, goddamned idea what any of this is for, or what it means, if anything."

She nods. "I know. I think we all feel that way."

"We're strangers."

"We are also connected. Stay. Find out."

I shrug. Why not? What have I to lose? I have my stuff in my car and they have a private apartment. Why the hell not?

Except that this woman beside me is an enigma that I can't begin to figure out or understand. She asks me to stay, yet I really believe in my gut she doesn't want me to. Then why ask me to stay? I don't get it. But maybe, my staying here is the perfect punishment for her, and one which she deserves. It would be so much easier on her if I refused to stay and just left and went back to where I came from. I straighten my stance and push my shoulders back. Screw Jessie Hendricks! I'll take pleasure in their hospitality for a week, especially if all I accomplish is making her endure my continued presence. I'm the baby she rejected. And never wondered about. And never would have come looking for. But surprise! Here I am.

CHAPTER 9

AM

SHOWERING HELPS. I DON'T stink anymore. My breath is still sour, but I hope enough mouthwash and tooth brushing will change that. Dustin folded and added to the clothes I threw into my duffel bag. I dress in my suit pants and button–up shirt, no tie or jacket. My confidence slowly starts to return as I shave, groom and wear the clothes I once used as a shield, pretending to navigate this new world I occupied, worked and socialized in. These clothes that formerly allowed me to pretend I was totally comfortable and successful.

Dustin nods and stares at me. He could have turned on me. I nod back. I owe him. "Could you tell Mom for me? She'll need to know. Especially since I'll be gone. I don't know how long I'll be. I can't—"

"No, Sam, I won't tell them. You need to."

Right. My mess. I have the work to do. I nod. Dustin adds,

"There's a flight to Spokane, Washington leaving tonight at eight. If you hurry, you can make it. From there, you can take a smaller plane to a small airport not far from there. Or you can drive."

I can make it. I can't wait. A rush of feelings I've never had overcomes me. Purpose. Commitment. Hope. Fear. Anxiety. Helplessness. I've never really felt the last ones before. What didn't go my way? Not much in my life.

But now? Everything is wrong. And it's all my own doing. "I'll hurry. I'll call Mom and Dad… and Dustin? Thank you. I might not deserve it, but I really needed someone to help me today."

"You don't often need it. I'd never deny you that. No matter what, you have to know that."

I shake the hand he puts out before grabbing the suitcase and my wallet and leaving.

Later, I land at a small airport, and all my clothes are in my carry-on. I feel free and unencumbered as I hastily hire a rental car with GPS. I have to find my wife in a place I've never heard of. I drive until I enter a small town that looks more like a flat stretch of pancake. It's nothing like the steep, hilly city streets of San Francisco, wafting its cool bay air and fresh, salty scents. Here it is endless sky, not ocean.

My wife could be here… or not. It's crazy that I came here. I start to realize that while cruising on Interstate 90. It's a pretty easy drive of straight-a-ways and light traffic so my mind wanders. She could be anywhere. She might not even be here. She could have already come and gone. Even if I find the town, I already discerned the population is less than twenty thousand people. Still, there are lots of places to look for one Christina Hendricks. Of course, there are other, more efficient ways to find someone, but I haven't had the time to try that yet. I might have to do just that. Lacking confidence, and with nothing else to lose, I drive on towards Ellensburg with absolutely no real destination in mind.

~

"Aren't you Sam Ford?" Hearing my name, I whip around, completely astounded, almost jumping with shock. My recognition of the voice behind me is instantaneous: the kid with Christina, Max. He's staring at me and his eyes seem interested, yet not all that surprised. His slight hesitation, and because he's not totally shocked, tells me he must have seen Natalie. Quite recently, Natalie probably met him again. I order my voice to stay calm and casual. I dare not express my complete and utter excitement that I could be close. I might find her. My crazy–ass idea just might work. I was walking listlessly around the tiny main part of town, the college district. Spotting a small coffee shop, it seems the most logical place where people would eventually spend their time in a small town. So I go there. And low and behold, I am recognized.

I put my hand out to shake his. "Hi, Max. Yes. It's me."

"What are you doing here?" Max asks as he waves his hand toward the coffee shop. He's perplexed, no doubt, about the reason I would be mindlessly wandering through town.

"I just got here. I wanted to see Natalie. Obviously. But I got lost. I thought I'd get directions here. My phone's dead." I hedge. He nods, as if understanding. He knows where Natalie is. My heart is tripping. I want to shake him, and demand he tell me where she is.

Max shakes his head with a small smile. "This is a coincidence I ran into you. I'm sure Natalie told you about yesterday. Crazy stuff, huh? I mean, after all these years? Now she's staying there? She didn't mention you were coming too."

Yesterday? Crazy? Obviously, Natalie saw Max. Therefore,

131

I must assume, Christina and her mother did too? I am salivating for answers. I want to grab Max and grill him. I nearly beg him to take me to her. My anxiety makes my hands fidget so I tuck them into my pants pockets. I'm still trying to pull off the façade that I'm here casually and fully expected by Natalie.

Instead of showing the way I really feel: despised, distrusted and hated.

It takes a prolonged moment for Max's words to fully hit me. *Staying there*? Natalie is staying with her long-lost mother? That is bat–shit impossible. Natalie is more apt to tell her off and be promptly escorted out of town than acting so nice she ended up staying there. I am speechless.

I go for it, hoping I can con Max into believing I'm the caring husband he thinks I am. "I decided after hearing all that stuff, and because she decided to stay, she could probably use my support."

"I thought you were traveling for work, or something?"

"Cancelled it all." Or quit. All the same now. "But I still don't know how to get there, even with the address. I wanted to surprise her by just showing up. You know." I shrug as if I'm no more than a helpless, sweet romantic for my wife.

"Sure. That's because it's in middle of nowhere. Not like where you're from. I'll take you."

"Thank you, Max. You can't know how much this means to me."

Max shrugs. "Car's right there. I pulled over when I saw you. I knew it was you. Hard to miss you. You're tall."

"I got a rental car here."

Max waved it off. "We'll come back later for it."

I follow Max to his car and get in. He makes a quick U-turn and drives us quickly out of town, and yes, into the middle of nowhere. I make idle conversation, but don't even listen to his side of it. He says something about where he goes to school, or what he's studying, et cetera, et cetera. My heart lodges in my throat. My tongue starts to swell as my raw nerves make my palms slick with sweat. Then, I see a house. We stop the car. It's a nice, big rambler. Welcoming and pristine. We get out and Max waits as I grab my lone duffel bag. I rarely travel so light, but I don't have even a book or a backpack. Fresh underwear and jeans are about all that's packed. I follow Max. There is no need to knock. My stomach starts to cramp as we head up the three steps to the front door and Max casually opens it. Comfortable. At ease. He's thinking it's a good thing he found me and brought me here. I grip the nylon straps of my bag tighter and step behind Max before entering the house.

Where Natalie should be. Natalie, who has not seen me since... I can't even stand to picture it. Not now. Not while I feel like hurling. I can't think about all I have to fix. Or how she might react. I have to be glad, for once, that we're surrounded by virtual strangers, who are more than strangers and possibly mean more to her now, so maybe she won't throw me out. Maybe I can somehow get a few minutes alone with her.

The living room has only an older woman and a young, blonde girl sitting in it. They both turn when we walk in. The house is one giant, open room so there's no sneaking up on anyone. Here we are. I quickly take stock of the room and don't find Natalie.

I'm guessing the attractive, fifty–ish woman before me is Natalie's mom. She glances up from where she's sitting on the couch with paperwork spread around her. The teen is laid out comfortably, watching the TV.

"Max?" The woman rises to her feet. She is wearing what look like work clothes and stockings on her legs. A pair of heels lie casually to the right of her. I can hear the question in her tone; she might as well just ask, who is the strange guy behind Max?

"Hey, Jessie. You won't believe who I ran into coming home from school!"

Jessie? Natalie's mother has a name. I put my best, most pleasant smile on.

Jessie blinks in response. "Ah, who? I don't have any more long-lost children."

I beam a full smile at them, and Max laughs out loud. She sighs and shakes her head. "Sorry, I shouldn't have said that. I'm thinking, however, you must be Sam."

There is no strange tone to her voice. Is she shocked by my presence? Does she think terrible things about me? Do I represent no more to her than a cheating asshole? But I see only pleasant curiosity in her tone and facial expression.

"Uh, yes. I am Sam." I wince. I hate saying that. It usually comes out before I can stop it. It reminds me too much of Dr. Seuss's *Green Eggs and Ham* book. Been teased about that more than once.

The teen perks up on the couch at the sound of my voice and notices me. She was almost catatonic to my presence before. Her eyes grow larger and she swings her feet to the ground while smoothing her blonde hair back.

Jessie puts her hand out. "I'm Jessie. I'm sure you figured that out already." She has a warm, pleasant tone that is also kind and genuine. I can hear her uncertainty at the situation, but I appreciate her realness and the humor she interjects. I am surprised at the woman Natalie's mom turns out to be.

"It's very nice to meet you, Mrs. Hendricks." I assume she has the same last name as Christina. I hope so otherwise it will be obvious I have not spoken to Natalie. It would be pretty unbelievable to almost anyone that a woman could meet her biological mother after twenty–eight years and not bother to call her husband and talk about it. Or analyze and dissect it. Or rant, rave, cry or express something about it. But the crazy part is, I ponder as I shake Jessie Hendricks's hand, I'm not sure that Natalie would have called me to talk about it. Or asked me to help her cope. Or help her figure it out. More people enter the room, and Jessie turns as I do. There is another teen and a man.

They stop and check me out. "This is Natalie's husband, Sam," Jessie says quickly to catch them up. My hasty introduction to Will and Melissa leaves me thinking they are all very nice and pleasant and interested. As far as first impressions go? This is a good one.

Still, Jessie abandoned her firstborn. What could make a woman do that and then go on and raise an entire family that, at first glance, appears so nice, mannerly and even pretty? But as I often observe, appearances are crap. They are no more than a cover. A pretty manhole cover over a sewer pit. Open it up and the stink and crap might burn your nose as well as your eyes.

I slide my duffel to the floor, hoping my action will trigger one of them to say where Natalie is. I need our first meeting to be in private. I need a moment to try to get her to talk to me. I fear she won't hold back in front of these strangers, and I am growing desperate for any chance to talk to her.

Something. Anything. We have to start somewhere before we can go anywhere.

"Natalie is coming in any moment; she—"

But Jessie doesn't finish her sentence since Natalie is suddenly at the sliding door, opening it and entering. I know by the relaxed position of her shoulders that she hasn't seen me yet. I stare at her. My heart swells. The sight of her punches me in the gut. I want to fall to my knees and scoop her up. Kiss her. Hug her. Beg for her forgiveness. I want to do something, anything to get her to hear me.

Her gaze is on the rest of the family, scattered around the living room. I am off to her left, near the front door and out of her line of vision, until I move shifting my feet, and that slight movement alerts her to my presence.

Her gaze lands on me. Time stops. Everyone else disappears. It's us. Only us, Sam and Natalie, staring with shock, anger, hurt and devastation at each other. We are both speaking volumes with our eyes. As her brown eyes slightly enlarge, I glimpse the emotions that fill them. She usually has iron control of her emotions and facial expressions, but for a second, a split, half second, I see the naked hurt, betrayal, horror, anger, rage, and... love. I see it all in that moment just before she blinks and regains her composure. Now, it's gone. The honesty is gone. She shuts her mind down along with her expression and her emotions. She's about to go numb. She'll deal, however, but only because of the strangers surrounding us, witnessing our interaction.

"Sam? How? Why are you here?" she barely whispers. I nod and watch her glance around. I don't miss the vulnerability in her gaze. She is unsure of these people, and me... but at least she has history with me.

"Max found me in town, wandering around lost, and he gave me a ride. Lucky break," I say, keeping my tone casual and a half smile on my face for everyone else's benefit. My eyes, however, are locked on Natalie. I stare as deeply into her gaze as I can, trying to pour my feelings inside her and let her know how I feel. *Hear me, feel me, see me, sense me, Natalie.* I'm ready to beg her, *Forgive me.* I want her to yell and reprimand me. Do anything except look at me with those hollow-eyed eyes as if I were a terminal cancer she once vanquished, and now returned to ruin her remission.

"Wow. *You're* her husband?"

I glance off to the left at the older teen's comment. She's staring at me, her eyes big with appreciation. Natalie glances at her too and finally rolls her eyes. "Yes, he's wow. Been hearing that his whole life too; you're not the first."

Somehow, hearing the teen's infatuation with me breaks the ice. I can hear Natalie's exasperation mixed with patient tolerance of the teen. She usually rolls her eyes with visible amusement at any other woman's tacit appreciation of my appearance. I have good genes. I've been told often enough to get that. But the one thing about Natalie? She never allowed me to get away with anything by using it. For some reason, young and old women alike invariably fall for my particular brand of flirting. Natalie says it's because of my *too pretty* looks. Natalie usually just laughs it off.

The family. These strangers. The Hendrickses and Max, are all laughing. They find her funny and probably consider the two of us amusing and cute. People often enjoy listening to our banter. We used to be better at it. Rooted in fun, our sarcasm and humor became more like a source of hot foreplay for us.

There is a semblance of comfort I hear in Natalie's voice as she speaks to these strangers. I don't hear any loathing. Is she giving them a chance? It doesn't ring right to me, or is what I picture from Natalie. Not for the woman who so wronged her. But here she is. And they seem to like her being there.

"I'm sure you're anxious to put your stuff up with Natalie's. Please, don't let us stop you." That comes from Jessie again. She seems pretty attuned to odd situations. I nod gratefully at her. She probably guesses any couple in this situation would want to have a few moments alone, to touch base, or hug and kiss, or just to speak freely about the awkward, massive impact of finding Natalie staying at the same house with her biological mother and sisters.

"Thank you; that is most appreciated." I lean down to heave my things over my shoulder. I intend to be an ass and force Natalie to deal with me. I hope since we're here, she'll comply with my wishes, if only out of duress. I clearly see she hasn't told them anything about me, or what I did, or where we are relationship-wise. Oddly enough, these total strangers just might be my only chance to find a way to save my marriage. Otherwise, I will eventually receive divorce papers in the mail. No kidding. If I can't convince her to hear me out now, I think that's exactly what she will do and without ever again seeing me.

Being trapped here together, under these unique circumstances, could mean I might manage to persuade her to talk to me just once. Without that pressure, however, I don't think she would.

Natalie turns from me. I see her grabbing the door handle, but missing it in her haste. She is visibly shaken. I've upset her and made her lose her composure. My heart squeezes in pain to know that I'm the source of her unhappy reaction. But it doesn't hurt enough to change my plan.

She finally grasps the handle and slides the door open. I follow her and shut it. Just like that, we're alone at last. Silence fills the space before she glances up at me. Her face is still impassive as her newfound family can still observe us. "You low-down, pissant son of a bitch! I have no idea how you found me, and the gall it takes for you to come here... like this and corner me? This is low, even for you." She speaks in a low, simmering tone. Her teeth are locked together and her jaw seems hard as stone.

"I know."

She whips around and walks away from me. I follow her across the deck, and down the stairs before crossing about two hundred feet of lawn. We're heading toward a wood-framed structure that I'm guessing has a mother-in-law apartment over it. Up Natalie goes, stomping on the stairs before nearly jerking the door off its hinges.

She doesn't turn towards me as I enter, so I lower my bag and gently shut the door. She leans her hands on the small counter in the kitchen. She is hunched over, and breathing hard; I can see the rapid rise and fall of her back as she breathes. She stays silent for several minutes, until finally, her head starts shaking. She doesn't turn towards me, but says, "How can you do this to me? Haven't you done enough?"

I want to withdraw immediately and disappear. I start to cower because she's right, and I have no way to fix what I've done. I've never been in the wrong like this before. I don't even know how to begin. But I think of Dustin. He said I had to "start somewhere." I can't do anything unless I start. I'm here now, and I'm doing this to try and keep our relationship alive before she ends everything.

"Because I was wrong. Because I'm sorry and because I love you... We have to talk. We..."

Her face whips around and I see the tears streaking her cheeks. "No. Actually, we never have to talk again. Get out, Sam. I don't know how you possibly managed to find me or got here, but, typical Sam Ford, luck always seems to go with you. You manage to accomplish the impossible. But not this time. Not this time; you can't fix it because there is nothing to fix. We are broken. Over. Done."

"We haven't even started yet. We haven't even discussed it. We aren't done. My God, Natalie..."

Her entire body straightens as she draws in a deep breath. "You were... I can't even think about it. I saw you! I relive it every moment I close my eyes, and revisit it every morning! Started? It's already finished me, Sam. Just get out. Now. Forever. I don't ever want to see you." Her voice and tone are audibly destroyed. She leans on the table and breathes deeply again. I squeeze my fingers into fists, trying to restrain the urge to touch her. I can't let her go either.

NATALIE

I can't breathe right. Used air is stuck in my chest. I lean on the table again, trying to force it out of my mouth, but it keeps catching in my throat. It feels like something is holding it back. My peripheral vision perceives the world closing in around me. Am I having a panic attack? Never before have I had one, until now. My heart is palpitating in my chest way too fast. *Because Sam is right behind me.* I shake my head and lean all my weight towards the table. I can't believe this is happening. I was simply returning to the house full of strangers and there was Sam. I never pictured that. It never occurred to me he'd figure out where I was. It's incredible in some ways that he's here. He's talking to me. He's apologizing. He says he loves me. And he found me somehow.

I close my eyes, trying to stop the tears. "Please, Sam. Just leave. I can't do this. I can't do this here, not with these strangers."

"No. I can't. I just can't leave things how they are. I know what you'll do if I don't use this chance to talk to you. You'll run away from here now, just because I showed up, and keep running from me, from us and from them. You'll send me divorce papers at some point and erroneously think that's it. Done. Forever. But it's not! We're not done yet. If nothing else, we have to talk. We have to do this."

He's right. So what? So what if he's right about the suddenly compelling urge growing inside me that says *Go! Leave. We're done here.* So what if Sam knows me so well? It doesn't change what he did. Or what we no longer share.

"Ask me, Natalie. Ask me why I did it. Yell and scream and rage at me! Demand to know how I could do it. Please, just say something. We have to start somewhere." His tone is quiet, as he pleads behind me. He's watching me. He's calm. He sounds tortured. I have to squeeze my eyes shut because he sounds so normal to me. He sounds like the man I once loved and chose to marry. He sounds like my friend again.

"*Why?*" I scream, injecting the frustration and anguish into that one word. I suddenly scream again out of nowhere. "Why you did it? What the hell do you think I care about *why*? No explanation can change my knowing that you did it. It doesn't matter to me *why*. It only matters that you did! And I witnessed it for myself. There is nowhere for us to go from there."

"I didn't set out to do it. I never once set out to cheat on you."

His tone is so calm. I want to turn and gouge out his eyes with my fingernails. I feel like grasping both of his eye sockets and digging his lying, cheating eyes right out of his skull. My arms start to shake as the anger overcomes me. Now it is rage. The adrenaline races through me and its power, combined with how much I want to hurt him, scares me.

I shove the table, and stomp around it. I grab the first thing I see, a picture frame, and hurl it against the wall. It dents the plaster and falls to the ground, breaking the glass in a long diagonal crack. I am shaking everywhere. My head hurts and I feel like I might throw up. My emotions are so overwhelming now, and I thought I managed to put a little distance from it in my mind. I thought, I really did, that I wouldn't fear my desire to physically hurt him.

He moves. I hear his shoe sliding on the tile flooring and jerk my face up to his. I put my arms out while shaking my head. "Stay back! Stay away from me. Don't come near me. Ever. Ever. Don't come near me, you two–timing, cheating bastard!"

I'm screaming… and hysterical. Somewhere in my brain, I realize that, but I've gone too far now to stop or control it. My sobs become deep, gulping gasps. I'm trembling and a dull pressure blinds me as it starts building behind my temples. He ignores me and grabs me, pulling me against him as he tries to hold me there. He's saying something in a soothing tone. Soothing words. I push at his chest. I'm strong, but not strong enough to push him off me, especially while gasping for air and with my tears blinding me. I feel myself weakening.

"I hate you. I hate you. I hate you." I'm still hysterical, screaming and punching his chest. I do it hard. Hard enough to bruise him, and I use my fists. I may be losing it and hysterical, but I'm still strong and I know how to fight.

That's what makes my heart hurt so much. It feels like it's been slit open and blood is pouring out of the gaping wound. I don't want to hurt Sam. I don't want Sam to hurt me. I want... Sam. I want to love him and be with him, but he ruined it all. I can't understand my odd reaction. I don't grasp why he did it, or why I'm crying on him, even after it happened. Nothing is clear–cut for me. Nothing is easy.

Inexplicably, I quit hitting him, I clutch his shirt in my fists as if letting him hold me up before burying my face in his chest. I can feel his mouth on my hair as he whispers and clutches me closer to him. How can I quit fighting him? How can I let him touch me? He repulses me, but I also repulse myself. So I cling to him hysterically.

How can you love and need the same person who hurt you the most? And whom you most detest and hate and curse?

"Why are you doing this to me?" I finally whisper, my head hanging down. My voice sounds odd and weak, even to my own ears. The unexpected onslaught of emotions finally wanes and I start to feel numb. Cold. I'm totally depleted of everything. From my energy to my emotions. I feel hollow and empty. Drained.

I push him off me after I finally regain control of my tears and rage. He barely loosens his hold on me. My legs are trembling. He gently places me back on the couch. He sits down in a chair close by and his butt rests on the edge. Bending his legs, he rests his elbows on his thighs. His head is down and his shoulders are drooping. I sit up, finally calmer.

"I don't want to end it, Natalie. I don't want you to divorce me. I'll do anything. That's it. The reason I'm here. And why I had to find you."

"You already did enough."

"I know." He stares at his hands before him. There is nothing about his slouching, defeated demeanor that I recognize. His tone is as hollow as my insides feel. He might as well have carved me out like a knife in a pumpkin, and scraped out all my internal organs. I have nothing left inside me. I am empty. Devoid of all life. I almost have an out-of-body experience, feeling like I am someone else sitting there now as I *almost calmly* talk to him.

Silence falls between us again, and I am dumbfounded by it. After the shocking display of my anger and tears, along with Sam's own apologies, and all the things we need to discuss, or end, or deal with, a thick silence engulfs us? It's incomprehensible. But there it is. We are both staring down at our fingers. Is this how our marriage ends? Our apathetic, sad, hollow emotions hopelessly trying to draw any kind of sense from it?

"You threw your phone out your car window somewhere, didn't you?"

I glance up at his quiet question. Startled, I nod. *How could he know that?*

"How did you figure out where I was?"

"I lay in bed for days, trying to figure out where you might have gone. I thought and thought. I even went to see your dad. But I knew you wouldn't go anywhere near work, or my family, or our friends. I realized you'd taken off for parts unknown, of course. It finally dawned on me while I was trying to convince Dustin to tell our mom what I did. I don't... I didn't want to tell her."

"What did Dustin say?" I picture Dustin's indignation over Sam doing that to me, but I know Dustin would still have been there for his brother. He is that kind of a man.

"Grow up. Do it myself. Start somewhere."

That's where he got the "start somewhere" mantra that seems to be his holy grail. Does it make it easier for him to sleep at night? Or face himself? He's picturing how to charge in and fix everything. He has a plan, an end goal in his mind. I know how much that would comfort and empower him. He can't handle ambiguity. He thinks he can do and fix anything. Too bad; this time, he finally fails.

"Anyway, it got me thinking about family and with you already running, it seemed like the perfect time for you to go after Christina. I know you, Nat. Nothing changes that."

"You don't know me."

The pervasive quiet lingers. He shakes his head and leans forward. "I *did* know you once. I used to know you better than anyone. We used to—"

No. Oh, my God, no! He's not going to blame this on me. Yes, things changed last year. Yes, we grew apart, and were having problems, but nothing like this. Nothing that was as bad as this. There was no smoking gun and I was never so horrible as to lead Sam to do *that.*

"Don't you dare blame this on that!" My voice sounds low and raw.

He glances up and shakes his head, holding my gaze. "I never have. But since then, you have quit trying to talk to me."

"I didn't talk to you enough? Or have enough sex with you? Somehow, poor, neglected Sam earned the right to go screw another woman?" Wow, my anger rises fast. I jerk the strands of my hair behind my ear.

"No. The point is, I know you. I know you better than yourself, and have for years. For a couple of decades now. You don't always know your true self, Natalie. I won't allow this to become the one thing I did that erases everything we had previously."

"The one thing you did?" My mouth hangs open in disbelief.

He sighs. "This sin. This lie. This terrible, evil, horrible deed that I committed. I know what it is. But I found you because we need to talk. We need to talk about it. All of it. If we're done, we need to at least talk about it. You can't run forever. You can't freeze me out forever. If you're hiring a lawyer the minute you return to San Francisco, I won't be surprised. But don't we owe it to the kids we once were together? Or the teens and newlyweds we once were to at least talk about it? We have to at least acknowledge what we once had and were, and how this happened. I, at the very least, need to say the right words, *I'm so sorry*. Do I think you will accept them? No. I don't. Do I expect my apologies to help you at all, or do any good? Again, no. But I still have to say them. What kind of uncaring monster would I be otherwise? I am so panicked and worried about losing you that I have to at least say that to you."

He's compelling. He can argue points with cool logic in his warm, deep baritone voice. And he makes so much sense. Somehow, Sam, in this critical moment, makes sense.

But that doesn't mean his actions make any sense to me.

I lean forward, resting my aching forehead on my knees as I stare at the floor. Tears blind me again. I'm so sad. It hits me like someone is pressing on my back, trying to force me to the floor.

"You found your mother," he states finally after a long, terrible silence.

I shrug.

"She's not what you pictured." I want to ignore him. But he's the only one I've ever voiced my thoughts to in regard to my biological mother and father. He is the only one who knows for years how I wondered about my origin. He knows that after my mother died, I got so depressed, I had to take antidepressants as I tried to learn the identity of the woman who gave me away. But I didn't get anywhere. He knows all that. Sam knows. He knows me. Which makes his betrayal that much more bitter. He knows it never occurred to me that my biological mother would be kind of normal and nice, much less raising a decent family.

"Natalie, I'm here. I want to be here. You were never going to seek out your biological family, but I think you need to face it, just as much as you need to hear me out. Let me be here for you. Let me help you face this. I can do that. I can support you. When we go home—" His voice falters and he clears his throat. "When we go home, you can decide what you want to do about us. But I don't think you can handle this alone right now. You've had too much happen at once. You are the strongest woman I know, but even you will break at some point."

"Just leave right now and I'll be a whole lot better."

"I could just stay. Here. With you. I'll sleep on the couch. I won't... I won't talk about it again unless you want to. I'll listen. I'll just be your friend. For this. Because I know, Natalie, I know what this means to you."

His tone is caring, and so seductive. There is no one I ever let my guard down with, except Sam. And I am exhausted right now. My ragged emotions feel like they've been dragged over a barbed wire fence. I'm shredded. But I can't just run. I'm here. And he's here.

146

"I don't think I can ever be your friend again."

"Just be my friend here. How long did you agree to stay?"

"A week."

"What's one more week for us? We've been together since we were kids. Please, just let this go for one more week. Then…"

I shake my head. "I hate you." I whisper as my eyes scratch and ache from all the tears I've cried.

"I deserve that. But who else knows you as well as me? Who else is here?"

The loneliness I feel makes my heart drop down into my stomach. He is manipulating me, of course. He knows how much I miss my family, and how devastating it is to watch my father losing his mind and me to dementia. He knows how I ache for family again. How I cling to his family. But he ruined that. How could I go running to them with my broken heart? They'd have to take his side, or at least, try and reason with me to accept his apology.

It's not like I consider these strangers my family. A week is nothing compared to a lifetime. There is no recapturing that. Or creating that kind of deep bond. There is, maybe, being pleasant or friendly. There are some answers. But no connections to compensate for the ones that were abruptly severed from my life.

"I don't want you here."

"Let me stay. I'll stay at a motel. Just let me be here for you. Let me do this one last thing for you."

"I don't want them to know. And what would be more obvious or strange than my husband staying in town at a motel?"

He tilts his head. "Okay. You're right. Let me stay here. They don't know us yet. They won't know anything. And… you're not all alone. It's not you against them. It's you and me against them. I was your best friend once, Nat. Long ago.

Years ago, I was your best friend. Let me be again for just a few days more."

So reasonable, isn't he? So freaking correct too. He was my best friend once, and facing all this alone makes me feel less anchored in a world where nothing and no one is familiar. It's a bit disconcerting to leave town and have no one other than Sam worry about me. Sam is the only one who would know I'm gone. Sam is the only one left with that kind of connection to me, and feels that kind of concern.

"Let's call a truce. For this week, let's call a truce and when it's over, we'll figure everything out. Either way. We'll do this together. But right now? Let me just be here for you."

I drop my chin. I can't believe I'm even allowing him the same air to breathe in my vicinity. But here I am. I'm confused, unsure, and at least he's familiar. He feels normal. Even if there is nothing normal about us anymore. "One week." I close my eyes, my chest feeling tight and constricted. "Then it's over, Sam. It's all over."

He nods. His expression is bleak. "One week."

CHAPTER 10

*N*ATALIE

I DON'T KNOW HOW to deal with Sam being here. But he
is. He somehow conned me into a truce, of all things. I leave
the small apartment immediately after dabbing some
makeup on my eyes to reduce the appearance of tears, and
hastily find refuge with the strangers inside the house. So far
today, I've hung out with the three girls who are my *sisters.*
The morning was spent driving around their small town.
They took me to one panoramic point that overlooked the
town and a long stretch of land that faded off like a smudge
in the mountain. It was a stunning vista revealing the flatness
of the area, but also the endless sprawl of farms, ranches,
houses, trees, and rivers. There were huge, white fan-
looking things in the distance, the blades of a wind farm.
There was nothing really to see, but also everything. We
walked the university campus and browsed the few places
dedicated to the students. They showed me their aunt's

house and where Max lived. I saw their elementary school and their dad's office in town. It was a tour of their childhood roots in a town that they obviously were proud to be connected to despite making so much fun of it. I got the distinct feeling the older two would never leave it. Emily? Who knows? She can't look at me without her cheeks burning up with embarrassment or confusion. She has no idea what to say to me.

And now? Sam is here and I have to avoid him. He comes into the house where the family is. They are all home from work and their various errands as the dinner is being prepared. I help this time. Although not a great cook, I can follow directions. Sam comes up behind me and offers his help, winning Jessie and Melissa's grateful smiles. I grit my teeth. He is such a suck–up! And why are women in general so bowled over with pleasure when a man offers to help with dinner, or the dishes, or any other domestic chores? With women, it's kind of expected. If I didn't offer my services, they'd have most likely commented about it behind my back. Yet no one really expects Sam to help.

Sam knows how to read people and how to react to them. He knows how to play them too, but not in an evil way. He's just so damn charismatic and likeable. I watch him work his magic on these people with whom I am still stiff and unnatural. He's wearing his usual designer shirts that cost ridiculous amounts of our money. It drives me crazy how much he spends on his clothes. I used to fight with him over it, but eventually had to give up. Despite all of our fights and my protests, he still bought them. His reasoning was obvious: he made that much money and "needed" to look the part. *Whatever.* But here in Ellensburg? It's totally wasted. He rolls his sleeves up to his elbows in precise folds and digs into the dough Jessie wants him to put on cookie sheets to bake for dessert. All the while, he makes casual, easy, funny conversation with the Hendrickses. No one can resist him. I wish I were kidding. He's completely magnetic. Yeah, where I'm the reliable, safe Volvo, he's more like a Porsche, or a Jaguar or a Ferrari that everyone marvels and drools after.

I say little to Sam, trying to avoid glancing up. He purposely comes behind me, blocking my body with his as he pretends to reach around me for a hand towel, and later, a wooden spoon in a container in front of where I diligently chop the vegetables. His body wraps around me, and his warm chest touches my back. His hand casually extends as his face approaches the side of mine. My breath catches and every nerve ending reacts to his presence. He is deliberately trying to remind me of us. Our sexual chemistry was never in question. I finally step back, and using the heel of my boot, I step on his toe. He jerks with surprise and steps back, releasing me from his almost hypnotic captivity. When he's close to me, oh hell, close to *anyone,* we sort of lose our heads around him. He's just that attractive. His innate animal magnetism has always affected me strongly, far stronger than any other man's presence.

Dinner tonight is much easier than the night before was, and it galls me. The reason it's easier is because Sam is here. Sam sits next to me and engages in three different conversations, one with Jessie, one with Will, and all the while teases the younger two Hendricks girls. All too easily, he ingratiates himself to them. The two teens stare at him with big, curious eyes and almost tongue–tied crushes. He's lively, smiling and easy to relate to. There is not a single day when Sam carried a chip on his shoulder. He is always wide open to the world and the people around him. He loves strangers. He loves meeting people and hearing their personal stories. His voice is full of warmth and honey. Yet he is totally appropriate with the girls, and can effortlessly switch over and be just as serious and interesting with Jessie and Will. He is well read,

151

and makes a huge effort to stay that way. Naturally, it's part of his image. No one but me knows how much time and effort he puts into trying to cover up his true history and roots. It irritates me how much he tries to cover up that which I am most proud of.

We also discuss some of my cases, the funnier ones. Actually, there are more tragic and sad cases than there are funny ones. But I stick with the funny ones. Like the time a guy pulled into a drive–through at a fast food place with his gun in hand, and ski mask on, demanding cash. The quick–thinking sales clerk simply shut the window and ducked down. The perp was caught a few blocks away. They also ask about the strange calls that I investigate. Like the man who reported a stranger lurking on the porch, and I kindly asked him if he'd done any on-line shopping of late. Yes, the man had and I handed him the package, after explaining it was the delivery man. Another time, someone reported a baby in a trash can at a local discount store, only to discover it was actually a breakfast burrito. On and on my stories go. Sam keeps staring at me, pleased to see me smiling, laughing and somewhat at ease. I must admit I feel a companionship we haven't shared for a long time.

I soon have the entire table rolling in laughter, which leads to a discussion of some crazy things Jessie saw pet owners doing to their pets. She tells about some lady who had a taxidermist stuff and mount a dozen cats. As if that weren't odd enough, she then tried to bring them in to Jessie for their exams once a year! The craziness of that had us all laughing. Later on, her sister, Lindsey, and her husband, Noah, come over. I am swiftly introduced to an attractive couple, both tall and lean, with dark hair. Lindsey has a quick smile, and seems worldly. She has a world–weariness about people, however, and is somewhat reserved, which I totally get.

But eventually everyone leaves and it is time to go to bed. I walk with Sam in total silence to the apartment. I shut the bedroom door without a word that night. The next day is simply more of the same until Max gets off school and shows up. He and some friends are playing a softball at a nearby field. "Any takers?" he asks, glancing around. Sam glances at me and I don't fail to notice the gleam in his eye. I give him the death stare. *No way.* I have no desire to play sports with these people, and especially with him.

But Sam stands up. "We will. You won't believe the arm on Natalie."

Christina gets up as Melissa squeals, "Oh, I totally suck. But can I come anyway?"

"I want to too!" Emily glances at me before making a rude face at Melissa with her lip curled up and her cheeks squished weird. "Except I totally don't suck. You'll be dust under my heels."

"*That* sounds like Nat," Sam says with a grin. So it's a sister thing. Sam is daring me. I can feel it in his gaze and raised eyebrows, as if to say, *Your call, Nat.* "What do you say?"

"Fine." I keep my glare at bay until everyone else is busy getting up to grab their shoes and change their clothes. His smile expands even wider. How can he be such a cheating, two-timing ass and still have the nerve to smile at me like that? Even worse, how can my heart still thump so painfully in my chest over him?

The baseball field is well-tended. Short grass, raked dirt and the lines are decent enough to delineate the diamond. The back fence has no graffiti. Farther off, kids are climbing on toys and being pushed on swings. People are walking, picnicking, and enjoying the pleasant sun and air. The sky is clear blue and goes on forever here. I breathe in the smell of freshly cut grass. Is there any scent that makes one feel more like it's spring? Or more alive? I have a borrowed mitt on my hand. I'm wearing sneakers, leggings, and a t-shirt, and a baseball cap completes my outfit. There are a bunch of young people here. All of them seem closer to Max and Christina's ages than ours. Friends from high school, I learn. They must know the entire school; how many kids could there be? But the teens are all lithe, slim, athletic and most of all, young. *Youth.* In the last week, it feels like I've completely lost the last remnant of what I once considered my youth.

Whatever. The teams are chosen and I make sure I'm on the team opposite Sam. Oh, Sam... How predictably the young teens and twenty-somethings start fawning over him as he gives them pointers. He even does a few physical demonstrations, instructing the girls to widen their stances, or showing them how to properly grip the baseball bat. Does he miss the one who's rubbing against him suggestively? Honestly? I think that might be possible. His gaze remains on her feet as he intently tries to position the girl from nearly standing on home plate. But she's too busy trying to rub her body on him to notice his instructions. Sam and I take our recreation seriously. I know her lack of seriously trying irritates him more than her sexiness could possibly interest him. Finally, we start to play. After three innings, we're tied, so we play through to four. The weaklings are done. Sam and I make eye contact a few times, both of us slightly annoyed when the others decide to cut the game short. We don't do that. Never. But we're quiet and hold our tongues politely, being guests and all.

Christina is terrible, but Melissa is worse. They can't hit, run, catch, or throw. They pretend to try, but look like typical, uncoordinated, stereotypical "girls" doing it. I play first base. I throw accurately and my catches are spot-on. Playing sports starts to warm me up, and gives me more confidence. I know how to do this stuff. I hit a double, then a triple, and finally, a homerun. I make the most of the outs, or at the very least, instruct and coach the other teammates on how to improve. I watch Sam attempting to do the same thing with his own team, although with more finesse than I possess. I catch him tightening his lips in annoyance, despite all his seemingly supportive instructions and calls. He's as intense in sports as I am. He likes to win as much as I do. And right now? Even with all the shit between us, he won't let me win. I almost respect him for that. Because another man might feel so haunted by fresh guilt, as Sam claims he is, he might be tempted to just let me win. Out of respect. Or care. Or just trying to please me. Not Sam. I nod at him with genuine respect for not doing that.

"Damn, girl. You are something else," Max says to me when I tag him out at first. He's yet to get past me.

I grin, until I see Sam is up next. He stares at me, kicking his feet against the metal bat. That's his ritual. He taps his right, and then his left toes, and then each heel. Every single time. In that exact order. Since he was ten years old, he has done that exact ritual before he bats.

He takes the position. A girl named Jayne tosses in a lame, underhand, slow pitch. I ache to grab it and lob in an over-hand fast pitch. That's the kind Sam, Dustin and I always played. That's why I'm not pitching. I can't take this slow crap. It's like listening to an orchestra play a symphony when all I really want is some damn rock 'n' roll!

But the next pitch is good enough and Sam easily hits it and connects. I see it and back up from my position, hoping his famous hook comes my way. He hits it mid–field. The fielder misses and goes after it. Sam is running hard with a huge grin on his face; heading for home. I know it. I run to home base and yell and scream to the fielder to throw the ball to me. He finally manages to grab it and throws it to me. I catch the crazy, too-high throw with a jump as high as I can stretch. As Sam's barrels down at me. I land on the base, just as his foot crosses it.

I had it! I'm sure I landed a millisecond before he crossed. I grin triumphantly to tag him out and glance all around. No one else is cheering. They aren't sure if I got the out or not, and there's no umpire to rule. Or anyone who even knows the damn rules. Max kind of shrugs, acting as an unofficial judge. "Uh, wow. Close. But I think Sam had it… just barely. I think we won."

Throwing my mitt down, I rail, "Are you blind, Max? Jesus H! I had that. I caught it! He is so out. I can't believe this shit…" I begin to rant. Max's expression goes from amiable to shocked. He glances around, looking for help, or perhaps an explanation as to why this is suddenly happening to him. I feel a hand on my shoulder. It's Sam.

"Hey, Nat. It was close. Fair call. We won."

I whirl on him and push his hand away. "Bullshit! You did not."

"We did too. It's fair."

"Fair, my ass. Let me tell you what's fair. And this? This is not fair. I had you. You are out. You didn't win. Unless, of course, you insist on cheating? Always the preferred method, huh?"

We are staring at each other. Outside noises, colorful flashes of clothes on the other players, the sun on my arms, all of those things fade as we stare each other down. I am transported. I see him. I see him with her. Doing with her, what he should only ever do with me, exclusively. My nostrils flare, my eyes widen. I become wild. The familiar rage bubbles just beneath the surface of my skin. All it takes is one little scratch or prick before it gushes out of me.

"I had no idea you were so competitive. Okay, we'll replay the point." Max's voice chimes in behind me. It's a fair, level–headed solution, but I can hear the falsity in his tone. He's probably wondering why anyone would care that much. But since I do, fine! I get to have my way. I close my eyes as I realize I'm standing amongst a bunch of kids, all strangers, even my sisters, with my fists clenched, my lungs heaving, and my eyes on fire. All while participating in a deadlocked staring contest with my husband over a single point in a for-fun softball game.

Only it was not just a softball game. It symbolizes my entire life with Sam.

But no one else realizes that. I look and sound crazy, stupid, competitive, and belligerent. I act like the poorest sport in history. I open my eyes and exhale a deep rush of breath from my mouth. *Calm. Act calm and normal.* I must not be like that. I loosen my fists and glance around finally. "Oh shit. I'm sorry. Sam and I have an ongoing competition. We've been playing since kids, keeping track of who wins, he has four more than me. It's stupid, really. A contest. A lark. I got overheated for no reason. You all won." What I say is true. We do have an ongoing tally of our wins. But my over-heated poor-sportsmanship is actually no more than a sad cry for my husband, as I mourn my devastation at his betrayal.

Max cracks up. "Holy shit! You two are hilarious. And damn, Natalie, you are one chick I would never mess with!"

I turn and sock him in the shoulder. "Don't call me *chick*. It's degrading and juvenile. Haven't you—"

His grin is huge. "Yeah, I got your number. You are so easy to get going." Now, he is full on laughing. I see nothing but fun in his gaze. He's razzing me. He's doing what I usually do, trash talking. Competitor dissing. Not too serious. But enough to end a good game.

Christina finally laughs and comes over to me. "I thought you were going to punch Sam, or maybe even Max. And not like I punch. If you punched them, they'd need first aid."

The tense situation is defused as I dip my head in a small smile of acknowledgement. I know that I've overreacted and shown my way-too-competitive side. Sam uses the opportunity to swing his arm around my shoulder and pull me closer. I push away, but he's got me firmly. It looks casual, but it's not. He grips the back of my neck and presses his lips into my hair. I try to push him off me, but he holds me steady. I can't get away from him without being super obvious. Why should I cringe and fight my husband's affections?

Then he whispers into my ear, "Fight me. Keep fighting me. Because that way, I know you haven't given up on us." He lets me go and keeps walking to grab some water off the bleachers. I stare after him, but no one else notices me. He likes my unattractive attributes? I get so heated about games and competition, especially winning, I'm ridiculous sometimes. How can anyone find me tolerable? Let alone attractive? But I know I've given myself away here with Sam. I might hate him, but nothing can conceal the fact that he's broken my heart and I don't know how to deal with it.

THE GROUP of teens we're with decides we should all hang out; and Christina is Sam's and my ride. I can't believe I'm stuck with them, hanging out like a damn high school freshman with the wrong crowd. They eat and laugh and joke. There are a lot of jokes about Max and Christina, so their cousin thing doesn't earn my comments alone. There's joke after joke of family inbreeding and they take it all with smiles and good humor.

We eat hamburgers and fries at a favorite local place. It's good and I like the special sauce. I hear a bunch of stories about my sister in high school and the trouble that Max got into often. His famous stint the summer before last in illegal fighting managed to raise him to god–like status with the guys his age. Even Sam perks up and asks all kinds of questions about it. The most offensive is, how could short Max win his fights? Max merely laughs off all the innocuous ribbing.

We stay there for a long while until another couple wants to go to the beach, wherever that is. Max and Christina consult with us, explaining how it used to be their hangout, and since this is the first time they are all home together since last summer, do we mind?

I do. *Extremely.* Because it prolongs my presence in Sam's company. But I smile and nod as if it's just another way to spend the evening. Melissa and Emily get permission to come also and we are soon out on a darkening beach with a rushing river nearby. It makes lapping background gurgles. We are on private land and people are sitting around a large bonfire. It's a relaxed atmosphere as they reminisce. There are even a dozen or so lawn chairs available. We sit for a while. Finally, the crowd depletes until it's just Sam and me, my sisters and Max. I sit on the ground, drawing my knees up while staring into the fire. Sam sits in a chair near me. I've had enough of his presence. And close proximity. I can feel every single time he moves his arm, or leans forward. I am hyper-aware of every single move he makes and all the words he says. I am acting almost like I used to with him.

It felt a bit like being a teenager again hanging out together the way we are surrounded by them. However, we never found a secluded beach in the middle of nowhere and had a bonfire, of course. We usually went to the field near our apartment, or behind one of the old, abandoned buildings on the block whenever we wanted to hang out undisturbed. We still had the same idea.

"How did you two meet?" Christina asks Sam. My head is down and I am nearly hypnotized by the waning fire's glow. I don't raise my head. I feel Sam rustling his butt back and forth before he finally leans forward to rest his elbows on his knees.

"We were childhood friends. Always."

"So were we. The best of friends," Christina says, her voice warming up. I see her glance at Max and he at her.

"Nat and I were always close too."

"How old were you when you met?" asks Emily, who rarely speaks. Her gaze is fixed on Sam, and I don't fail to notice the pink flush in her cheeks. She has a total crush on Sam.

"I was eight. Nat was five. She was walking with her parents, and my brother asked her why her skin wasn't the same color as her parents'. I boxed him on the ears and called him something…"

"Twerp. You called him a twerp, and told me not to listen to the 'bottom feeder.'" I jerk my shoulders back. I was not intending to speak. But there I go, joining in with all the pointless and hurtful reminiscing. Stupid, right? What better way to sadden me more and make everything hurt even worse?

Lifting my gaze to Sam, I see the small smile of nostalgia on his lips. He nods at me. "Yes, that sounds right. Anyway, from that day on, Dustin and Natalie followed me everywhere. I was their babysitter for years at a time. But Natalie quickly outshone Dustin, as well as every other boy in our neighborhood, with her speed, coordination and agility. She and I started to compete when she was eight. For a few early years, we were well-matched, until puberty gave me a biological advantage."

I bristle. It still annoys me. "That's the only damn reason. Stupid boys," I mumble.

I notice Melissa smiling from across the fire at us. Sam's warm hand is on my shoulder. He's taking advantage of my unwillingness to let anyone know how much I currently loathe him. So now he thinks he can touch me? To try and... what did he say? *Start somewhere?* Well, screw him. No amount of pretty memories could ever undo the horrifying one I now possess of him with another woman.

"When did it change for you guys?" Christina directly asks me.

I stare hard at the fire, trying to ignore Sam whose focus narrows on me. I casually dig my hands into the sand and let the cold grains run through my fingers. I do it again and again. I'm stalling, and letting the repetition slow my racing heart.

"The summer he graduated from UCLA. He came out with an inflated ego, he was so high on being a frat–boy idiot and so smug and sure he was better than all of us. But by then, my mom was dying and he was my oldest and best friend... so I told him about it. And..."

"And?" Emily urged. I had her complete attention. She is always hanging on what I say, like a hang glider grasping the wind. Our story entrances her. She probably envisions Sam as the noble hero of a romance novel. She also, no doubt, thinks we are some kind of *happily ever after* story. She has no clue of the tragedy that now taints my whole life with Sam.

"And she told me about her mom one night in my parents' apartment. And I think that was the first time I saw her as a girl. She was always a friend, sure, as well as a competitor. But a pretty girl? No, not to me anyway, which was crazy stupid because she *was*. I remember more than one of our mutual friends making a play for her."

I sharpen my gaze on his. He grins when he notices my stunned look. "You didn't realize that? Sure, Ty and Jackson and Asher. I shut them down pretty quick. They noticed you before I did, when you blossomed and turned from a rival to... a girl they wanted to date. I never told you that?"

I nod in the negative. He lifts one side of his mouth. "Anyway, until that night, when I saw her so hurt and trying to remain so strong about her mother, that was when I first realized she was all grown–up. I was no longer her big brother friend, or protector or the guy who's always trying to poke fun at her just to see her reaction. Suddenly, she's a beautiful young woman and I didn't know what to do. It was never that way for us before, not until that exact moment."

"I was always the tomboy; never once did I become the graceful swan," I add with an impassioned tone. "And I still haven't."

Melissa nearly claps her hands. "That's so awesome. I can't imagine having so much confidence in myself. For me, it's almost impossible to be… comfortable. I always want to be the way people want me to be. You know? I mean…" She stops talking and glances around. Only then does she realize all of us are listening to her. She drops her head, shaking it, letting her long hair fall over her face. There are obvious self–image issues with her. My heart aches. I remember that age. It was so hard. Young girls are so beautiful, but they never believe their beauty is the right or desirable kind.

"I say, if a guy doesn't like you for exactly who and what you are, especially when it comes to your looks, then fuck 'em, Melissa! They don't deserve even a skinny slice of time from your brain. Discard them along with any rude comments as if they're no more than trash you're tossing away. Got it?"

She lifts her head and we stare at each other. I have a strong personality. I know that. Especially about women in general, and how I think we should feel about ourselves. I might come on a tad too strong, but Melissa's eyes fill with tears as she nods in agreement.

"I try. But I can't always."

"It takes time to figure yourself out," Christina adds more gently.

"No. It doesn't." I fight this common stereotype often. Young girls erroneously believe they shouldn't be self–confident and strong, or announce to others exactly who and what they are. "You know, even now, what feels right to you. I mean it, Melissa—"

"Missy. Everyone calls me Missy."

I pause. I know everyone calls her that, but I don't call her that. In an almost bashful way, she hides her face and mumbles that softly. I can almost feel hot tears pricking my eyes. She wants me to call her by her nickname. That means something. It means something real has started to form between us. My heart swells.

"Missy," I say while holding her stare. She smiles a girlish, soft smile that instantly connects us. "Don't let anyone give you doubts when your gut knows something is true. No matter how cute, or pretty the boy is. The old advice that if he doesn't like you as you are, just screw him, is so true." I glance at Sam, scowling. She notices and laughs too. She doesn't know my expression is not just a flirt or banter. I am doing it, in reality, because of what we are now.

Holding my gaze captive, while speaking to Melissa he says, "She's right, Melissa. Guys are dumb at your age, but when they grow older, they sometimes figure it out. Don't let them tell you who or what you are." Sam earns a smidgeon of my grudging respect.

"How old were you two? When you got together, I mean?"

"I was twenty," I reply while shaking my head. At the time, it seemed like Sam took years to notice me. I thought he would *never* notice me as anything but his tomboy friend. But looking back, I realize what a baby I was even at twenty. Unprepared for life or adulthood, I was amazed at how fast it all passed. I fell in love when I was still young, and maybe...

it really wasn't all I thought it was. Maybe in the end, it came to this; and we were just too young. For all my tough talk and tomboy ways, I felt so sure life would always go my way back then. I still had plenty of hope and optimism. I didn't consider all the ways life can beat you down. Or your love. It seemed so simple at twenty. It was all about love. Attraction. Sex.

"What happened to your mom?" I am jolted out of my reverie by Christina's question, which she asks in a kind, empathetic voice.

"She had cancer. Colon cancer, and it was stage four before she finally went to the doctor, so there wasn't much left to do for her. She died when I was just twenty."

"When I was first looking for you, I had a family friend hunt down information about you. I read in the stuff I got from him that your mom had died just a few years ago."

"No. That's about when my dad first started to show signs of dementia. Your fact checker had some things wrong."

"You've lost a lot in the last eight years. Both parents? Twenty? Oh, Natalie, that's so young. That would be me losing mom *now*. I can't imagine that. I'm just... *so* sorry." Christina holds my gaze with her tiny smile, and her eyes big with compassion. I feel her apology. I sense she really is sorry for me. I nod and accept her sympathy.

"Thank you. It was rough. It was terrible, actually." And it still haunts me, even today.

"Is that what brought you two together?" Emily asks.

"Yes." Sam answers for both of us. His gaze finds mine when I turn towards him. He holds it and we share a brief moment of familiarity, like we always used to as we both remember. Together, we are remembering Mom's unnecessary death. How hard it was to bury her. How I clung to his arm, leaning my entire body against his side to just hold me up. We both cried as after everyone else left, we watched them completely cover her coffin. And Sam let me sit there for hours, in the cold air as I tried to grasp what was right before me. My mother was dead. He didn't make me leave until I finally said I was ready. We missed all the formal funeral reception stuff. But he got that I needed this cold, harsh reality to start facing my grief more than I could play hostess at my mother's funeral.

After that summer, Sam was supposed to leave to earn his MBA at UCLA. He left for three months. My mother died just before he left, so we were barely official as boyfriend and girlfriend. During those three months, I lost my mind. I got so depressed, I didn't get out of bed. Dustin called Sam and told him what I would never have confessed. Even in my depression and grief, my pride prevented me from ever telling him. Sam promptly quit school and came back to the neighborhood. He entered my bedroom and swept me up in his arms. He held me and promised he'd never leave me again. And he didn't.

His presence, however, wasn't enough to cure me. He insisted that I see my doctor and I was on antidepressants for a while. It was a real illness. I almost *couldn't* physically get out of bed. But until then, I never had a mood disorder. That would have made me look weak. I felt weak for needing the pills to cope, but they worked. I eventually found myself again. And Sam was right there for me. He was there beside me when I buried my mother, and when I tried to pick myself up afterwards. I wasn't much of a crier. But the sadness weighed on me like concrete being poured through my blood vessels. I didn't understand what was wrong with me. Sam saw through it, however, and helped ease me into accepting professional help.

Meanwhile, after calling a friend from UCLA, he got a job in San Francisco. It wasn't at a big or prestigious firm, like he originally wanted, and it wasn't L.A. either, but it *was* with me. Or so he said. He and I moved in together not too long after he returned. We lived in a crappy, little studio apartment on the fifth floor of a building. No elevator, and lots of stairs. I was in limbo, wanting to become a cop, but still too young to start. So I worked odd jobs. Finally, the following summer, I began the brutally comprehensive interview process. Later on, I eagerly started with the academy. All the while, Sam worked insane hours, the equivalent of two full-time jobs. Under extreme stress and high expectations, Sam earned his MBA from the University of San Francisco. We were married about two years after our first kiss.

I shake my head now. It doesn't matter. Not any of this. This history of those two people no longer exists and the relationship they once shared no longer has any future.

I banish all those memories now in my head. We are no longer those two happy, carefree, connected and in love kids.

CHAPTER 11

NATALIE

THE CONVERSATION TURNS TOWARDS more banal things and I stare once more, like I'm in a trance, at the fire. Christina and Max get up and so do the girls; they are ready to leave. We are all quiet as we pull into their parents' house. I glance around. It feels so surreal still for me to be here. We exit the car and they go into the main house, even Max. Sam and I say goodnight before silently heading towards the side of the house to the apartment. The moon is big and round tonight, providing almost a spotlight effect to guide us. We are walking towards Will's shop and less than ten feet separate us. Just before the stairs, Sam suddenly stops. I step back, unwilling to get close to him.

"Do you remember that first night we spent in our own apartment? We had no furniture, so we had to lie in sleeping bags on the floor, thinking we owned the world? We giggled like teenagers with our pizza and pop, thinking we were so grown up, and out on our own. Remember that night? How we talked until three about all the things we wanted to do and be?"

Of course, I remembered how it felt to lie on the hard floor as we sat cross–legged, talking until we stretched out. We were so excited to be all alone, we talked for hours on end. We could have sex anytime we wanted! That was a huge revelation for us. Until then, we had to deal with his parents, as well as Dustin, trying to hook up around them without them knowing what we were doing. I step back. "I don't want to do this. You can't talk away what happened by bringing up fond memories we once shared. Our past can't make up for the now."

"I never thought, not even for a second back then, that we wouldn't be anything but perfect together. We were such a good team. We were so honest, and we totally got each other. I remember how you so completely understood me. I never had that before in my relationships. You were volatile, and quick to anger at me, but I could trust you to do that. I could always be honest, even if you got mad. Knowing that was freeing somehow. You were the only the person I never had to perform with. Not perform, actually… just…"

"Not be the so-perfect Sam Ford."

He sighed. "You always got that about that about me."

I don't want to be drawn into a conversation of any kind, especially alone with him. He is staring listlessly down at one of the wooden steps. They lead up to a door on the outside of the little apartment.

I sigh and cross my arms over my chest, rubbing my bare skin even though I don't feel cold. "I tried not to get jealous over all the women who threw themselves at you. I saw how many wanted you. I took comfort in knowing that none of them actually knew you. None of them knew that when you came home from work, or from one of those insufferable country clubs, or formal dinners you dragged us to, you were far from perfect. You fart in your sleep. You dribble pee around the toilet seat more like a squirt gun than a man. You tell me things, both little and big, that no one else knows. I thought I was the one person you felt safe with."

"You were. You were the only person I was real with. My parents always wanted me to go so much further in life than they did. They knew Dustin wasn't ambitious either, but I was. I could do it. But to do that, I had to sacrifice my youth and my early twenties. There were no clueless parties that lasted nights on end for me. There was simply work and more work. You managed to break the monotony of it for me. Only you."

"Let me pass." I start to step around him. I don't want to go backwards to remember the Sam I first fell in love with and dated. I can't forget the way he seemed to grasp me whenever we managed to steal some moments alone. He needed me so much and I reveled in his need.

"We should talk about what happened. We should talk about all of it, not just my infidelity." His voice sounds low and weary.

I stop and with exaggerated motions I sit a few steps above him my actions jerky with anger. "Okay, fine. How was she? Good, wet pussy? Or dry and small? Did she moan a lot? I don't remember. Honestly, I was so shocked, I don't even remember what she looked like. She was blonde though, as usual, until me, of course. I was never relegated to that stupid box."

I know that's not what he means. He lets my sarcasm fall like an anvil between us. He doesn't react and I shift forward, running my hands up and down my leggings. The powerful images that fill my brain are still so distressing. I tuck my hands under my armpits and squeeze my torso.

He sighs loudly, but walks a few steps above me and sits

too. "I don't remember what she was like. I remember looking up and seeing you. Staring at me. Everything else is irrelevant."

"Oh, my GOD! I don't actually want to discuss *it*. I was being sarcastic."

"I'll answer whatever you want to know. If you want to talk about it, we'll talk about it for the next five hours. I won't hide anything from you. I won't insult you, or ask if we can just move past it. I will tell you anything you need to hear."

"Would you have told me? If I didn't have the pleasure of witnessing you myself? Would you have told me?"

I don't look up where he sits above me on the stairs, but I hear his shirt rustling as his legs shift. "I-I can't say. I honestly never considered that until just now. I hope so. I hope I would have told you, Nat."

"Don't call me that." He nods. I can see him through my periphery. "Nat" was my friend name. The name he used when all was good between us.

"And 'talking about all of it,' I assume you mean the baby situation? Are you saying that somehow led to this? Is that your theory? Your excuse?"

"Looking back now, I think we were starting to drift before that even."

"Well, then! Surely, you are justified. After all, any good counselor would first ask how long it's been since we had sex. And our answer is… what? Six months? I'm sure you have it right down to the nanosecond, and that's why you needed extramarital sex. Sure, it's all my fault for not doing it more with you. Why—"

"I didn't want to either," he cuts in. I stiffen my back. Well, yeah, great. I need to hear he didn't want me, but her? Some faceless, blonde bimbo?

"I—"

"I meant—" He interrupts me, his tone now gentler. "I was confused and upset all that time too. I was working insane hours. I wasn't thinking about sex. I never consciously thought about how long it had been. I knew we needed to talk and work things out... I just kept putting it off. I made excuses. I was busy. We were both busy. It could wait. That night, I was there strictly to work, Natalie. Like every other night of my life. *I was working.* I was blurry-eyed with sleep deprivation. She came in. Her name is Chantal. She's a stupid secretary that used to flirt with me during office hours. I never... and I know you can't believe me, but I never flirted with her or considered her someone I even wanted to have sex with. She was just another pool secretary to me. Nothing I obsessed about. I looked straight past her. I ignored her. She came in, came on to me, and I got up to throw her out. Do you want me to stop?"

"No. Finish. Tell me." I somehow need to hear his lame explanation. I need to re-experience and hear all about what I saw, except through his eyes. I need to understand that it was real and that's what I want to see him admit. I glance back to meet his gaze for a brief moment. He nods. His jaw is locked, and his expression is grim. He knows how badly I need details before things make sense to me. Before I can leave and turn my back on him, I need to hear all of this.

"She tried playing coy, asking dumb questions and telling this lame story of why she was there so late. I opened the door and was standing there, waiting for her to leave. She started to go past me and stopped right in front of me. She put her hand directly on my dick, and pressed while using the other hand to pull my neck to her mouth. It was only a matter of minutes before you came in. One moment, I was pushing her out, and the next, she was lying on my desk. I don't clearly remember any conscious decision to do it. I didn't stare at her with lustful desire or anything. There was no great moment when I felt any kind of urge or impulse to have sex with her. I didn't want to. Or at least, I didn't set out to. I just... Fuck!" He suddenly stands up and leans heavily on the railing as he shakes his head. He runs his hands over and over in his hair, then puts them on the railing and pushes his weight on them. "This is hard. You really want me to say more?"

"Yes." My voice is glacial. Of course, the picture he paints is nearly tearing my heart out of my chest. He might as well be using a scalpel and forceps to ruthlessly yank it out. He's painting his side of the story so real, I think he may succeed in making me throw up. But then again, I know I need to hear his side. That way, Sam's charms, apologies, and circular logic can't change what the real picture is: the end of us.

"I just remember her being on me. Okay, she turned me on. But it was fast and cold and it could have been anyone. Her voice, her face, and her body? None of it registered with me. She pressed herself on me and wanted me so I responded. I pushed her onto my desk. I ripped off her underwear and she helped undo mine. She had a condom. I was inside her and it was no more than gratuitous sex. It was just sex. It wasn't even good sex. And then—" his voice catches, but he clears his throat and continues, "and then I looked up and there you were. I felt—"

"Stop. Don't tell me how you *felt*."

He is staring out into the Hendrickses' farmyard. The night air is cool now. The animals create the only disturbance. Trees loom in shadowy forms beyond us. It's very quiet and country. I find it almost hard to believe how we can be here now, doing this.

"What do you want from me, Sam? I have to ask. You know what I witnessed. How could you think I'd want to see you again? Or want you here? There is no going back from that."

His head hangs. "I want to talk. I want to talk to you. The way I used to. Honestly. For real. The kind of realness we shared when your mom died and your dad went away. But then, isn't that the start?"

I leap to my feet. "The start of what?"

"The end." His tone is chilling, and final. "That's when you started to withdraw. I know what losing both of them did to you. Your dad was your last link to your family and identity. And you felt a large amount of resentment after realizing that I was all you had left in the world, and my family. It made you feel abandoned. And trapped."

I lean back against the cool wood of the building, my hands gripping the rough-hewn lumber. "You never said that to me before." He was right. I did feel both things.

"I wanted to give you space. It was so unfair how he faded from you—from us. I loved him too. And then we found out that—"

"Screw off, if you're going to say what I think you're trying to say."

He shakes his head. "I wasn't going to blame you; I was going to say, we never dealt with it. Not together anyway."

"Because there was nothing to deal with. We can't have kids. Or more accurately, *I* can't have kids. So what, Sam? It makes me less of a woman? Less desirable to you? Because fuck you! It does not. I refuse to let it define me as a woman or a failure. If I can't have kids, I don't need kids. I don't need—"

"I do though, Natalie."

He stops me dead. His quiet statement is almost a whisper between us, and far more significant than my heated outbursts. "You said you didn't care that much."

Right when my dad started getting worse, we thought about having kids. We tried for over a year, and nothing. I always had infrequent, unreliable periods. I casually

173

attributed that to how much I'd always exercised and lifted weights. Sam and I both got physical exams, just to rule out other things, never dreaming there would be anything. We were both so young and healthy. But there was a problem. I suffer from abnormal ovulation, meaning my eggs don't release. Consequently, there is a significantly lowered chance of pregnancy for me without, what I consider, super–heroic measures. Drugs. Artificial insemination. In vitro fertilization. We considered the available options, and most have forty percent or better success rates for infertile couples, such as we now are. But I wanted nothing to do with any of it. I decided I didn't need to have kids. Sam was shocked too by the news. For a few days, I felt like a failure, but then I realized it was just how I was built. There was nothing wrong with me. I was merely unable to conceive babies. It wasn't the end of my world. I figured we could keep having unprotected sex, and if it ever happened, then it was meant to be. I heard stories of couples who did everything they could to have a baby, and then, low and behold, out of nowhere, when they were finally relaxed and stopped actively trying, they got pregnant. That sounded like the best option to me. I wasn't averse to having a child, but if I didn't, I was fine with that too. I certainly didn't want to start a journey down the road of "infertility options."

"I read up on it. I read all that literature the doctor gave you. I listened to their explanations for how you might feel. I was ready to be there for you. To reassure you that I loved you no matter what. I didn't need for you to get pregnant. That I—"

"Your feelings were hurt because my self-esteem didn't take enough of a hit to suit your liking?"

His shoulders deflate. "No, Natalie, I didn't want to press you, or make you feel like you should react another way. Besides, you didn't want to talk about it. You didn't ask me about it. You decided that was how God or nature made you and intended you to be, so we weren't meant to have kids. You never asked me my personal opinion."

I push into the building and stare at him, my jaw dropping. "We agreed. We had our careers. Our very important and very fulfilling, at least to us, careers…" I whisper, fading off in stunned silence.

"Yes. We did. And we do. But I wanted to discuss the option of having a baby another way or adopting. But I knew what your thoughts on adoption were. No. No way. Hell would freeze over. You would definitely not adopt a child. The adoptee would not be the adopter of another. Those were your words. I didn't understand it then; I mean, your life was good with your adopted parents. You did and do love them. Why couldn't the adoptee become the adopter? It worked for you. Why not pay that goodness forward? I thought maybe it was God, or nature, or destiny's remedy: we should adopt a child just like you were adopted."

"You didn't think that."

"I did," he says softly. His gaze finds mine. "I wanted to talk about a lot of things. But you became… fierce with me. With everyone. You seemed to need to prove how strong you are. Which I admire, Natalie. I didn't want you to feel bad, or down, or sad. But I did want to talk *to you*. Not be *talked at* by you. But I was afraid to say anything… I was afraid if I tried, you might think I was criticizing you or something. But I simply wanted to talk about someday in the future, and how we might still be able to have kids. I don't know. Maybe I don't want them either. I just wanted the option, and the chance, to talk about it. Maybe compromise or…"

"You can't compromise. You either have a kid or not."

He shut his eyes, and seemed so weary, as if he could not handle standing there another second. He shook his head. "I just wanted the right to talk about it with you. Maybe you didn't need me then, but I needed you. Yeah, duh, you're the strong one, I guess, in this. But you didn't seem to notice me. We talked less and less… about that, about our parents, until eventually, I can't remember the last time we talked about what we were doing for the day, or having for dinner. This is the first time I can remember being honest with you in a very long time."

He shakes his head. Eyes still closed. "I wronged you. I hurt you. I betrayed you. I hate myself. I hate who and what I've become and done to you and to us. But there was something missing and something gone, and you refused to stop and notice. Or talk about it. Or even to acknowledge me." He opens his eyes and his gaze pierces me. "And I didn't tell you, so it's my fault too. I know that. But my mistake did not come completely out of a vacuum. I was frustrated, angry and hurt. And I swear to God, you never once considered if I'd have any kind of reaction to it."

"You just wanted a perfect, barefoot and pregnant wife in your kitchen. Four or five kids and a good little wifey who didn't cause you any trouble or embarrassment. No challenges. Or at the least, a polished society wife who could carry off your insane need for rich snobs to like and be impressed by you."

I spit it out at him, and my venom is toxic. My rising anger makes it easy.

"No," he says simply. Sharply. He keeps shaking his head. "No, that's not what I wanted. I wanted *you*. Police Officer Natalie Ford. I just hoped we could make decisions about our life and our family together."

"Well, you certainly, epically managed to do that, now, didn't you, Sam Ford?"

He stares hard at me. We are close, barely two steps apart. He is above me. His shoulders fall and his mouth turns down in a deep frown. "Yes. I did."

Pivoting on his foot, Sam goes up the steps and inside the little apartment. I stare after him. I don't expect such an abrupt end to this. It was the most honest we've been with each other in months; okay, maybe a year. I am shaking. My hands are trembling and I bury my face in my hands. Did I do that? Did I never ask him? Did I, in my pride over how I dealt with it, never consider how Sam was dealing with it?

But typical me, my anger always trumps my sentiments. The emotions hurt and choke my throat. The anger? It's quite refreshing. Easy. It clears up my throat and head and just blurts out.

But at what cost? What is the cost for being right?

CHAPTER 12

 AM

I LIE THERE HALF the night, just staring at the ceiling where the reflection from the outside yard casts odd shapes in shadows. I throw a tennis ball up and down repeatedly as I relive last night. I also relive the last week along with the last years.

Our final conversation keeps playing and replaying in my head.

I had pushed Natalie into having kids. I wanted to try for a baby. I talked her into doing it. She wanted to wait until she was older and had been on the job more. About this same time I pushed for us to move. It was too much. I see that now looking back.

She liked the small apartment that was only a few blocks from where we grew up. Our days as newlyweds were perhaps the best, but I was too clueless and busy back then to even notice. She worked a lot of shifts and crazy hours, but then again, so did I. After being hired at BorderLine, my entire focus centered on my career. We spent what little spare time we had together, usually around the mission, or at different bars. We enjoyed the music culture that thrived around there, as well as a smattering of different hole–in–the–wall restaurants serving everything from oyster bars to burgers. We often walked or took the BART to different districts of the city on the weekends to hang out. We were never bored. There was always something to do, or some-place to go. Chinatown became one of our favorites and we spent most of our Saturday afternoons down there, brows-ing, and of course, getting dinner. It was always over-crowded, thriving with tourists, and seeing so many colors and traditional lanterns only enlivened the atmosphere. There are endless restaurants, teahouses, temples, fish and fowl markets; not to mention all the merchants peddling almost every kind of herb or other strange merchandise. We always felt like we stepped onto a different continent and were on a vacation, when all the while, we remained within our own city's limits. We thoroughly appreciated its unique sights, tastes and colors.

I look back now on all those memories and wonder if I appreciated what I had then. Because at the time it wasn't enough for me. I wanted more. I wanted it *all.* The company offered me a promotion, which came with a Victorian house on Dolores Street, where we now lived. It's hilly, quiet and truly spectacular, being so close to Dolores Park. When we first moved there, we often played tennis or soccer at the park. It was a substantial improvement over the lot we remembered playing sports together in. But as time went by, we went there together less frequently. It offered great views of the city and the East Bay, but Natalie was not one to sit around enjoying the vistas. Our house was one of the smallest on a street of grand, old Victorians. We could never afford to live there on our own dime. Natalie didn't want to move there. She said it was too big and pretentious, and it didn't match anything about her or her taste. She didn't like all the gentrification that had taken place over the passing years in many parts of the city. She also didn't like living in what she felt was a "freaking postcard." People imagining San Francisco housing pretty much see the very picture of our street. I personally decorated and furnished the house. Yes, typically, the wife would've been assigned such chores, but it worked for us. Or at least, I believed it did. However, there was really nothing typical about Natalie ever, and that was what so attracted me to her.

About the same time we were getting moved into this bigger house, I pressured her harder to try and have a baby. It would come in the way of her job, of course, but I argued that it would have to do that at some point anyway. Biology, right? Not my fault. She always tried to resist the biological constraints of being a girl, then later, a woman.

So we started trying to conceive, and nothing happened. I grew impatient. I was ready. I wanted to do this *now.* I was always like that once I decided my course of action. But duh, there was no controlling this. I did my research, and even questioned my own mom about conception and the like. I know for a fact I drove Natalie nuts. She had no one to consult, and just wanted to let things go on as they were. I insisted we get checked out medically. I don't know if I regret that now, or not. I mean, if we'd waited another two years, we'd still have heard the same news. News that devastated me. Natalie took the results with complete calm. She had solid control of her emotions. The first few days after the revelation, I assumed she was merely denying what was going on. I even thought she might be holding in her true reaction.

Or not. Really, she didn't have a strong reaction to it. She shrugged it off with mild disappointment and said she was fine. She simply accepted the news that we could not easily make our own babies.

We got home from the doctor's office and several days passed before I finally asked her to talk to me about it. I remember that conversation as clearly as I can see the sky outside the window right now. She sat in our living room and finally told me how the news affected her. She shrugged and said she was sorry, but at least, we knew now and we could deal with it. She gave me kudos for insisting we dig deeper into the problem. It was a relief for her just to know. There were no tears, or anger, or further discussion.

And that was it. That was our only conversation about her problem conceiving children.

I was stunned. Not because she could not have kids and I was married to her, but because I realized then what a relief it was to her. She didn't really care about having kids. She thought it was a sign we just weren't supposed to. She accepted that without grief or hesitation. The decision was already made for her.

And therefore, for me.

I cared though. I remember how my heart squeezed when we met with her OB/GYN. I held her hand tighter and tighter as we heard the news together. I can still feel the sinking sensation in my guts. I turned to her immediately, thinking she needed me to be strong. I was determined to do that.

But she didn't need my strength. She shook her head with intensity at the doctor, listening with a sober expression, taking in the news with a seriousness I can't deny.

I thought we both needed some time to let it all sink in, and to deal with our separate emotions and opinions on the matter. She portrayed, and pretty convincingly, how well she accepted her condition as her new reality. She didn't want to sit around crying about it, or even discussing it. It was part of who she was and she could accept that without any problem.

The thing is, I could too. I could accept our inability to conceive our own natural child, because there were options. Adoption. Surrogates. In vitro fertilization. I don't know exactly what, or even how far I'd be willing to pursue parenthood, but I wanted to explore it. I wanted to find out. I figured we could start collecting information and talking about the alternatives before we made a decision together.

I wanted to have a child. I still do. But Natalie didn't ask me. She accepted her diagnosis as *our diagnosis* and acted like I had no feelings or thoughts about it. I felt like a monster for being so disappointed in her body. I wasn't trying to change what reality was; I wanted to discuss our goals together, and what we wanted, if we dared to try another way. I wanted her to acknowledge how much it affected me too. She didn't open the discussion up to me. She expected me to be fine with the knowledge that we most likely could not conceive. That was the new reality and I had better get on board.

I grew to resent her for that. She so cavalierly decided I couldn't be a father. I wanted then, and still want to be a father. But more than that even, I wanted to talk to her, or fight with her, or cry with her, just to feel *something* with her about it. For me, it was a startling development in our life together. But I wanted to deal with it *together.* I wanted her to care about what I felt and thought. I just wanted her acknowledgment that it affected me too.

But she wouldn't. Natalie refused to talk about it. She didn't want to tell anyone and she asked me not to. Including Dustin and my parents. It was *her* body, and I needed to respect *her* decision.

I understood that, so I didn't tell anyone, despite the slowly growing black knot inside my heart. I was angry. She shut me down. She didn't even try to find out how I felt. So looking back, I guess I shut her down too.

She started to irritate me more. Every little thing she did started to grate on me, and since I could comment on those things, I did. Natalie being a mess? Always. Only now I nagged at every little thing she didn't put away, and cupboard she didn't close. Looking back, I see I used all the petty stuff to argue and pick fights about, when really, it was the bigger issue she forbade me from discussing that I wanted to fight about. That was the source of all our bickering. I wanted to argue, fight, cry, or voice my thoughts. I'm not sure what I needed to do. I just wanted for us to deal with it together.

But I picked at her. I criticized the long hours she worked being a cop. And repeated how dangerous it was. I acted as if everything that gave her a strong identity was somehow not good enough for me. I complained that I wanted her to be a more traditional–acting woman than she was. I blamed my career and socializing as the reason I needed her to change. So naturally, she chose not to come with me to anymore dinners, or meetings, or charity events, or even nights out at Davies Symphony Hall to hear the San Francisco Symphony, which used to be the one thing Natalie liked to do. That was a favorite of Jayden's too and therefore, something I was frequently invited to.

Each time she refused to go to one of my work outings I harped on her for days afterwards. I dissed her about being a cop, and claimed that was half of why not having kids didn't bother her.

I let things go, but I actually did not let anything go. She started to freeze me out when I got too rude about her job, or pressured her to be more supportive of mine. I listened to Jayden razzing me about my image. I insisted I needed to bring her to those stupid, pointless socializing events that happened outside the office. And there were a lot of them. I usually went alone and resented every single moment of them. BorderLine has a rabid, crowded and vicious internal political scene. Jayden's dad, the long-time CEO, likes things that way. He thinks it keeps his executives and managers in stiff competition, trying to improve and outdo each other. It is like a micro-capitalistic society inside the company. Image is very important. There are a lot of client schmoozing involved with our jobs. Hence, the parties, dinners, symphony, and concerts that I had to attend. Natalie wanted nothing to do with any of it. She attempted to at first, but the last year she didn't even try.

Things deteriorated rather quickly after that. We lived in the same house, and we were together, but not at all. We led completely separate lives. Sex became something ferocious between us. A lot like one of the old sports competitions. Now we were trying to best each other. The crazy part is, we did it a lot and the sex was fantastic. Hot. Almost to the point of being unable to move or walk after going at each other so hard. Both of us were trying to dominate the other. Not exactly a loving expression for how we felt about each other. The bed was just another arena in which we competed. Right up until the last few months, when it completely stopped.

I get up off the couch, my thoughts drowning me. Standing before the window, I am looking out over the quiet, rural country of the Hendrickses' small farmyard. I didn't have sex with Chantal because Natalie and I hadn't been intimate in a few months. I also didn't do it because she can't get pregnant. I didn't do it because she is a cop either. I didn't do it because she wasn't girlie enough for me, or willing to play the good little wifey role that my job functions tried to peg into her becoming. I realize now, why I did it, as I stare into the yard. I finally have words for why I did it.

I hang my head as the truth glares at me. I did it specifically to hurt Natalie. I did it to punish her because she wouldn't listen to me. I felt ignored and trapped by her decisions. Like I had no right to voice my feelings.

I shake my head as if we're in a pretend conversation. That last conversation was the factor in helping me formulate how I could do something I never intended, or even considered doing. I don't cheat. I don't have trouble keeping my shit in my pants ever. Contrary to my actions, being faithful has never been hard for me, or even optional. I just was that way. I was happy to be faithful.

Now? I was not. I cheated once and would always, to Natalie anyway, be a cheater. I lean my head against the cool glass. I allowed legitimate concerns and problems between us to exist without dealing with them. In ignoring them, anger and resentment began to grow. A wall of total separation soon came between us, isolating both of us. Feeling alone made me even angrier. It made it easy when another woman grabbed my dick and I thought it was okay to have gratuitous sex with her. I did it to punish Natalie. I realize that as I stand here. I didn't know it at the time. I could not understand what provoked me to do such a thing. Now I think I do. Hearing even now how she won't listen to the possibility that my opinion could be valid, or even my POV about her condition and not having kids, makes my anger pulsate and burn.

"I got a call that night."

Her voice startles me. I turn toward her. She's a shadowy figure in the apartment. I'm shocked she's gotten up. I settle my shoulders back to lean against the window and cross my arms over my chest. "From whom?"

"Jayden. He said I should go to your office. That you were working too long, and he was worried about your stress level. He said he knew how hard things were for us at home and he just wanted to make sure you took care of yourself.

So I came as soon as I got off my shift. I was thinking maybe we should talk. I had no idea how you felt about anything in months, and I didn't know you were feeling so stressed."

I let my shoulders fall and snorted. *That bastard.* "He set it up. He hired Chantal to come onto me. Apparently, she does that kind of thing. She gets paid sometimes for screwing the guys in the company."

"That's disgusting."

"Yeah, it is."

"You still did it with her though?" Her voice is full of reproach.

"No. I mean, yes, I did it, but I didn't know Jayden hired her then. He told me later. He really called you?"

She nods. Of course! It makes sense. Why she came there in the first place, and why her timing was so epically bad. But it still doesn't change the fact that I did it.

"I told you he was a sociopathic, psychotic asshole who wants to destroy us."

I nod. She did tell me that. If only I'd listened. "I didn't see it. Not until now. But it doesn't change the fact that I did it. He might have set us up, but I took the bait. I did the foul deed. I let you catch me doing something wrong."

"Yes, you quite easily took his bait."

"Why are you up?" I ask finally when she just stands there, glaring at me.

"Because I can't sleep. I think about it all the time."

"I do too," I agree, my tone defeated.

She stares at me from across the room. "Do you hate me? Is that why you did it?"

I slump as I cross the room and flop onto a chair. "No. I wouldn't be here if that were the case. I have been so angry, but I never told you. I just sucked it all in, and it turned me sour and awful. I acted bitter and angry about your job. That's why I was blaming it for all our problems, and why we didn't have kids, why you didn't care, why you didn't ever accompany me anywhere. But I think I'm starting to see the truth now. I did it because I wanted to hurt you, only I didn't know that at the time. I didn't set out that night to hurt you. I was presented with an opportunity and I used it to hurt you. I took advantage of it. I don't know what that says about me. I was thinking maybe I should just go. Maybe you are right. We are done. I can't undo this. I can't undo what I want."

"What is it you want? If I asked you what your ideal outcome would be for your life and your spouse, what would you say?"

"A kid. I want to have a child at some point. And I'd like to have a wife I can talk to. But after what I did? I see and understand now why you can't forgive me or trust me again. Duh. I get that. Clearly. But I came anyway."

She is different now. The anger isn't percolating beneath her skin, threatening to burst out of her. She is quieter, and more subdued. Now she seems almost willing to actually talk to me. She steps forward and leans on the back of the couch. "I was thinking about everything we said. I wonder, Sam, did you come here because it seemed the right thing to do, since that's the kind of guy you usually are? You're the guy who doesn't do stuff like that. The guy that everyone likes and respects, and now you have to try and fix this mess?"

I rub the ache between my eyes. There is some truth to what she says. "I came because I was so ashamed by what I did. Because I'm that sorry, and I was panicked to tell you. I know I love you. I just don't know how living with you went so wrong."

"Do you think there's a chance we shouldn't be living together?"

I suck in a breath. Her statement is so soft. So sincere. Not spoken out of anger. I finally glance up and hold her gaze. "Yes," I say simply. Honestly. "I think there is a valid chance that we shouldn't be living together. We want different things. But knowing that, I also find so many things I want in you. You challenge me. You make me think more clearly. I used to consider your obstinacy, and your ability to do things no other woman I knew could do or handle, to be the hottest foreplay ever."

"When did that change?"

I stare back at my hands. "I guess when I realized that talking to you would make me a pussy in your eyes. Except, I really needed to. The anger built. The resentment and I—"

"Can't admit you feel those things about anything, especially me, so you never really told me. We just started to argue and continued to do that."

"Yes. Strangely, I just came to that deduction in the last hour too. But it doesn't change anything; you can't un-see what you saw. No matter that Jayden's an asswipe, and what he did sucked, it still worked, and that's only because of me."

"I can't stop thinking about it. I see you in the daylight, and yet, my brain keeps flipping back to that moment and nothing can excuse it."

"No, you're right," I concede, my tone as flat and heavy as my heart feels. There really is no excusing it. I see the hopeless endeavor our marriage has become. Perhaps no real answer exists. This might be the final act for which we've been leading up to in the past year.

Silence stretches on and on. There is still so much left unresolved and more to be said. But we both relish a moment of peace right now, and I'm afraid to shatter it. I don't want to fight with her. Or hurt her.

"Your sisters are very nice girls."

She nods. "Yes, they are."

"Doing this? Being here? It's huge for you, I know. I think it's good. Really good."

Silence again. "Will you do anything about Jayden? Or

will you just keep on with him as if he hadn't set this all in motion?"

"It's fair to say he'll never speak to me again. I quit, Nat. That night, I walked out and I never intend to go back. I called in finally while drunk and formally quit. Didn't go over too well."

"You quit?" Her tone is shocked. She stands up straight and her jaw drops.

"What else could I do? I knew what I did. I lost everything in that one bad decision. You. My self–respect. My job. The woman works there. I didn't know at the time that she was for hire, of course, and therefore not likely to sue me for sexual harassment. But looking back, it didn't matter. I had to quit."

"But Jayden set you up. You can go back now. The woman is neutral in all of this. You worked for so long and so hard. You can't just quit."

"I can and I did. Do you think I can look at myself and be proud of what I am? What I've done? But life goes on, and I can't undo it all. All I can do is change what got me there. That job was half of it. So I started there. I quit because I should have long ago."

"What will you do now?"

I shake my head. "I have no idea. Hence, why I lay awake most nights. Thinking of you. Of when we go home. Of what I'll do for work."

"When you talk like this? You sound like the Sam I remember. The Sam I see now, I haven't heard from in a very long time."

I shrug my shoulders loosely. "Yeah, you haven't. I haven't either. I lost track of myself, my values, and you. I mostly lost track of you."

"What led us here—?"

"I don't expect you to forgive me because I was lonely or hurt over the original issue."

"I don't. But there are times, I don't totally hate you."

My smile feels old and tired, like it doesn't know how to work. It stretches my lips as if they might split. "But there are times you do."

"Yes."

"I want to stay. I think it's important you see this through with Jessie and your sisters. But after we go home, I'll move. You won't have to deal with me again."

"We'll both have to move. The company won't let us stay in that awful Victorian."

"Fair enough. But I won't fight you. You can have whatever you want."

She stares at me. I feel defeated as my gaze falls to my bare feet on the floor. I don't see any other choice. She might have done things wrong, but what I did was much worse.

"Sam—" she whispers and her eyes look huge across the distance.

I let a small, tentative smile curl my lips. "Maybe someday, you'll find a way to look me in the eye again and not hate me. Maybe... maybe that can happen... someday."

Reality is something I've avoided for far too long. Starting with the baby I wanted, and ending with the job I put ahead of everything else. This is my marriage and its logical conclusion. It's time I accept it. My heart seems to have a knife stuck inside it, projecting from my chest. Or at least, the sharp pain I feel right there seems like it.

NATALIE

I scurry back to bed. Sam's defeated posture speaks more to me than any of his apologies could. There is no way I can sleep. This subdued version of Sam is not one I recognize.

I've never known him to admit defeat; and that's what this last discussion, or maybe we should call it *our first discussion* about what happened, was. I lie on my side, staring at the window as daylight barely starts to break through the closed mini-blinds. Sam said a lot of things. New things I've never heard from him before. Or if he did tell me before, I didn't understand what he meant. But I probably didn't hear it from him before now.

The baby thing. It was a shock at first. I mean, what healthy, physically fit woman wouldn't just assume she could have a baby? Yes, I assumed that. I remember distinctly sitting in the high-backed green chair in the office of my OB/GYN as she started to explain ovulation. She used such a gentle voice, as if preparing me for death. I was taken aback. But no, I wasn't devastated to the extreme by the news, not like I now think Sam was. I felt weird. Like my body had betrayed me just because I am so physically fit. I can run miles, and pretty fast. I lift weights. I've more than once caught up to male suspects running away from me on foot. For a girl, and later a woman, I'm strong and healthy. Learning I can't perform one of the basic functions of a woman, something even a fourteen-year-old girl can do, was totally disconcerting. I admit that. I didn't like hearing it. It's not like I left there doing somersaults, or cartwheels with glee. Of course, I prefer having the choice of conceiving our own baby. But that day, we learned my body has no choice. My body said a resounding *no*.

And yes, I call that a sign. I don't really want to take extraordinary measures to have a baby. I don't want to be poked, or prodded, or put on miscellaneous medications. The little I read about fertility options was expensive, complicated and time-consuming. So no, I don't feel too passionately about pursuing it.

I flip over onto my back. Did I ever ask Sam how he felt? I

remember a few conversations, but we talked about me, and how I felt. He was pretty damn good at convincing me it wasn't my fault, and telling me I had nothing to feel guilty about. But did I ever once ask him how he felt? He brought up adoption. And other options, but I was adamant I wanted neither. I found the irony of being adopted and then being unable to have kids cruel, and it struck me hard. All I wanted for so many years since my mom died was to have a family. I wanted to feel connected to someone. Now I find out I can't even have my own children who share my blood? It completely shocks me. I always assumed I would someday have my own kids. So, no, I didn't want to adopt. I wanted my own kids. Biological. I wanted to freaking belong to someone, which is so strange because I did belong to the parents who raised me. I really did. I didn't grow up lacking things, or feeling like I was a guest in their home. We were a real family. As I lie here now, thinking over what Sam asked me, I wonder why I didn't think of adopting a kid like me, one who wasn't wanted. Why don't I think that's a good idea? Why wouldn't that be the only thing I want to do? I honestly don't know.

We both went back to work after that. We didn't tell anyone, per my request, and we started working harder, and spending less time together. I don't think I comprehended how much Sam was hurt and that changed how he treated me. Sure, I realized we weren't getting along or talking... but it shames me now, and almost makes my body burn up with rage to realize that I just didn't see it. Not to the extent Sam expressed. I had no idea he resented me so much, or how thoroughly I ignored him.

Oh, my God! He thought I would consider him a pussy if he talked to me?

Could I be that bad? Is that how I've become? So focused

on my own insecurities and making all the decisions that I won't even allow Sam to talk to me?

It rings true. I groan as I bury my head in the pillow. He did grow increasingly angry and rude towards me. He started to pick and nag at stupid, pointless things. They were always small things we fought about. I blamed it on his wanting a girlie-girl. A woman who wasn't a cop.

A woman who could easily bear him children.

I sit up in the bed. For God's sake, is that why I let it go on and on? I never once initiated a conversation, or invited him to talk to me. I was so afraid he'd reject me because I could not give him the one thing I did and do know he wants: kids. I'm not all wet in that notion, nor am I wrong. Sam wants a society wife with lots of kids at home to take care of, or a high-powered corporate wife with no time for kids. I was neither, and therefore, was an annoyance to him. A *hindrance*, as that asswipe, Jayden, so eloquently referred to me as.

Now here I am, surrounded by at least four women who share my blood, and I still have no idea what that means. And Sam is here, although he's almost given up on us, and I have no idea where I stand now in any of it. Or how my life reached this point. But what's scarier to me in this moment is how little I realized. I didn't think that anything was wrong with my life. How clueless and removed I was from Sam, myself and our life together.

CHAPTER 13

$\mathcal{N}$ATALIE

I GET UP FINALLY and slip on my clothes and go into the house. Sam doesn't stir on the couch. I don't think he's asleep, but I completely understand him wanting to pretend to be. In many ways, it's too painful to talk. Or even look at each other. I don't want to contemplate what he said last night.

Jessie is already there, eating breakfast. We greet each other and I move around the kitchen, almost feeling confident and comfortable. I pause as I start to pour coffee. *I'm having coffee in my mother's house.* I grip the countertop. I never foresaw this in all my wild imaginings.

"Natalie? Is everything okay?" she asks me quietly. Jessie has a soothing tone. A calm tone. A good mom tone. I sigh and tears fill up my eyes. I turn to hide my blurry eyes while pretending to scrounge around for a spoon to go with the cereal I've just selected.

"Fine. Why?"

She lets the quiet stand before saying softly, "Because you're tearing up. I might not know you well, but I've experienced enough of you to know you don't just tear up. You don't get sentimental at sappy commercials, or feel–good movies, or songs. I think, or at least, I'm willing to surmise, that you only get upset when something is actually wrong."

I keep my back to her, but reply with a single, precise nod of affirmation. I hear the tap of her setting her coffee cup on the table. Then, the slide of the chair, and her clothes shuffling as she stands and her hand touches my shoulder. "What is it? You can talk to me. You could look at me as a stranger who doesn't know about your life, and whether or not you ever see me again is all your choosing; so why not talk to me? You look exhausted and pale. Your face is drawn and your eyes are puffy; that tells me you have been crying and haven't slept. Is it you and Sam? I know you just might tell me to go to hell, but I sensed something the first day he was here. Your face, for just a split second, when you realized he was standing in this living room, was total shock and almost awe, and I deduced then that you did not tell him to come here. In fact, I daresay you didn't expect him to even know you came here. So that makes me wonder. I mean, under the circumstances of extreme stress and upset at finding me, who wouldn't call and tell their spouse? Unless the spouse is someone whom you aren't getting along with."

I told no one what I witnessed that night at Sam's office. I talked to no one about the person who might as well have taken a serrated knife, and cut into my chest to yank out my heart and set it before my eyes to examine. Watching Sam have sex with another woman sickened me and twisted up my insides. Since then, I've suffered from perpetual stomach aches, and intermittent throbbing of my temples. I came here and had to endure more emotional stress than I've ever felt before; and now Sam is here. The tension I feel is all exploding out of me. I expect steam to be coming out of my ears, mouth and nose. I feel so overwhelmed and I have no one to talk about it with. Granted, I'm not a touchy–feely kind of girl. I don't have heart–to–hearts with my BFFs and I abhor a frilly girls' night out. My friends, which yes, I do have, are basically men, or other women cops. I have several with whom I meet every Wednesday night for drinks at seven o'clock. We vent and blow off steam about what we have to deal with all week at work, or rag on some of the more pig–headed, chauvinistic guy cops we work with.

But a girlfriend I can call and say, *Hey, I can't have kids* to. Or *Sam was having sex with a girl right in front of my eyes?* No. There is no one to whom I can utter those words.

Yet here is a woman asking me. Someone who knows nothing about me. Someone I could tell my point of view to, and maybe release some of this awful pressure building in my chest and shredding my heart. I threatened Sam when I said we were done. When this week ended, we were forever done. But scarier still? Sam said something entirely too similar last night. I think I'm reeling even more this morning because it truly never occurred to me that Sam would be the one with the power to say those things. I thought I held the power between us now, but hearing him speak like he did last night nauseates me and makes my head ache. It might not just be lip service or rage, but the ugly reality that my marriage to Sam is over. The sad part, and yes, the biggest surprise is, I don't know how I feel about that.

"I can't have kids."

I whip my eyes up to Jessie, shocking myself that I said *anything,* and even worse, shocked about the subject I chose to tell her. I intended to say, Sam cheated on me and that's what spurred this crazy trip, out of nowhere, to meet you all, never mind staying on to see if I liked them.

Jessie leans back against the counter as if my news physically pushes her. "Oh, Natalie, I'm sorry."

I straighten up. "Are you? Why? Why do people automatically think that means there is something wrong with me and I must feel like crap? It doesn't make me less of a woman, or less of a person. It doesn't mean the purpose of my life is over. I have a thriving job that contributes far more than most people do to my surrounding community. I have a lot to offer, even if I can't help overpopulate this already overcrowded planet."

Jessie's eyebrows rise and her lips turn up just enough to suggest a smile. "O-kay then. I agree; it doesn't mean anything is wrong with you, but since you told me after tearing up out of nowhere, perhaps it's an issue for you. Not to mention that your voice rose about three octaves higher when you said it."

I wilt and back up to lean on the opposite counter. "I've known for over a year."

"Are you at all angry and wondering why I could so accidentally have given birth to you, because you and Sam can't do the same thing?"

I hold her gaze. Her eyebrows are again raised. She isn't challenging me, her voice is kind and honest. She's opening up so I can say something to her. "The thought did cross my mind."

Jessie nods. "I can't answer that. Life isn't fair, and it rarely makes sense. I know, however, you already know that. I agree with you; it's shitty luck, these circumstances. I can get pregnant almost the first month I try to; and all it takes is one time when I'm not even trying. So if you're angry at me for that, I get it. It's fine. I think you can fairly add that to your list of reasons to resent me. I have to give it to you though, you don't transfer your resentment onto the girls. The younger two think you're awesome. A hero, really. They don't know any other woman cop, or a woman who is as capable, strong and confident in her toughness as you are. They were awed by your sportsmanship. They said you could challenge any man out there."

That little, gossipy tidbit lifts something in my chest. It's nice to hear. I've never had anyone look up to me before. Hearing that these little girls do is pretty amazing to me. "Not one thing about you, this place, or your daughters is what I could have anticipated."

"I know." Jessie and I eye each other. There is a strange undercurrent between us. We can't quite reach friendly, and we don't fully connect, yet there is a streak of honesty that, I have to say, doesn't exist with anyone else. "Can I ask what your childhood was like? Was it something that makes you consider adoption a terrible alternative? I don't have the right to ask, or even know, but I guess I am anyway. I want to know. It's the first thing I wanted to ask you. Are you okay? It's maybe none of my business and you can certainly tell me to go to hell, but here I am… asking."

I clear my throat, and consider her request. No, she really doesn't deserve the reassurance I can almost guarantee she is seeking. She wants me to tell her about my happy childhood to alleviate her guilt. Four days ago, I probably would have told her to screw off. Now? My perspective and overall compassion towards another, even this woman, has matured and blossomed in a way that probably never before happened in my adulthood. I sag against the counter. "My parents were an older couple who could not have kids. Ironic, huh? I have the same affliction, yet we share no genes. They married late in life and adopted me. They were hardworking, honest, rigid, and caring, and I was their only child. We didn't share the level of money and possessions and the nice home you have here. We lived in a modest, two-bedroom apartment in a generic, kind of ugly block building. But I didn't know any better. I was never bitter about it. I had everything I needed, and I fully understood when I couldn't have all the stuff I wanted. They taught me about hard work, discipline, setting goals and having the tenacity to strive for them. They loved me too; I never once doubted that. Even if they weren't terribly demonstrative, or said it very often, I always knew. So, no, in answer to your question, they did nothing except show me how people should treat a child who was not theirs."

"But that isn't something you and Sam want?"

"Sam might. I don't. I grew up feeling there was something missing from me, or my life. There was something I wanted to know. I doubt if I want to go through that again."

"But that understanding might make you the perfect candidate. You get it. You could be sensitive to it, and maybe more than most mothers, help a child deal with it."

I shrug. "I haven't seriously considered that."

"But somehow, I get the feeling Sam has."

I can't find the strength to hide it, or pretend otherwise. "Yes. But I don't think I understood how much he did until now."

"Were you fighting? Is that what propelled you to come here?"

I stare at her and she stares as intently back at me. "Why should I be honest with you? About private stuff?"

Jessie throws her hands up. "I honestly don't know. I don't know why you would, or what I could say to convince you to, I just know that I do want you to."

"What actually propelled me to come here was, I pretty much freaked the fuck out after I walked into his office and saw him having sex with another woman on his desk. That's what made me rush out of town. I was escaping that. He somehow figured out where the hell I was headed and because I didn't want you all to know about it, he used that ploy to stay here."

I let out a rush of breath after my litany of words. I have to unclench my fists. I can't believe I just told her all that. I raise my hands to rub my tired eyes. The thing is, stress and exhaustion have made me lose my mind. Why would I tell her that stuff? I just can't begin to explain it.

"But the worst of it is, he has an excuse for it. He said I didn't even listen to his concerns about not being able to conceive a baby. And since I would not listen to him, he felt shut out. Like he was living with a stranger who wouldn't let him speak, which made him resent me. Of course, he claims he didn't intend to sleep with the woman; but in ways he never realized until now, he did that to punish me because he was so angry. And crazier still? He's right! Not about doing it. But I didn't let him talk about it to me. I didn't consult with him. I acted as if it was all my problem and not half his. I just didn't see it…"

"Until now, when it smacks you right in the face. I get it. When I was young, my God, I could not compromise, or talk, or even remotely tell Will what was wrong. I get that."

"I'll bet Will never cheated on you."

"No. Will never cheated on me."

"Did you ever cheat on him?" I ask bluntly.

She hesitates for just a moment. "No. Not since we fell in love. Since we've been in love, I'm not sure I've even noticed another man in that way. But the way we started, there was definitely a time when I tried."

"I thought it was that way for us. But I sense there is more to your statement, like there is something you're not saying. Is there?"

She nods and purses her lips. "Yes. You are intuitive. Comes in handy, I guess, for being a cop. Will and my relationship is pretty complicated. Especially at the start."

"You seem so perfect."

She snorts. "Our beginning was anything but."

"Because of me?"

She shakes her head. "No, actually, it wasn't because of you. I was immature and scared; and well, my father was a general in the Army, which further complicated matters in my life. He wasn't a nice man. Will married me the first time just to get me away from him. At that point, it was a marriage in name only."

I straighten up as I listen, totally rapt, to Jessie. I never expect this twist to their story. Not at all. From what I've witnessed, they are a loving, respectful, almost youthful–acting couple who manage their lives and parenting with fun, work, hobbies, honesty and love.

"We eventually fell in love and got married for real... Then we went on to have a family and got good jobs. But years ago? I was not destined for this at all."

"I never dreamed Sam and I were destined for where we are today."

Jessie's face contorts in sympathy. It's not faked either. "Marriage is hard and long and it is so easy to take each other for granted and not even know you are. But it doesn't mean it's over. One mistake might just be what makes you try to make the changes you wouldn't have made otherwise. It's easy to walk away, Natalie. It's a lot harder to stay and make it work. Especially when you have such polarized views on a very important topic."

"How can we compromise about kids? You either want them, or you don't."

"True. But you have different circumstances. You have to go to a lot of effort to have a child in your life. Maybe you can't compromise, but you can hear each other, and care about each other's opinions and thoughts, even if you don't change yours. My experience? Communication can't just be a pretty buzz word. It has to happen for real. It requires two people who mutually choose to be uncomfortable until they find a solution they both can live with. If it turns into anger, resentment, bitterness... all those things only lead a person to feeling completely alone, even though their spouse is right there."

"You're saying, I caused him to seek someone else?"

Jessie's mouth puckers and her eyebrows draw together. "Oh, hell no. No, he doesn't get a pass because you two had problems. He doesn't get to have an excuse. His behavior is still his. His choices are still his own. I don't know what I'd do if Will ever cheated on me. Lose my mind a bit, yeah. But would I let that decide whether or not to lose him? I can't honestly say. But that's me. I don't know you and Sam. No one can tell you what to do with your marriage. I just know it's hard, complicated and never as obvious as anyone thinks."

"What does it say about us when the first real hard choices and decisions we encounter make us end up here? Like this?"

"Is he a womanizer? I mean, is it something that he does often? Or has he done it before?"

"No!" I say as surely as I do my name when being introduced to people. I know, even now, that Sam is not a player. Sam did that, but I know it was not done lightly, and he's not blowing smoke up my ass in fake apologies, or promises never to do it again. In all honesty? I pretty much believe he won't do it again. I physically see his distress, horror and guilt. He doesn't like to feel like a failure and this makes him one in his eyes.

"Then you have to decide what you want. You have to decide to trust him again, and determine how much love is left."

"Please don't tell anyone."

"I wouldn't."

"Somehow, I believe you." We share a long look across her kitchen. It makes me feel uneasy. We're no closer to crossing that distance and hugging in bonded, mother–daughter understanding, but there is something real here. It is something very much like my own mother would have done in this situation. That startles me as I think it, but my mother might easily have reacted like Jessie did about Sam if she was the one I had consulted. I shrink back as I realize I'm talking to Jessie, my pseudo–mother, because I just want my own mom to tell me what to do. To guide me and help me. I'm desperate for her advice. And now I've unloaded my burden on a near stranger just because she asked. Because she's a motherly figure to me. I regret the words that spewed from my mouth. I'm usually so circumspect with my feelings. I can't believe I've just let so much out of me.

"I'm not looking for a new mother. I lost mine. She died of cancer when I was twenty. There will never be another mother for me," I add when the guilt over comparing my two mothers fills my head.

She nods. "I'm very sorry about that. And I don't expect anything from you."

Emily comes out and we both turn towards her. We both greet her. I swear I can hear the relief in both of our voices at having a buffer between us in this strange, intense, amazing conversation, and the oddly strong feelings that surround us like an aura.

"Hey, Natalie, wanna go exploring with me and Missy today?"

I smile at her. She is still so shy with me. I swear I can see her chest rise and fall in a deep breaths as she musters the nerve to speak to me. I try to keep my tone easy and encouraging with her, so she feels like she can talk to me. Melissa comes with us and we spend the day going to the Columbia

River. We take something called the Old Vantage Highway, which looks impossible to find unless someone is familiar with the area. It goes through a stunning, desert–like landscape of basalt bluffs that tower over the Columbia River. The road physically disappears under the Columbia River. Weird thing to see. Of course, it's blocked off, but it is kind of a cool thing to witness. The pavement literally vanishes under the water. A new bridge and the I–90 now replace the old road. We explore some of the Ginkgo Petrified Forest State Park, regarded as one of the most unusual fossil forests in the world. In the middle of nowhere, I learn something new about the world. And I never experienced a landscape like that. It's all carved rock, remnants from some long-ago ice age.

Later, we buy sandwiches and pop at the gas station by the Vantage Bridge and go to the state park just down the road, where we watch the dramatic sunset over the tranquil Columbia River. The darkening hills turn black against the stunning colors of the sunset. We are at ease and the conversations are real. The two girls talk about everything from their friends at school to more intimate descriptions of their experiences growing up as Will and Jessie's daughters.

The next day, Christina joins us to go hiking along Taneum Creek. It's a five–mile hike through thick woods. We see a scattering of elk, which I never witnessed in the wild, and it lifts my spirits. I finally feel like smiling after all the stress of the last few days. Emily is an avid hiker and five miles is nothing to her. Missy is breathing hard and complains at the last of it. She and her dad often ride motorcycles around there, she tells me, and she just doesn't see any reason for hiking when a motorcycle can do all the hard work. Emily shoots back with an argument about the disturbance to the wildlife and the way it cuts up the area... on and on, they bicker. They constantly go at each other or call each other names, and sometimes, it makes my heart ping. You can only be so mean and annoying to a sibling you love. But the minute anyone else intrudes or bothers one of them, they instantly have each other's back. There is something pure about their rivalry, their annoyance, and their love of each other. Each day we are together, there is something real growing between us. There is a presence to us now. We share a few laughs and jokes now and I know something is building here. I can feel it.

I do not know what to do with my marriage. But somehow, these strangers, *these sisters* of mine, manage to make me feel a little better today.

CHAPTER 14

SAM

I AVOID BEING ALONE with Natalie for the next few days. We hang around inside the Hendrickses' home with her "family." It is completely surreal. There we are in the middle of nowhere in a strange state with a strange family, and yet she fits in. She and her sisters, especially the younger two, spend a lot of time going off together, exploring the area. There isn't much in terms of culture. There are more natural things. They go driving and hiking and Natalie gets quite animated about the elk, the wildlife and the history around the Columbia River. I don't go along very often, despite how hard the girls try to persuade me to come. I wave them off and willingly give Natalie more time with them. I spend a lot of my time wandering around their farm. I talk to Will a lot. He is an interesting guy, with plenty of war stories to tell. We spend a lot of time just talking. He is into motorcycles, something I've never done before. I grew up in the middle of a city and never moved away from it. He is pretty amused about that and gives me a lot of shit. Enough that I finally try it. I nearly crash at the first little rock I ride over, but I keep at it until I am zooming around their track. I use a lot more caution and have a lot less speed than Will, but at least, I am doing it.

We are invited to go with the Hendrickses to the local fair, which is in town for the weekend. They set it up in the park we played softball in. There are small carnival rides, game booths and prizes, as well as overpriced stuffed animals. Emily asks if we can go in her shy, endearing way when Natalie and I are both sitting at their table, eating breakfast. We are across from each other, trying to maintain the illusion that we're together. I glance her way, but she doesn't look at me. She smiles at Emily with a warmth I haven't seen directed at me in months, and agrees, saying we'd like to go. Sure, we'd *love* to go. So I guess I'd love to since this is why I'm here: to substantiate the façade that Natalie is happily married. And to be there, at least in theory, for her.

So that's how I end up at a country fair for a rip roaring Friday night "out" in Ellensburg. I am watching a dessert contest. People actually enter their own kitchen creations and compete for first, second and third place prizes. There is even a large crowd amassing around the results. It is hard to keep my smirk in check. I can't help feeling amused at all this really small-town stuff. There is the usual farmer's market, featuring organic, locally grown produce, as well as local artists showing their wares. There are small-time local authors too, with their printed books for sale, along with several artists' paintings and ceramics displayed. Emily and Melissa squeal in delight over the handmade scarves and each girl purchases one, even convincing Natalie to get a matching one. They all wear them together. She hems and

LEANNE DAVIS

haws, rolling her eyes as if they are forcing her, but I notice the genuine interest in her eyes. She is not only appeasing them, but also becoming a part of them.

We pass several booths and I get myself into a pissing contest with Will after the girls goad me and say I could never beat their dad at the small Shoot the Duck game. Well, as it turns out, Will's history as a Special Forces soldier… yeah, I can't compete with that. I spend a butt load of money and have nothing to show for it but my wounded pride. Natalie steps up to the plate, being a cop and all, and soon beats Will. She takes a lot more pleasure in showing me up than in beating Will, who graciously gives her the victory. I finally win by sheer luck at one of those toss-the-coin-in-the-can games. I give the sad, pathetic, ten–cent stuffed animal to Emily, who smiles at my corniness. There is plenty of junk food for Natalie and me to sample while she glares at me discreetly between bites. We walk loosely together, but never actually together. We never touch each other physically either.

I notice a beer garden with great pleasure, and by nine o'clock, I decide it is the perfect spot for me to alight. Natalie is more than occupied with her budding, positive relationship to her sisters and all I am doing presently is providing a target for her to glare at. I am sick and tired of perpetuating it.

There is dancing, too. Outside, they have a make-shift dance floor, below the little stage they set up, where, all evening long, the town's musical talent is on display. Everything from the accordion, to guitars, to folksongs and serenades, not to mention plenty of oldies were featured. A few of them were quite talented. By now in the beer garden, the crowd is growing exponentially. Kids are running all around the area, and white, twinkling lights create a festive atmosphere. The warm weather means we only need light sweatshirts and can still be comfortable wearing our shorts. Jessie and Will dance. I watch them swaying together, talking, smiling into each other's eyes, or just quietly embracing. Max and Christina dance too. Melissa and Emily find a group of local kids around their own ages; and I wince as they blatantly flirt with boys who are way too old for them. I almost get up to intervene, but Will notices what's going on about then and charges over to end it.

Chuckling, I glance up to find a woman sitting on the stool near me. There is a large bar set up and I've been here for a while now. I am enjoying the ambiance and drinking, while trying to relax. I was an uptight mess in Ellensburg. Self-induced. And well-deserved. But tonight, I am trying to remember that I am not the devil. I have to learn to live with what I've done, so I drink and watch the town. It is quite pleasant, in all honesty. I don't want to talk, but the woman on the stool starts asking me direct questions. I'd be rude not to answer, so I do, as best I can, without really turning towards her. I contemplate the dark amber of the ale I am drinking. It is provided, I learn, by a popular local brewery. That information first comes from the bartender and then from the woman who sits next to me. I sip the dark ale and pick out a pretzel from the bowl before me.

The woman beside me has long hair. It falls on top of the bar whenever she leans in to talk to me. She is young, attractive and her breasts are unfortunately quite large. They keep spilling from her top. I don't look, of course, trying to stay focused on my beer. I want her to leave. I'm not a freaking idiot. My wife, the one I cheated on and want to prove how sorry I am to, is somewhere around here. The last thing I want is for her to see me with another woman, as if this is how I really am. Or what and who I truly am. But the blonde refuses to disappear. I turn my back just a smidgeon, trying to convey the vibe that I'm not interested. She freaking switches to the other side of me and moves over to sit there. She's very grabby too. She touches my hand. Then a little rub of her shoulders against mine. Her hair keeps swishing this way and that. Good God! She will not give up.

"Do you want to dance?"

I slam the mug of ale down and the foam slips over the rim. "No! My wife's around here and I'm waiting for her," I finally just grumble at the woman. Then I wiggle my left hand at her, flashing my wedding ring. Yup, I still got it and I plan to use it for as long as I can legally justify wearing it. *Jesus H. Have a bit of self-esteem*, I want to say to her. When I finally glance at her, she's not bad–looking. Other than a patch of acne on her chin, she's pretty attractive. There is no reason she can't find a guy. But it's not me.

"Oh." The woman's face falls, and I resist the urge to roll my eyes. As if our five–minute, brief interaction could cause so much disappointment. "The good ones are always taken."

"You barely conversed for five minutes with me. You have no idea if I'm a good one. You don't know if I've just cheated on my wife, or embezzled a million dollars, or injected a fresh dose of meth into my arm. *You don't know me.*"

She jerks back at my verbal attack. I realize how grumpy I must sound. I'm fast losing my patience. This is what my future holds? Dating. Being single? Simpering girls looking to me for validation? I can't; no one can validate another person's exis-tence. I can't stand clingy, needy, crestfallen women who blame me for their own shortcomings. I rub my already pounding temple. This glimpse of my future gives me a headache and the ensuing pain zings down all of my nerve endings. *No.* I don't want clingy, needy, annoying females. I want Natalie.

Natalie who never once needed any validation. She told me what was up. She is hot and she knows it. She is smart and knows it too. We could talk for hours and I never once felt this level of annoyance with her. Or the need to censor my words to avoid injuring her fragile self–esteem.

"Sam?"

I hold in a groan when Natalie's voice comes from behind me. The question in her tone is not weepy. It's not like, *How could I be flirting with another blonde right now?* No. It's more like, *Sam, what the hell are you doing now?* I nearly lay my head flat on the bar. I can't catch a freaking break.

NATALIE

I'm buzzed. The beer that I ingest warms my stomach and spreads further from there. I am not giggly when drunk, but more open than I usually am. I'm hanging with Christina, and she is acting a bit drunk as well. I ignore the fact she's obviously snuck some beer. I suspect her parents know she's having it, as I saw her sipping some of her dad's drink. Seeing as how she's six months from being of age and her parents are right here, I take their cue, and ignore it. We talk. Like, we really *talk*. Sister–to–sister kind of talking. We discuss her relationship with her parents, and sisters and Max. I tell her about my own parents and even Sam. There is no simpering, or giggling, or slang, or selfies taken. I think I like Christina. She's tough, intelligent, rational and funny. And hell, her boyfriend is an ex–fight clubber with a complex. There are edges to her that one might not think she has at first. She's isn't nearly the namby–pamby wuss I initially pegged her to be.

So I'm feeling pretty good as I get up for another beer. That's when I spot Sam, sitting at the bar, and turned toward… a freaking blonde, of course! Always the blondes. She's twirling her hair around her finger, and touching his hand. Then his shoulder. She leans in towards him, creating an effect of intimacy, acting as if they are the only two seated at the bar.

She seems to miss all of his signals. My gaze instantly zeroes in on him as I watch him pulling his shoulder away, and sliding his fingers away from hers. He's leaning farther back to avoid her face being right in his. I know what's happening then and I have to laugh: he's being hit on and doesn't want to be, but the woman refuses to take no from him.

I should be annoyed. But somehow, this feels so much like the usual. I have to laugh again to myself as I remember the countless times I came to his rescue. Lots of women, from the young to middle–aged to old, try to pick him up. He's that freaking good-looking; but also that much of a gentleman. He knows how to make a person feel like the only person in the room, or the world, for that matter. He has no idea he's even doing it. I can see by his body language that I'm right. This is Sam being himself, trying not to attract the woman. Somehow, knowing this truly helps my confidence: I do know Sam. He hasn't completely morphed into a monster, despite what my heart often considers him to be now.

As I approach him, he mumbles something to the blonde; something about *not knowing* him. The girl, who's probably in her early twenties, looks crestfallen. I lean on the bar and smile as I say his name.

He jerks to attention, his back going ramrod straight as his head whips around. He lays his head down flat on the bar for a moment, as if totally defeated, before he suddenly jumps off the stool. In an impassioned tone, he exclaims, "She came on to *me*. I told her to leave!"

I bite the inside of my cheek. He sounds like a typical guy who just got caught cheating right now. It makes me laugh a little bit. Insecurity was never a part of Sam's personality. Assuming I don't know what happened here is new too. I don't know how many times I rescued him from such lame pick–ups. It's kind of our thing. I enjoy seeing him squirm. The poor girl looks from me to Sam as she shifts her feet and backs up. Then she spins around, almost running away.

"I swear, she kept coming on to me. I wasn't... I mean, I don't..."

I burst out laughing. He's staring at his feet, shuffling them like a little boy caught peeing in public. "You can't help being so pretty. The girls just lose their minds. Always the victim, aren't you?"

He glances up and holds my gaze, finally breaking into a grin when he realizes I'm kidding him. It's a smile that sends rockets of emotion zinging down my nerve endings. Even my toes curl in my shoes. God, I'm so cynical and competitive, almost as bad as a guy, not to mention I half hate this man right now for betraying me. It is such an ugly, disrespectful, disgusting thing to do. Really, it is. And yet, even I am almost swooning at his feet, under the power of his grin. And his dark eyes studying me.

My teasing smile starts to fade along with his grin. We stare at each other, both buzzed, I'm pretty sure. At least, I know I am. He steps towards me. A tentative, almost unsure step. I feel his hand reaching out towards me. I look down at the hand wearing the ring that I put on his finger. He is waiting for me. My tears replace the smile. I close my eyes. *Sam.* I just want Sam. How do you hate and love someone at the same time? It is so unclear and it makes me feel unclean. I should hate him. But all my nerve endings ache for him. I lift my fingertips and let them touch his. He closes his eyes as if the sensation of my contact overwhelms him. That's how he gets me. He always makes me feel like our love, and how we feel about each other, are so much more than the way other couples feel.

He pulls me forward, and that quickly and easily, I fall

against his chest, looping my arms around his neck. I cling to him, as needful as the blonde he just turned down. We start to sway to the music and slowly meander closer to the other couples. There are no words, just music. I relish the warm feel of his body against mine. I love his hands on my back. The white lights strung from poles twinkle and sway in the clear night sky as I pretend and remember how easily it is to fall back in love with Sam.

As if it never stopped. Not even for a moment. Not even in that terrible moment did I stop loving him. I hated him; and I still might. I resent him. I want to hurt him still, even in my fantasies. But the line separating love from hate is very undefined for me right now.

We cling together for so many songs, I lose track. I have no coherent thoughts. I forget. I let myself forget temporarily that we are over. Done. In many ways, this should be us saying goodbye to each other and letting go of one another. Clearly, there are big problems for us. Maybe our personalities are too strong individually to mesh together. Maybe we are too polarized.

He takes my hand at some point and pulls me toward him. We disappear into the darkness. I let him walk us to a private spot, away from the twinkling lights and crowds. There is no one around. He stops and pulls me against his chest. My heart suddenly pounds as my bloods starts to pump with eager anticipation. Something painful drums in my chest, and releases me when his lips touch mine. I let his mouth press hard, his lips and tongue completely tasting mine. I stand up on my tiptoes and lean my head back to reach him better. It's incredible. On and on, we kiss and his hands entangle my long, thick hair. His lips travel from my mouth to my cheekbone, and under my jaw, down along my throat. His hands leave my hair and he suddenly lifts his mouth from me and hugs me tightly.

"I love you, Nat. I love you so much," he mumbles into my ear. I know. My heart is screaming at me and at him, I know he loves me. But if that were sincerely true, then how could he cheat on me? How could his body dive into another woman's? How could he allow her legs to wrap around him? Moving their bodies together. Her head thrown back, her hair trailing down on his desk, and her long neck, a curving C... I so easily see that image again in my mind. I witnessed too damn much to gloss over the details, or for any of it to be abstract.

I shove him away. "I can't. I can't tell you that now. Not anymore. Just... I'm going to catch a ride with Christina. I'll see... you back there. Later." I fumble for excuses, along with my footing as I push away from his heat. I head back toward the lights and people, my heart tripping in my chest. I am buzzed enough that I want to turn around and fling myself at him and pretend. I really want to pretend that everything is so different than it actually is.

I find Christina sitting on Max's lap. Her eyes are quite bright and her cheeks are red. She's sloshed, I'm guessing, by the open way she's hanging all over Max. He keeps trying to gently push her away a little bit, while glancing frequently at her parents. I take pity on the poor guy for trying to do the right thing. "Hey, Christina, do you mind if I ride back with you? I've had enough fun for tonight, and Sam wants to stay awhile longer."

Although I highly doubt she's ready, she consents to let a sober Max drive us back to the house. Christina is chatty and buzzed, but I'm coming down fast. I listen to her cheerful chatter as Max and I readily exchange glances and snicker. She keeps trying to hug him when we sit down on the deck together and Max lights a fire in the fire pit the deck is built around. No one else is back yet. As she tries again to hug him, he finally grabs her arms with his fingertips in a tight grasp, saying, "Damn it! Stop it, Christina."

I am a bit stunned. I jerk to attention at Max's tone and the rough way he is gripping her forearms. I don't like it one bit. But to date, I've only ever heard Max being considerate, if not a little unreal, about her. He seemed to adore her until this very moment. She immediately stills and quits fighting him. Her voice crumples, "Oh, Max, I'm sorry. I'll stop." Her voice sounds way too serious. What harm is there in the little bit of flirting she did?

I stand up. "What's your problem, Max? Quit strong-arming her." I put my hand on her arm and she turns towards me. I can see the incident sobers her up almost instantly.

"It's okay, Natalie."

"No, it's not. He doesn't have to act like such an ass over nothing. Don't let guys just grab or manhandle you at their will, Christina."

She shakes her head. "It's not like that." I notice Max releasing her. He backs up and hangs his head, as if in shame. My stomach knots. Does he ever hit her or anything? They appear to be such a nice, cute couple, but is that just a gimmick to hide something more sinister? And Christina saying the typical excuse: it isn't his fault for having a temper? She thinks she provokes him? Does she really believe that? Does Jessie know? My head is leaping to conclusions. I feel ready to get my gun and empty a clip into Max. I think I have some serious aggression concerns with men right now. "He has this thing about being touched. It's a condition called by many names, one being haphephobia. You can look it up if you don't believe us. I usually... don't push him like that. But I was drinking and.... Well, it's not what your cynical mind is thinking, Nat."

Rarely does anyone but Sam call me Nat. It makes my heart bump. I like the unexpected familiarity. And how she seems to know I'm cynical. We stare each other, and I start to think, *Holy shit, we might have connected a bit over the last few days.*

I'm startled, however, by her quiet statement and Max's subsequent, obvious embarrassment. He finally lifts his head up. "I can't handle being touched. We... Tiny and I usually work it out, but sometimes, she goes too far for me. I don't mean to react so sharply. I just.... It's a real phobia."

I nod. I have heard of it. It must be tough to carry on a sexual relationship when you hate to be touched. I look at my sister with new eyes. The privileged, kind of selfish, bratty image she first projected easily vanishes in the depths I'm beginning to see inside her.

"People generally aren't what we think they are. It's okay, Max. Sorry I thought...."

He gives me an understanding nod. "I'm glad you reacted like that; and I know you would never let something like that happen."

"Must be tough having such an unobvious aversion, especially when everyone comes at you, touching. I'm not a real touchy–feely–let's–hug–because–we–met–once kind of person either, so I get how much you must endure your discomfort. Except I'm nowhere near the extent of what you suffer from."

"It's embarrassing."

Christina shakes her head. "No, it's just how it is. No big deal," she says, her tone crisp and matter of fact. She gives me a little smile when I catch her eye and we share a look. I'm slightly startled, it's our first communication through body language and eye contact. Like what she does with Emily and Melissa, her *sisters*.

I'm a little buzzed still. That's probably why I see our sisterhood in every single interaction we share. I lie back on the chaise lounge. Max gets up at some point and goes inside, leaving Christina and me alone.

"Did your mom tell you about me?" I'm curious to know if Jessie told her little clone about my defunct marriage and abnormal ovulation.

"About you? Never. Not even that you were born. You two don't do more than nod hello at each other. You're saying you actually had a conversation with her?"

I catch the bitter tone in Christina's voice. She thinks I'm too hard on her mother. I get that. She's protective of the ones she loves. As she should be.

"I assumed since you two share so much, she might have told you."

Christina scoots over on her side now and stares at me. "Okay, with that lead-in, you can't leave me hanging, what did you two discuss?"

"How unlike her, I can't have kids." It just pops out of my mouth. I shut my eyes and smack my own forehead. Way too much alcohol tonight.

Christina gasps appropriately and gives me the usual *sorry* and *how terrible*. I nod and wave her off. "I found out a while ago. I keep thinking about it when I'm here. That's probably because of my own paternity search, and that gets me thinking about adoption, and never mind... I've been drinking too much."

"Yeah, you don't give much away about yourself. But I get that. Max is a lot like that. I've learned to interpret the signs and translate what neither of you are willing to say."

"Are you two serious?"

"Yes. Forever kind of serious. But we know we're young and have lots of time. We intend to try and stay together through all of our separations and through all the obstacles before us. We're committed to each other, but we also have goals and ambitions we both want to attain that are on slightly different paths. We're not getting married anytime soon, or anything."

"Good. You are very young. You can't imagine how hard *forever* actually can be to live with."

"Because things like not being able to have kids can happen?"

I sigh and squeeze my eyelids shut. Shit. How did I get into this depressing conversation? "Yes, because sometimes things you never expect can happen."

"Is it something you and Sam fight about?"

My eyes pop open. No! No! Damn it! We never fought about it. Or talked about it either. We never dealt with it. I realize that as I stare up at the stars high above me. I try to swallow the lump lodged now in my throat. "No. We didn't deal with it before; and now, I don't know how to start."

"I'm glad you came here, Natalie. I was scared the first time I met you, and mad you blew me off and when you decided to acknowledge me; but I'm really freaking glad now you found us."

"Why?" I have to ask. What have I added to their lives? They didn't need me. I'm not a bright ray of sunlight that inspires those around me. I'm grouchy, grumpy, competitive, tough to know, tough to even talk to. Like Max, I'm not warm and fuzzy. Why would this kind, energetic, well-liked girl be so glad to meet me?

"Because we're sisters. I think that means something."

"I have to admit it's nice to just know more. I have some answers now. The things I didn't know used to drive me nuts. I can deal with the truth. Even if I don't like it. Even if it hurts."

She snorts. "Says every person until they hear the worst news of their life. Then they wish for blissful oblivion and ignorance."

I tilt my head and stare at her. It's rare for her to speak

with so much gusto, let alone, so much sarcasm. "What? What is that in reference to?"

"Oh, nothing. Nothing at all. I was just talking."

She refuses to meet my gaze. I feel her concentrating harder on the sky. She is purposely not meeting my eyes for fear of what I'll see in hers. She knows something more about me. I realize that with an almost tired jab of *What now?* What more do I not know about my life?

"Christina? You just lied to me. You just fed me bullshit. I'm not so buzzed I don't know that. You're buzzed enough that you slipped something out. So since you already have, what is it? What truth should make me grateful for blissful oblivion and ignorance?"

She slowly turns her gaze to mine in the fire–flickering dark shadows. She shakes her head just slightly as if to say she's sorry. Her eyes are huge, and almost liquid in their intensity.

"Tell me," I whisper softly. "Truth over lies."

"Are you sure?" she whispers back. I like how she doesn't simper, or waffle, or pretend she doesn't know what we both know she's hiding.

"I'm sure." I stare right at her and nod. I sit up, swinging my legs around so I'm sitting on the chaise lounge, leaning my elbows on my thighs and waiting for her to spill it.

She does the same until we are facing each other and just a few feet apart. She clasps her hands and keeps folding and unfolding her fingers together.

"Mom. She… didn't tell you the truth about how you were conceived. I don't know if it matters. I don't know if you should know. But I get what you said about secrets and stuff. I hate them. She thinks she's protecting others from her story. I agree. Except… it would change how you think about her. It could totally change how you feel about her. And maybe, goddamn it, maybe I want that because it's so unfair.

You scorn and almost hate her and your disrespect is just a reaction to what you think is true. If you only knew how wrong you are. And how far she went to protect you. If you only knew what she really suffered."

She meets my eyes finally, and nods her head just a fraction of an inch. I nod with her and shut my eyes. I get it immediately. My stomach heaves as the alcohol turns sour and Christina's words stun my heart.

Rape.

There is no other reason for Christina to talk that way. I know for sure then that Jessie was raped and I'm the result.

I go numb. I don't feel anything right now and I'm glad for that. I keep my voice neutral. "She told you?"

"My dad first told me. But I didn't know about you then. Not until I dug further into it. But later, yes, I learned the whole story. I—it's a bad story. But it will change everything you think of Mom. And that's the only good that I can see in your knowing. But that seems huge. You could really use her in your life. Maybe not as your mother, per se, but as a friend. Someone you can trust. Someone who is your sisters' mother. I hate how you resent her and dislike her so much. I just want you to know who she is and the truth before you judge her. It's not what you've been told, which isn't flattering. She did what she did, she lied, to protect you. She also tried to lie to protect me. But you should know the truth."

"Tell me then."

"I can't. I found it out from some letters Mom had. I was never meant to know as much I know. You should hear it from—"

Right then, the rest of the Hendrickses funnel into the house. They all come storming out to the deck as soon as they notice the fire. They are smiling, chatting, and eager to talk to us, but something about our conversation must be evident, because they instantly fall silent. Christina and I barely spare them a glance. We continue staring at each other, unsmiling. Unhappy.

I hear Jessie's sharp intake of breath before she says calmly, "Girls, why don't you go off to bed?"

Will seems to take her cue and follows them, leaving the three of us. Jessie keeps her hands at her sides and her stance wide, but her voice is strained as she says, "You told her?"

"Just that things aren't what they seem," Christina whispers, plopping her head down in shame.

"No, they never are," I finally mutter. I'm thinking of Sam. Of me. Of us having kids. Of us, period. I slowly rise to my feet, crossing the deck and leaving them alone. Maybe I'm not ready yet for anything else to not be what it seems.

CHAPTER 15

$\mathcal{N}$ATALIE

I STAND HERE, GRIPPING one of the posts that holds up the stall with all my strength. The wood feels smooth and cool under my palm. The interior of the barn is gloomy, cast in shadows and smelling of mothballs, and lit by a single, bare bulb. Never in my life could I picture my retreat into a damn barn sounding good. But I doubt anyone would think it is where I'd be either. I'm hiding. Physically and emotionally. Before the last few weeks, I never hid from anything or anyone. But I can't seem to regain my mojo, or my equilibrium. One thing after another keeps knocking me off the proverbial balance beam I keep trying to walk. That thing that makes me tough and cool, sometimes even cold under pressure? It's not here anymore.

I am leaning against the stall. The horse outside nickers softly from the pasture. The barn's strong scents singe my nose. Dried horse poop is just a few feet away from where I stand. I turn my back and fall onto my butt, my knees pointed skyward as I slump down. Christina's words are echoing inside me. My entire life seems to be falling apart and even this turns out to be all a lie. I should've known it though, right? Jessie's story didn't add up to the woman she seems to be. Her love for her children, her daughters... I knew there was more to the story, I just didn't want there to be. I didn't want to be what I am: the product of Jessie's rape.

A shoe squeaks on the floor. I know she's coming after me. I'm surprised she finds me so quickly. I don't look up. She steps forward. She waits a moment, but I don't glance up to acknowledge her. She sits on a step stool just across the aisle, still wearing gray slacks and a white blouse.

"You were never going to tell me, were you?" I finally whisper.

From the periphery of my downcast eyes, I see her nod. "No, I was never going to tell you."

"Christina and Max know?"

"They know. Christina found out by accident. It's what made her come after you."

Jessie's back is straight, and she isn't fidgeting. There is something resolute about her.

"The letters she mentioned?"

Jessie sighs. "Yes. They were never meant for her eyes. She stumbled upon them and read just the first one. Figured out some stuff, and here we are."

"You were raped? I was the result?"

"Yes."

"Was it anyone you knew?"

Her black hair flies around her face as she shakes her head. "No. No one I knew."

I lift my head up to her. "Why did you allow me to go full term? Why didn't you get rid of me before my birth?"

"That was never an option to me. I said it a few times, but

never once looked into it. Then I heard your heartbeat, and that was it for me."

"You never wanted to find me because I reminded you of it?"

"It was never that cut and dried. I was... not well at the time. I was not strong, or even sane, really. It wasn't you, Natalie. It was me. And unforeseen circumstances."

"You thought you couldn't mother me without seeing him, didn't you?"

She let out a strange, small laugh. "I wish I was sane enough then to have that clear of a thought. No. I was suffering from post-traumatic stress disorder. Only I didn't know it at the time. No one really knew it, except maybe Will."

"He was there for you?"

She nods. "He was there for me."

"He doesn't hate me?"

"No. He feels nothing but compassion for you."

I stare at her and Jessie stares at me. "That's why you act so odd with me, isn't it? You can't look at me without thinking about it again. Feeling it. And hurting."

"Maybe. I can't say. It was hard to look at you; and know I should have been better, stronger, and more sane. I could handle it now. If I had you now, I'd keep you. But back then... I could not. I would have ruined your life. I can't even express to you how true that is, but it doesn't excuse giving you up either."

"I need to see the letters. I need to... know."

"No. No, you don't. No good will come from it. It will hurt you. Far more than you deserve. And you didn't do anything wrong. You're not responsible."

"But my father is a rapist."

"Yes. But he was never your father. Just as I was never your mother. So it's just genetics. Nothing is different about you. Nothing has changed since the day you stepped foot in here. That is the only reason I didn't want you here. I didn't want you to know."

I stare at her. She doesn't flinch. "It's that bad. Whatever happened to you was that bad, wasn't it?"

"Yes." She doesn't keep speaking, or try to qualify the why or the how. Somehow, her simple, inexplicit answers tell me more about how bad it was than if she elaborated in a longer monologue.

"I'm a cop. I've seen a lot. I've had to witness a lot. I can handle it."

"No. I'm sorry, Natalie, I won't tell you anymore. You know the truth. I'm sorry for it. So very sorry for it. But I won't tell you anymore."

I'm hungry for details. And context. I want to know what she suffered. What she went through and how I came to be. I want to understand this woman before me, with whom I have a connection, although we can't seem to ever connect.

"I'm asking you to tell me. I'm asking you to trust me enough to tell me."

She shakes her head. "I won't tell you. No matter how much you think you're owed, or for whatever reason you think you should know. You know why I gave you up. That's the truth. The rest? They're just morbid details that won't help you."

We stare at each other. The light is bare and minimal. She is unyielding. I see it in the set of her jaw as I set mine. We might share one trait: stubbornness.

"I'm sorry. For whatever happened to you, I'm very sorry."

Her head bobs up and down. "I am too. I'm sorry it happened. But then again, you wouldn't be here. I never had a face to connect the baby to as the result of the rape that nearly ruined me. Seeing you now, I don't know, Natalie. I've always wondered so much about why. Why me? Why do things like that occur? Could God really want that to be my fate? But then, here you are and I don't regret it. It's confusing. And I'm sorry. But it's why I could not be and am not your mother."

"You surprised me. You seem like such a decent one. A good one, in fact. I pictured so many reasons why you gave me up and so many different situations. I thought you were really despicable. Or sad and weak and broken. Or an alcoholic, a drug addict, or even married and living a life that dictated you deny you ever had me. I thought I was a mistake you buried and wanted no one to find out about. I once pictured you being raped. It occurred to me, of course. But you said, *no, it was just a one–night–stand.* That made me resent you a little more, but I was also relieved."

"There is nothing about this that has ever been straightforward. It took me years to work that out. I basically tried to pretend the pregnancy never happened. I moved on from rape, and married Will and we made a life together and I was so grateful for that. But I did wonder about you. I had to believe, in my core, that whatever your life was, it had to be better than what I could have offered you."

"It was, Jessie. I've had a good life. I don't have any regrets. I think if things were how you say they were, you probably made the right decision. I didn't find you because I wanted to replace my mom. No one could do that. She was and is my mom forever. She knew every little detail about me while growing up. She talked me through high school, and when Sam didn't want to hang out with me as much when I was twelve, and he was starting to date girls his own age. She knew I hated onions and loved asparagus dipped in hot butter. She hugged me every night of my life. She—" Tears are filling my eyes. I didn't know I felt so strongly about my mom. I let the tears fall. Jessie comes closer and slides down to sit nearer me. Not touching me. Just being there. I sniff in my snot. "I miss her. Maybe…. maybe I ran here because I miss her so much. And after what I saw Sam doing, I just really needed *my mother*." The word *mother* and all its inherent significance, as well as all of the pain represented by both of my mothers, makes my voice crack. My tears fall hotter and faster. I use the side of my index finger to wipe the wetness under my eyes.

Jessie nods. "Yes, honey, I think you need your mother. What about your dad? Is he still in the picture?"

"He has dementia. He stayed with us for a little while, but we both work and couldn't keep him supervised. We put him in a small group assisted living home that is run by a husband/wife team who act as caretakers. There are five other residents, who all suffer from the same affliction. It's clean and neat and homey, but they also provide the constant care he needs. He doesn't know me anymore, or himself. So in a way, he died too, although I can still see him. And touch his hand. It's very confusing."

"Oh, Natalie, of course it must be. I think you are searching for an identity. Since losing both of your parents, you must feel like a leaf, drifting away from its tree."

I glance to the side. "What would that make us even be? You have daughters. I had a mother. Mine is gone, but you still can't be her to me."

Jessie squirms around. "I wish I could honestly find a label for what I could be. I saw clearly, from the start, how easily you and the girls found a way to be sisters."

"That's why you encouraged this week to happen?"

"Yes. I think it started something for all of you. Something positive and better than what your lives were before then. But you and I? I don't know what we are. Not mother and daughter, because I lost the right to know all those things your own mother knew and nurtured in you. Yet, you are still my daughter. I don't know what that means."

"But we're mostly strangers."

"Yes. But maybe we could start by being friends? I don't know what else to do, or call it."

I lick my lips. I agree. I have no urge to throw my arms around her, or hug her for comfort, neither hers, nor mine. But just as strongly, I have no desire to walk away from here and never see her again. There is something here, something more substantial than blind hatred or resentment. I'm interested in her, intrigued by her, but I don't know how that will translate into a relationship. I feel genuine compassion for what happened to her when she was young. I now have a fuller understanding of why a woman would give away her daughter, her baby, her flesh and blood.

I do not know, however, where that leaves us.

MORE PRETENDING. We pretend again the next morning. Sam and I only really associate or talk to each other when we are inside the Hendrickses' house. Somehow, I manage to leave before he pretends to stir in the mornings. There isn't a whole hell of a lot of peace between us. It's Saturday and everyone is hanging around. Jessie passes by me and stops to ask me something, casually setting her hand on my shoulder. I neither flinch away, nor discreetly try to remove it, but let it stay. We meet each other's stares and share a look. It's the first time as mother and daughter that we touch so casually.

I am planning to leave here tomorrow. My stomach cramps as I glance at Sam. He is casually stirring milk into his coffee while he and Will discuss the advantages of the local wind farm. Sam is quite interested in the giant windmills. I forget sometimes how intelligent he is. How quickly his mind works. But as he gets technical with Will, testing in depth Will's general knowledge of the wind farm's inner workings, I remember the Sam of our youth. He always wanted to know more about everything than anyone else ever bothered with. I think I've forgotten how attractive his brain is. He catches my stare and gives me a small, polite, yet almost nervous nod. He seems to sense I feel something different from yesterday. I don't know how I feel about all of it: Jessie, the sisters, him, or us. But tomorrow, when we go "back," something has to be done, or faced, or decided. I know what must happen, and it makes my stomach churn when I try to picture the reality of it happening.

It's mid–day when Christina finds me, I'm out towards the horse pasture, watching Melissa work with the mare. She's pretty good at getting the horse to circle her, then stop and go the other way. Her patience and endless kindness toward the animals impress me. Christina puts her foot on the fence rail next to me and nods at Melissa. "She's going to be like Mom someday with the animals. I just hope she can make it through school and go on and do something momentous with it. She should not waste her gift with animals."

"What do you mean *get through school*? She's fifteen."

"Missy doesn't like school at all. She barely gets Ds or passes. It's bad. But when you put her with an animal, she has so much patience, and endless talent. She can get them to do things no else can. She could be an amazing vet like Mom, or work in zoos or, I don't know… it seems limitless, if she'd just apply herself, or stick with something."

"She's got a lot of time to figure it out still. Most teens are apathetic, but they grow out of it. It's most likely just her age and a natural phase."

"I hope so. Look, Natalie, I know you leave tomorrow. I just, well, I got these for you. You seem to think you need to know everything. And I guess I think you earned the right. It's up to you what you do with them. Just, here…" She hands me a stack of letters with a rubber band around them. My mouth pops open in astonishment.

The letters! Jessie's letters are in my hand. I glance up at Christina, my eyes full of confusion. "You stole them from her?"

"I took them from her closet, yes. They will tell you the story I can't. It's a terrible story, Natalie. Be prepared for the worst. But then, maybe you will understand her better. And us. But it's not about you. Okay? This isn't the story of *you.* This is the story of Mom and how she decided to give you up in order for you to have a better life."

I should not do this. I'm breaking promises and my word. But still, I'm dying to sit down right there and start scanning them. Christina leaves and I do, too. I walk far from the house, past the horse pastures and into some trees. I find a pleasant spot to sit. A wooden bench that overlooks a small pond is perfect. I sit on it and grab the first letter. I take in a deep breath; here I go.

There are no dates. And no *to* or *from*. It's more like a journal entry. But it has the fold marks of being stuffed into an envelope at some point. They were written to Will because Jessie says his name many times. But it isn't the love notes of a husband and wife who are separated. It's angry, desolate, sarcastic and then... tragic. She calls her discomfort from the "monster" growing and forming inside her as a *mutated virus that won't go away.* That's what she calls me! My heart sits heavy. She detested me. I am the source of all the angry and awful words she writes. I flip to the next letter. This batch is consecutive. For more than forty days in a row, she wrote to him. Letter after letter depicting her discomfort, misery, and things about her father. Dear God, her father! I am shaking and starting to feel sick. Something deep and dark begins to grow in the pit of my stomach.

It isn't until the last letter of this batch when I start to understand. Her words haunt me. They're so few and yet… they say so much.

Will, I think about it. Every night. The pain. The pain. The pain. So much of it. Inside me. Around me. Everywhere. There is no hope for me. I lie there still tied up. Trapped forever. Like a rat to them. My life, and my pain have that much meaning to them. I mean nothing to them. I am nothing now. What you saw, if you had not come for me… I would have died. But I think, now, tonight, as I'm so alone here in this place, with you far away in the world, maybe that's what should have happened. It would have been so much easier. So much better for all. For you certainly. But maybe me, most of all. Who can go on after something like that? Who can live with that? Who can ever find something good in life again?

I set the letter down. *Tied up. Them.* The *them* has me shoving the papers away. I lean back, resting my head on the hard surface of the bench's back. My heart rate explodes and blood pumps madly through my ears. She was gang raped! I do not know the circumstances, or where she was, much less why Will was there and somehow managed to save her… but not before she was *gang raped.* Tears fill my eyes. They fall and I sit there, numb. I have no right.

I feel the pit of my stomach bottoming out. I had no right to pry into this woman's former life and read her personal thoughts. I slowly rise to my feet and gather all the letters in my hands. I hate myself and I know she will ask me to leave. I can accept that.

I deserve that.

But for now? The tears fall down my face.

"Natalie?"

It's Sam, of course. There is no missing his deep voice. Or the way my body trembles in response to him. The tears fall faster down my face. There is also no hiding the raw hurt in my eyes as I finally open them and find him standing over me. He doesn't hesitate, but simply rushes to my side and takes me in his arms. "How did you...?"

"Christina told me to find you. She said you needed me. She had no way of knowing that I am the last person you'd want to see."

I let him hold me. I cry against his chest, burying my face below his collarbone. I sniff deeply. He wears a soft cologne. Nothing obnoxious, just enough to tantalize me with his scent. It's soothing. Normal. *Sam.*

I don't know for what or for whom I cry. Jessie? Me? Will? Sam? Our history? Or now? I just don't know. Or for a wasted life and lost chances and rape and adultery? All of it swirls in my head with dizzying regularity.

There is nothing simple about my marriage, but he is here.

I'm still buried against him. I hiccup and finally mumble, "These letters... She was, she was raped. I am the biological result after she was gang raped."

His lips touch my hair in a kiss. "Damn. Baby, I'm sorry. I feared... something like this. There was a lot more to her story. There was a lot more there than the one–night–stand she claimed it was. I'm sorry for her, I am, but it's not your story. It's not you, Nat."

His large hand strokes my hair and the nape of my neck. He murmurs to me, but I don't know what he is saying. He leans back far enough to cup my face in his large hands. My cheeks fill them, and he runs his thumbs oh–so–gently over my lips. He presses his lips against mine and I can taste the faint salt from his warm skin. We stare at each other. Dark eyes to dark eyes. Tears to concern. Love to love.

"Why did you do it?" I finally whisper. There is no anger. Or recrimination. Just my broken heart. And my honesty. The depth of my heartbreak is evidenced in my tone.

He already told me, of course. We had this conversation before. I knew the reasons. I knew the discontent he felt. How I didn't need him and quit talking to him. And did not listen, or hear, or really even care about him for a year. I know all that. But why? My heart is screaming at me, and at him. Why did he have to do *that* to retaliate?

"Natalie..." His tone is tortured. It's a whisper. Like a prayer on his lips. He's sorry. I know that. I feel it in his touch and see it in his eyes. I know he's sorry. I know beneath all my anger and outright fury, the Sam I grew up with, dated, married and loved always is sincerely sorry. But he still did it. He broke us. There is no going back. We can't go home, or start living our lives again. We can't go back to working, grocery shopping, cooking dinner or living together as husband and wife. We can't go back to Dolores Street, or Golden Gate Park, or browse Pier 39, or stroll down at Crissy Field. We can't go back to the days when we explored the city together, mostly just to hold hands with each other. I know that so clearly, but my heart simply wants to try. We haven't been this connected in so long. And here, in this moment, we are.

We love each other. There isn't enough to erase it all. Or what we did to get here. Or what Sam ultimately did with another woman. Which I witnessed. We can't undo any of that. No amount of apologies or heated discussions can undo that.

His forehead rests on mine and his breath is warm on my nose as he leans down and kisses my eyelids. "Do you remember the first time I kissed you?" he whispers, his eyes so close to mine, we're almost cross-eyed. I inhale sharply at the memory. Of course I remember the night on his parents' couch. My heart was as hurt as it is right now, actually. My mother was dying. The shock and reality of that had not yet set in. Just the words. And he was home and acting like he never knew me. I all but kicked him in my fury for him to notice me. But then, somehow, we got close and I told him the news I'd yet to utter out loud. Then we kissed. We kissed and he instantly had my heart. Always. I just hadn't been mature or brave enough to admit it until that moment.

"I remember," I whisper. My eyes are still shut. I'm pretending that I shouldn't send him away. Pretending we are okay.

"It felt like the first time I ever kissed a girl." His statement is simple and sweet. I open my eyes to him. He smiles a boyish, almost shy grin. "I never felt that way with any girl before. I haven't since, either. I love you, Nat. I know, I know how much you think I don't. But I do. I would do anything to change what I did." His gaze is as compelling as a flame to someone suffering from hypothermia. "But I would never change you. You're here. I don't care how it happened. I'm just glad it did."

Tears cover my face because right now, that's exactly what I want to hear. I was born to an innocent woman who had to suffer unspeakable torture caused by other people's decisions. That doesn't make me feel glad I'm here and alive. I am a victim, but Jessie is so much more a victim than I am. I feel so alone, except for Sam.

He leans forward and his lips touch mine. It feels just like the first time. A sensuous meeting of lips, upper to upper, and lower to lower. So reverent and caring. He leans back and I know his gaze is fastened on my face. I keep my eyes closed. If I open them, I have to acknowledge where and who I am, as well as what year it is. I don't want to. I want to lose my head in my feelings and Sam. I don't want to think. I don't want to do what I should do. I don't want to remember *what he did.* I lean towards him. He tucks his hand behind my neck and firmly pulls me towards him.

"Look at me, Natalie."

I open my eyes at his tender command. I am captivated by his gaze.

"Tell me to stop."

I am staring into his eyes. We are inches apart, our breaths warm on each other's faces. My eyes are glazed over in tears. His are full of sympathy and I see something more. There is a fire glowing deeply in his brown, dark pools. My breath slowly escapes as I shrug and almost helplessly say, "I don't want to tell you to stop."

He holds my gaze hostage, leaning forward until his lips touch mine again. Almost as if it's the very first time he ever touched me. His lips are soft and wet, yet dry and perfect. He has a gift for exerting just the perfect amount of pressure and speed in his kisses. He starts slow, and builds it up gradually to create an even more intense burn. Or he swoops in fast and hot like a flash from a nuclear blast. Sometimes, his execution has me almost climbing on his lap, begging him for more. Sometimes, I'm so stunned I can't even move my limbs. He's just that good at it. And this time feels more intense than ever before. He comes in with a soft, tentative, almost insecure pressure of his lips on mine. When was Sam ever unsure of me? I'm filled with a power I've never felt before with him. I was always convinced I loved and wanted him more than he did me. I was crushing on him for years before he ever once noticed me. I watched him with girl after girl, all the same type. His type. And not one of them was anything like me. From their looks, to their coloring, to their personalities, talents, interests, opinions and thoughts.

I was the one he married. Sam was probably the only person on this planet that I felt insecure with. I cared about him so much that I doubted he could give that back to me. I was never totally, deep-down convinced I was the only one he wanted. He loved me. I didn't doubt that. He was attracted to me, and our sex was always hot and fresh. But I always suspected there was something missing. Maybe I wasn't really the love of his life.

Sam's cheating should have proven I was correct. That some deep dark corner of me had always been right. But shockingly, his reaction—running after me, trying so hard, apologizing over and over—has somehow touched something else deep inside me. I'm shocked he cares so much as to grovel. And to find me. Maybe he really does love me that much. Maybe I wasn't the only one who thought this relationship would be our end–all of everything emotional.

His hands slide to the bottom of my t–shirt before moving up to my sports bra. Never too girlie, not even in my underwear. He knows that as he slides his hands over the cotton material covering my breasts. The heat from his hands makes me moan. He knows how much I like this. His palms cup my breasts, and he lifts them while his fingers rub me. My nerve endings grow warm and tingle with heat before exploding when he swipes his thumbs back and forth, over both nipples, repeatedly. All the while, our lips are locked together tightly and our tongues fill each other's mouths. There is no finesse. And no slowing down now. We are messy, hot, lip–to–lip, mixing our spit, and *wild*. He grabs the edge of my bra and dips it down before tucking my small boobs on top and giving the bra a super support, push–up lift. I shift until I straddle him while he pulls away far enough to tug my shirt off. It goes over my neck and head, until my hair gets caught in the buttons. His eyes spark darkly as he stares at my uplifted breasts, as if being displayed at his feast. He leans forward, and this time, puts my bare nipple into his mouth. *Wet.* Oh–so–wet. The familiar, warm sensations start to percolate; they tug and strum my pleasure sensors until a deep, gnawing need begins to grow inside me. He tugs all my nerve endings and I respond by cradling his head to my chest. It feels like such a loving act, holding him close to me.

His dark head tucked against my bosom. I hold him, letting my fingers swirl through his dark hair. Overwhelming feelings rush into my chest. Love. Tenderness. Joy. Sex. Want. Need. So many emotions are swirling inside me at once. Sadness. Anger. How could he? They also speak from inside me as I cling to him. He causes all of this to happen inside me. And Jessie's story stirs up something deep and dark inside me too. It is more upsetting than I thought. I feel almost desperate for a connection. And Sam? *Sam is my connection.* Perhaps the only connection I have left.

Yes, I'm aware how vulnerable I am. So is he. I know when he stops and asks me. He's worried I'm using sex to eradicate my pain. The thing is, he might be right. I could be doing that. Jessie's story is so gruesome, I almost want to feel something that's good and real. Maybe that's twisted on my part, because her story centers on sex. But that sex was a very different kind than what I have with Sam.

He kisses my breasts and follows the curve towards my collarbone and my neck. I lean my head back, allowing him more access to my throat. His hands encircle my back as his lips once more find mine. He kisses me long and deep; but I feel a sense of desperation in his kiss, as well as in his grasp of me. His hands tremble as he grips my bare back. I begin to address his shirt. He has a button-up on so I quickly start unbuttoning it. He allows enough space between us for me to separate the sides of his shirt, jerking his shoulders forward and helping me slide it off them. He has a long, sleek torso, perfect for his tall height. Not an inch of fat on him, he is lean and trim. My hands slide over his chest and I memorize the feel of his skin against mine, the softness of his hair beneath my palms and his sharp intake of breath, letting me know how much he likes it.

He suddenly leans forward, and buries his hands into my hair, angling my head the way he wants it before his mouth nearly devours me. He's so anxious for me. His tongue delves deeper into my mouth and I moan at the onslaught. It's not like Sam. He's never so desperate or spontaneously unplanned. I feel his burning heat when I try to press my own aching body harder against him. He pushes me up, and I'm standing on trembling legs as his hands drop to my waist and he slips off the workout pants I wear. Unceremoniously, he drops them to my ankles, along with my underwear. I kick my sneakers off, but leave my socks on as he works his own pants down. I wait until they're far enough down and step forward to fill my hands with his hard, radiant warmth.

He stops instantly, almost in shock, like he'll scare me away if he dares to move or twitch. Groaning my name, he wraps his hands around me before pulling me closer. Then, we hug, of all things. My hands are trapped, and I'm virtually unable to move. I finally manage to slide them around his waist. He has me tightly against him with my head now resting on his shoulder and his on top of mine as he clings to me. We would probably make a strange sight to anyone that came upon us. We stand up, and I'm naked but for my white ankle socks; and Sam's also naked, but for the jeans wrapped around his ankles. He's rock hard and very turned on, pressing against my stomach, and yet, we can only cling to each other for several long minutes. The time presses on and on and on... yet nothing about it feels ridiculous. It is serious and intense. I feel just as vulnerable toward him as he does to me right now. Again, that sense of powerfulness sweeps through me. He finally realizes how much he needs me, and knows he loves me. His fear of losing me has changed his physical approach to me.

He gradually slides his hands down my bare back, landing on my butt, which he grasps with both hands. I moan with eager anticipation.

But then he stops and I'm briefly startled to find myself in his arms, as he slowly lowers me down. The ground beneath us consists of long, dry grass. It is also dirty, and certainly not a bed. We've never done the deed outside before. I feel the cool ground underneath me, and I don't care. The heat of his hands makes the rough substrate easy to ignore. He leans back, gently touching my thighs and spreading them wider, his gaze so hot, it's nearly blistering me. He watches me open wider as he leans forward until his mouth touches me. I buck up enthusiastically towards him. All the blood in my body seems to congregate right there. I swell in wanting. He moans before his tongue touches me ever so gently. He softly nibbles around my clit. It's so good. So fulfilling. I close my eyes, running my restless hands through his hair, tousling it mindlessly, while he satisfies yet creates something even deeper, burning inside me. On and on he kisses and sucks me while this radiant sweep of heat flows all the way down to my toes. I finally find sweet release and whisper his name gratefully.

He lifts his face from between my thighs, and kisses my stomach, moving up to my cleavage until he is hot and hard, waiting at my entrance. I'm so wet, he slides in effortlessly and fills me in a second. I hold him close to me, my nails raking his back as I lift up my knees and adjust the tilt of my pelvis, making us both groan in response. It's so freaking good. His hands cover my hands and he grasps them, entwining our fingers. I open my eyes and find his face right over mine and his gaze solely fastened on me. Deep. Unsmiling. Intense. He doesn't close his eyes, or break our connection, not even once. Then he shoves himself inside me over and over and over again and I feel him coming as my own body welcomes him in total abandon.

Only then does he lower his head and fall off me, to the side. Our bodies are hot and warm as we embrace, clinging to each other on the uneven ground. I finally open my eyes.

The sun is starting to slide across the tops of the trees. We are most unlikely to be seen or heard, but what if one of the Hendricks girls comes looking for us? Talk about eyesores and traumatizing them. I push Sam's shoulder to loosen his arm around me and sit up. My back is now to him as I clasp my knees to my chest.

I feel him wrestling up as he leans behind me and plants a gentle kiss on my shoulder. "Don't regret it. Not already."

He knows me too well. Now that I am no longer on the verge of hysterical crying, or a living mass of pulsating needs, I am thinking just that. *Way to teach him, Natalie.* He puts his penis in some other woman and I turn around and let him put it inside me again? I shake my head, getting cross at myself, and rest my chin on my hand.

Now, I'm not sure I should have done that. But when it started, nothing else could have felt more right. I don't know what to think now, other than I really can't decide while being naked in the woods. I pull my bra up as I slowly get back to my feet. At least it's Sam. There's no part of me he hasn't seen naked a hundred times and ways. I grab my underwear and pull them up. He gets to his feet and leans down to slide his jeans and underwear back on. He was never totally out of them.

As I take my shirt off the bench, I tell him, "This was just sex, Sam. It doesn't change anything."

He is shrugging when he stops dead. He reaches out and takes my shoulders, making me face him. "It felt like something more."

"Why? Because the last time you had sex, it meant nothing? Well, God, I hope it meant more than some strange pussy on your desk. But it's over. Us. This…" I flap my hands around, helpless and struggling for the right words to say. I don't feel total regret. I wanted and needed that. I required sex right then. I've always needed it. It releases something dark from inside me and resuscitates me back to life. So I don't totally hate myself. I really don't think, however, that sex fixes *anything* at all for us. "That was sex."

He closes his eyes. "No, it was more. But I know it fixes nothing. Even though you hate me, detest me, and wish I was castrated, while we were here, it's the first I've felt… like us. I've felt we were us again, where for so long, you became distant to me. A mirage. I lived with you, saw you all the time, but in so many ways, it felt like I didn't really see or live with you. I didn't even realize our connection was missing, until your anger allowed us to find some connection again. No apathy here in Ellensburg."

I want to lash out at him. But his shoulders are hunched and his hands are now buried in his jeans pockets. He hangs his head as he stares down. This is not a happy man. Or even a man at peace. This is a man who appears hopeless, as if he lost everything. I don't know if I feel vindicated by making him feel so low or not. I sympathize. I feel his pain. But I don't reach out to him. I don't know what any of that means.

"Apathy. I agree that was something we both used as deterrent and to avoid dealing with each other, and the straight fact that I can't easily conceive a baby. But the surest way to kill that was for you to have sex with someone else. It might have shaken us out of our apathy, but it doesn't suddenly shoot us back into being connected. We are… lost. I don't see any other outcome. Not one that will allow me to go on and live with myself."

"I'm glad I was here. Whatever happens with us, I'm glad I came here."

Strangely enough, I am too.

But that doesn't mean anything long term. Spinning on my sneaker, I slowly head back to civilization. I get in my car and take off for a while, needing the space. I need to think about what I just did with Sam, and how best to proceed with Jessie. I am riddled with guilt for betraying a woman who was so horribly victimized herself. I feel like I exploited her. I drive to a small park and walk for what seems like forever along the river and the picturesque farmland it follows.

CHAPTER 16

$\mathcal{N}$ATALIE

I TRUDGE BACK TO the main house. It's late and dark by then. My last night here and I haven't seen my sisters. The only illumination comes from the hood light over the stove as I enter from the deck. I stop dead. Jessie sits up. Alone. She is staring at her nails, and sitting at the kitchen table.

I walk forward and set the bundle of letters on the table. She doesn't grab them, or look up at me.

"I'm… sorry. I should have never…" The words get trapped in my throat. For a second, I almost understand Sam. Begging for my forgiveness and needing me to hear it. I feel that way with Jessie now. I want to beg for her forgiveness and I need her to hear me.

"I didn't read them all. I stopped." Her silence is unnerving. The house is so awfully quiet. A clock's soft ticking. The hum of the fridge. The spicy smell of tacos still lingering from dinner.

She doesn't answer, but finally pushes them back to me. "Maybe you should finish them."

I'm shocked. I fully expect her to storm away from me with them and never look at me again. When I meet her eyes, I turn away, ashamed. Her brown eyes are stark and cold. "They tell your story. Not mine."

"I heard Christina. I knew what she was doing. Somehow, I think I might have counted on her doing so. It's in her nature. No secrets. No lies. I'm glad she's that way. She's never had a reason not to be. None of my daughters do. I always had secrets growing up. I always knew other people's secrets and lies. So it's okay if she just wanted you to know the truth. Those..." She nods at the box. "Those are the raw, ultimate truth. There is nothing more I can tell you that will explain it. No one else but Will has ever read them. No one ever will either, if I have any say in it. But I realize if anyone has a right, it's you, Natalie. You just want to understand the reasons behind my decisions. I'll bet you blame yourself sometimes and wonder what was so bad with you, don't you? I understand that, Natalie. Needing answers. What I'm going to tell you is, your answers will hurt. They will make you feel sick and ill. But they might also provide the closure you've never had before. But hear me, okay? You have an idea now of what I had to face. But it was never your fault. I never blamed you for it, not even then. Even when I was broken down and toxic to myself. I never blamed *you*."

"One of them has the same blood as me. *That* disgusting, cruel vileness is in my lineage." I shudder and cringe. It's enough to make bile climb up the back of my throat.

"Yes, but the other half of your lineage is *mine*. I spent my youth figuring out I was a good, decent person. And you are too." She leans across the table, and for the first time ever in my life, my mother touches my hand with comfort. She has small fingers. Her cool fingers grasp mine and she squeezes them. "It is just a story of conception. The rest of the story is mine. But listen to me. Please, Natalie, hear me. I don't want you to waste any energy now questioning whether you are an inherently good and decent person, simply based on the identity of your father. Read my words. Read my story and you will learn how I spent half of my life falsely believing who my father was. I thought his blood was mine, too and it made me feel dirty and ashamed, because I let it. It turns out, he wasn't my father, but that didn't change much, since he was the father who raised me. We both share very bad fathers, but that doesn't determine who we are. It took me years and years to realize that. And believe it. It almost destroyed my mental health. I was never going to tell you because I didn't want any daughter of mine to suffer the pain of learning her father's identity as I did."

Tears fill my eyes. I had no idea. I finally grip her fingers with mine. She smiles softly and leans forward, touching my cheek with her other hand. "I'm sorry I could not be your mother. I think you are a lovely, kind, tough, strong, interesting and gentle daughter."

I push the papers at her. "I don't want to read anymore. I want... I want you to tell me about it."

She leans back. Our hands still gripping each other, she nods slowly. "I've never really told anyone what happened from the start to the finish. Will told Lindsey, and he also told Christina. Will usually tells it for me."

"How can he tell it for you?"

She sighs. Her lips tremble. "He was there."

My heart skips. Whoever expects that?

"How could he be there?"

"It's a very complicated and long, almost impossible story."

"I have time," I say after an extended pause. "I'd like to

hear it. To understand it, and you. I think I'd like to know you better. Would you tell me?"

"You think you'd like to know me better? You mean, who I was then?"

I nod and swallow, admitting, "Yes, for context. But I think more than that, I'd like to know you now. I-if that's okay with you."

She holds my gaze and then her slow nod answers me. "I would like to know you better too."

My smile is the weakest, most tremulous version of my mouth curling up. But there is no joy. Just a lot of confusion and conflicting emotions. "Will you tell me?"

"Yes. I'll tell you." She closes her eyes, takes a deep breath and starts to talk.

It is a long story and she takes hours to tell me all of it that night. Into the wee hours, we talk, ensconced sheerly by the dim light and surrounding darkness. I don't think we could have done it in the harsh light of day, or an evening lamplight. She tells me about a place in Mexico where she was kidnapped and held hostage. That was also where she was gang raped and I was conceived. She tells me how Will rescued her, not only figuratively, but also in every other way. I listen to her long, arduous journey through mental health and cutting herself. I hear about her own father and how he virtually sold her to his cronies for sex. She is right, her father is every bit as bad as mine. We cry many times. We stop, and start again. She tells me about the night I was born. She was in a hospital in San Francisco with her sister.

Not too long before I was born she came to Ellensburg to live with friends of Will as he wasn't in her life at that point. That was how they ended up here. She went back to San Francisco, however, to give birth to me. She had the help of a family friend, Will's ex-wife, overseeing her treatment. This woman lived in northern California and that was where

Jessie wanted to have me. She said she held me, looked at me, *loved* me, and let me go. She went back to Ellensburg and tried to move forward with her life without trying to destroy herself anymore. A task she said that took her years to complete. She thought she sealed her heart forever from me until the day I showed up on her doorstep.

She was exhausted afterwards. I could see the grief in her eyes. The thing is, I think she was more upset for me than for herself. "Christina knows this story?"

"She knows a lot of it. You can imagine how hard it was for her to hear."

"That's what made her come after me?"

"Yes."

"And why she freaked out a bit when I showed up. She was worried about you. Which I totally understand and sympathize with now." My gaze travels over this woman for whom I can't help feeling a profound sympathy and respect. Remembering the start of the week, when I might have completely rejected her, I never believed I could ever feel any of those things for the woman who gave me up. But I see now, life's events are so much more complicated than human actions appear. The "why" behind our actions, like cheating, or giving your baby away, matters just as much as the action itself. Recognizing the parallel of my own life right now isn't lost on me. I rejected all of Sam's *whys.* I told him it didn't matter *why* he cheated. But it does. It matters a lot why he did it. Maybe it doesn't always have to matter. Not if the person is a stranger or an acquaintance. But what if it's the only person you loved more than anyone else in your life? It feels like in those circumstances, maybe it does matter. Maybe I need to try and figure out or understand the *why* behind my husband's betrayal. It's a profound revelation that so easily slips into my brain. It instantly makes my spine snap straight, it's so shocking for me to realize. Judging other people is so easy. Understanding them? That's a whole different ballgame.

And understanding someone's motivation doesn't always mean forgiveness. It doesn't guarantee that I can let go of the offensive action either. But maybe someday, it could allow me to let it all go.

I've felt a lot of anger in my life. I formerly resented the concept of this woman sitting before me now, more than probably any other part of my life. And as it turns out, understanding her isn't hard at all… but forgiving her is even easier. Surprisingly, that concept releases something powerful into my bloodstream. Something that feels really good.

Silence, but a strangely content quiet, descends until she points up at my head. "Something happen with Sam today?"

Puzzled, I tilt my head. "How did you know?" She leans forward and her fingers clasp something in my hair. She opens her hand and shows me a small leaf. I blush and shrug. I oh–so–rarely blush about sex or anything else, but seeing that leaf immediately has me blushing. I grab the leaf and crumple it in my hands, smoothing my hair for more telltale signs. "Yes. I had a moment. After reading some of your letters to Will, and thinking about what happened to you… but that sounds disgusting. It didn't make me want to have sex. It made me realize how lucky I was to never have experienced something as degrading and horrible as rape." I groan, grasping my head with my hands. "I didn't mean to say anything like that out loud."

Jessie smiles and a small laugh escapes her mouth. She's pretty cool, even about that. Gotta give her credit. "No one can take in this story easily. But especially you. It had the most direct effect on your life. Don't ever doubt that. And feel free to say whatever you need to in order to deal with the stress of it, okay? It's not an easy story. Can I ask you something?"

"Sure."

"Do you love Sam?"

"Yes. I love him. But can I forgive him? I don't know."

"Whatever happens, you are always welcome here. Anytime. Any day. I will be here in support of *you*. I still don't know what we should call each other, but you know now. Everything I feared you finding out about, you already know. I never intended to hurt you, or make your life worse, but I guess I already did. I'd be very grateful if you came back for another visit."

"Honestly? It's hard to hear, but maybe Christina was right. She stirred up a sympathy and willingness to give you a chance with me that nothing else could."

"Maybe that's my point. No one knows what is right in how they react to things. Good or bad. We're all wrong. Whatever you decide about me, or your sisters, or Sam, you'll get no judgment from me. I just hope from this day forward, you'll feel welcome here."

"I feel like maybe I would like to come back."

She squeezes my hand for only a fraction of a second. "I hope more than anything that happens."

We smile very weary smiles and look away. Something strangely good came out of the worst story I ever heard. The story of my conception. The story of why I was subsequently given away. The story of my ancestry. It is dark, ugly, sick and twisted. And yet, here I am. I'm none of those things. I know that much about myself. Nothing will make me think otherwise either.

SAM IS UP EARLY and all packed when I come out of my room

the next morning. His gaze is weary as he tracks me across the too-small living room. "I would like to drive back with you. I don't want you driving alone across half the country again."

I yawn and scratch my leg. It's too early for me to hear this. I'm still in my pajamas and I was up late in one of the most emotional and intense talks of my life with Jessie. Not quite ready to go back to this dark, heavy and depressing stuff. I'm really not in the mood for it... ever. Right now, it isn't that important to me. I'm simply tired of all the drama and my emotions being roller-coastered in such extremes. I roll my eyes for effect. "I don't need you to drive me home. I'm the one who has the gun, for God's sake, Sam. I'm the trained cop who knows how to use it; I highly doubt I'll need your big, bad protection to keep me safe. And I can drive as well as you." I push my heavy mass of snarled hair off my face.

He is spic-n-span clean, shaved, groomed and ready to go. "I wasn't trying to protect you. But I think anyone is safer when there're two people."

"No. You fly home. I'll drive my car, same way I got here."

His shoulders droop. "What happens then?" His tone sounds tired; maybe he's as tired as I am of this.

"We separate," I reply finally after a long pause. "I think there is no other choice."

"There are other choices."

"Not right now. For me, there isn't any other choice."

"I'll move out of the house then."

"No. I will. I never really liked that place. It's too big and unfriendly for my taste. I already spoke to Dustin and he said there's a vacant unit in his building. He's going to get it for me."

"When did you do that?"

"I don't know. I called a few days ago, I guess."

"Were you going to tell me?"

"Yes. But then I got those letters… and we slept together and…" I trail off in my lame response.

His gaze searches mine. "Is it just over? Are you filing for divorce?"

"No. But neither am I pretending it didn't happen. Any of it. We feel impossible to me right now, and I honestly don't know what I want, or where it leaves us. But I need space, Sam. Real space. Not just a week spent with new acquaintances. I understand your urgency to find me. Maybe in a lot of ways, it was good this week happened. No other situation would have made me listen to you. I would have simply, and quite easily, hated you for the rest of my life. Yes, I was ready to divorce you. There is a lot here. A lot we've done to each other. My apathy. Your reactions. Whatever. It all arises from two people who are not happily married to each other. Otherwise, none of this would be as it is."

"You sound an awful lot like this week gave you a sense of closure."

I shake my head. "I honestly don't know right now, Sam. I can't give you an answer. What I can tell you is, I can't live with you. I can't go back to the life we formerly shared. I'm going to get my own place."

He closes his eyes and I can almost feel his weariness. "Okay. You'll need money. There should be plenty in the savings account."

"I know where our money is, Sam." *Our.* I flinch and so does he. One thing we rarely fought about was how we spent and saved our money. Neither of us ever monitored the other because we were both so good at budgeting.

Silence descends like a fog with the frigid chill of the future, the unknown, pervading it. It feels somehow like our entire relationship just comes down to his solemn acceptance of what I want.

Sam leaves before I do. He takes his rental car to the airport and I say goodbye to the women who are no longer a total surprise to me or total strangers. I easily hug the younger two. Christina and I also embrace and she squeezes my hand in support. "Come back, Natalie. Please, come back and be part of our family."

It's a seductive thought to believe this family wants to include me in it. Yet, I can't commit to such an invitation. This has been an intense week. Unprecedented for me. I honestly don't trust how I feel about anything right now. I need space, on all fronts, and time to process *everything* that happened to me and because of me. A long drive sounds like the perfect escape from everything. I finish loading my stuff in my car and slam the trunk before turning finally to Jessie, who's standing close. "That's it, I guess." I'm desperate to control the odd, uncomfortable energy between us. There is so much more between us now. Not just the anger or resentment of her being a stranger. We share understanding, sympathy and care even.

But still, we're almost strangers.

"Drive carefully. Please call one of us when you get home to let us know you arrived safely."

The maternal nature of her request makes my heart shift. I temporarily forgot what it felt like to have the presence of mom-worry in my life. Everyone ignores it, or rolls their eyes, but once it's gone, like after your mother dies, you miss it for every single day of your life thereafter. I used to think my mom would always be there for me no matter how busy or careless I was about calling or visiting her. I know now not to believe that. "I will. Besides, I promised Melissa I'd get her some pictures of me in my uniform. She doesn't really believe I'm a bad-ass girl-cop. Her words, not mine."

Jessie grins and steps forward. She sets her hand just below my elbow and her other hand on my shoulder. Pulling me towards her, we clasp in a half hug. She quickly lets me go. "Goodbye, Natalie, please don't be a stranger. Is… is it all right if I call you? You know, just to check in?"

I could so easily be done with her. I still harbor issues about us being strangers for so long. But the stronger urge is, I want to get to know her. To know… *my mother*. "Yes, I'd be glad to hear from you."

She nods, pressing her lips together. I see her physical release of breath. She's relieved and pleased with my answer.

I wave after I get in my car and start it. Heading down their isolated road, I realize I found things I never thought I wanted, or was looking for here. That opened up a bunch of possibilities for a future I never suspected. It also allowed Sam to find me. So many other things came out. I'm calmer than the day I pulled in here. But it's all too fresh and raw to say I feel any better, or can finally decide anything. For now? I'm going home.

The first thing I do when back in town is visit my dad. I hold his hand and listen to him ramble and ask me several times who I am. We have lunch and watch TV until he zones out, clueless, and eventually falls asleep. I get up and kiss his forehead, and my heart is heavy as my lips touch his wrinkled skin. Tears fall down my cheek. "Bye, Dad, until Friday," I say as I quietly take my leave.

That is my greeting from the world I left behind for over a week. No one really missed me or even knew I was gone. Other than work and Sam's family, I don't have anyone in my life. Loneliness fills me. I miss my mom and dad. I miss that feeling of safety from having your family there and present in your life. I even kind of miss the Hendrickses and the things I was starting to feel and experience with them.

I most of all miss Sam. But not the relationship I had with him over the last year. No, I miss the relationship with him I had started to remember while in Ellensburg. But I know there is no place now for those memories in what if left of us.

I go back to work. And back to my life. I am still trying to figure out how to live it now that Sam is no longer a part of it.

CHAPTER 17

AM

NATALIE TAKES THREE DAYS to return to the house. I learn from Dustin that she's in regular contact with him and subletting his friend's apartment. Voila! Natalie has her own place. We are officially separated. She stops by and gets some furniture, linens, and kitchen things that we split up. I'm generous, trying to push it all on her out of guilt. But she doesn't take advantage of it like she could, so I'll give her kudos on that. She asks that I not be there when she comes by our house. So, I comply.

I get the pleasure of facing my mother, who is beyond disappointed in me. No yelling, just that look and her plaintive, "Oh, Sam!" are enough to have me cringing in shame for the next decade. Mom is worried to death about Natalie and contacts her several times after she returns, while leaving me pretty much alone.

Everyone calls Natalie. I become a pariah. I have nothing

to do. No job to go to. I have no friends left because all of them were connected in one way or another to work or Jayden. During the week I disappeared, he pretty much blackballed me. What a juvenile prick! I need a new place to live. Everywhere at the house screams *Natalie and me*. And yet, I now realize the three years we spent here weren't happy memories; but rather, a lot of strained, awkward silences and petty, picky fights. We were two strangers occupying the same air space. I pack up my stuff, giving away half of it to charity. Suits, shoes, ties; all of the design wear is mostly gone. I keep a few suits in case I ever have a funeral to attend, but as far as I am concerned, I am finished with the corporate world. I have no idea what I will do. No one in my family particularly wants to hang out with me. I don't really want to hang out with me. I do nothing. I have hours and hours to think about what I did, why I did it and where the hell is my life going? I have no answers. It feels like nowhere.

There are days the stir–crazy becomes too much and I have to get out. I find myself sometimes wandering back to the apartment building we first lived in when we got married. Another day, I walk to the street we grew up on. And that takes me down to the lot where we spent all our free time.

The park. That park was Natalie's haven. It was fun for me. I spent most every afternoon after school there and many weekends. But I know it was Natalie's version of a backyard and a familiar place where she fit in. It was the place where she excelled and felt safe. She was accepted and applauded there.

I sit now on one of the dilapidated benches. It's askew, and broken on one end. Covered in graffiti like almost every other surface of the park, the lawn is overgrown, full of weeds and has ugly, bald spots. The baseball backstop is hanging on one end where a large branch took it out and no

one bothered to repair it. The lot is small. Just a dumpy baseball diamond, and farther off, double goals for soccer or
impromptu football games. There are abandoned concession
stands with broken glass and garbage as their only commodi-
ties. The small basketball court has more weeds than pavement, sprouting through myriad cracks. I'm surprised the lot
is still here and not torn down to accommodate the latest
version of median–income apartments like we grew up in.
The area has gone downhill from the working class residents
that occupied it when we were young. Now it's people who
are not working, but rather broken down and depressed.
This park seems like a reflection of the once decent, respectful, friendly neighborhood.

Who owns it now? Who allowed it to get like this? Does it
even matter? It doesn't seem like it matters to anyone at all.

Except me.

I sit there for two hours. Some teens wander by, razzing
each other as they walk along. They show no interest in
sports, or teams, or hanging here.

Not like we used to. I can picture the sun setting, turning
the park black against the peach sky as the breezes stir and
we; me, Natalie, Dustin and kids from the neighborhood,
pitch one last game, or play one final game of soccer. I see
myself racing Natalie home… and usually winning, despite
her angry reactions to my victory. A smile curls my lips.
Those were the best, and most innocent nights of my life.
Dustin, Natalie, me and a half-dozen neighborhood kids
ranging in all ages.

Teens nowadays don't seem to do anything here. They
pass by quickly, sometimes using it as a shortcut. They eye
me suspiciously for being here. The place is just a shithole
now, and more than likely provides a backdrop for drugs
than any other kind of recreation.

What a huge shame. It kept me and my friends out of

trouble for many years while my parents worked and couldn't always supervise us. It would have been easy to follow the wrong path. I glance around. There is nowhere safe. Or fun. Or even appealing left around there.

It takes me a week before I bother looking up who owns the lot now. It used to be owned by a now defunct youth center. A local landowner bought it, who already owns more than a dozen buildings, convenient stores and the like in the area. After a few days, I finally contact the owner.

"You want to know about what?" His tone is incredulous. "That old lot next to the abandoned rec center? Why the hell do you want to know about that?"

"Just curious. I grew up there and it used to be a pretty decent place for kids to hang out after school. The local sports teams played their games there. Why not anymore?"

"Gangs. Drugs. Sex. Take your pick. It ain't the neighborhood of your youth. I keep waiting for the area to turn around so I can sell it. Why? You interested?"

"In what?"

"The lot? You want it? You can have it cheap. It's a pain in my ass! Always having the cops contact me about some incident going on there or another. Be my guest."

What the hell would I do with an old park? I know nothing about it. The sum he asks for is also ridiculous, especially considering the condition of the land, the park and the area.

But somehow, all I can think about is Natalie and me, and the fun we had there. Young. Happy. Friends. The best of friends.

We have money. I made enough from BorderLine Solutions to grow a substantial nest egg. Considering we'll most likely be dividing it all in half, I could buy the land, but I'd have almost nothing left over to live in or on. I'm not sure if I should risk it.

After receiving notice from the company to vacate the house, I honestly can't wait to comply with their terse order. I find a craphole apartment and bring my favorite chair, the spare bed, some clothes and ditch the rest. Natalie says I could do whatever I want with what was left, as she'd already taken what she wanted. *Fantastic.* I am stuck with a house full of pretty furniture and a shithole to take it to.

That's why I give it almost all away.

I have figured out a lot of things. Everything I did before I cheated gave me a false sense of who I was and what I wanted. Everything that happened before was really what eventually led to this. So I decide to change everything about myself, my life, my occupation, where I live, how I dress and what I do all day.

So I set myself up with the basics and decide to buy the old park. I go over there with a rake one afternoon and get started. I rake the bald spots and rent a lawn mower to mow down the weeds. I get there each day a little earlier as I start to see some progress. I fix the fencing here, add new chain link over there, and bring in an entire new row of benches. I replant the grass and continue raking. I find plenty of broken glass, used needles, tin cans and other garbage. Bags and bags of it. I collect it all and start scrubbing out the graffiti. I scrub and scrub and paint and paint. There is a lot of it.

I look up one afternoon to find my brother, still in his uniform, his sleeves rolled up, standing there. He eyes me cautiously as if approaching a rabid grizzly bear or an escaped mental patient. "Sam?" His tone is curious and gentle. "What is this? What are you doing?"

I sit back on my heels and throw my hands up, as if to say, *Look around you.* "Duh. I'm weeding at present."

"I see that. But why? What are you doing? I know you told Mom you bought this place, but we can't figure out why. They are worried about you. You don't answer their calls.

Nor mine. You sold everything. You chucked a good job and lifestyle you've been chasing your entire life. Is this some kind of early mid–life crisis or something else?"

I stay on all fours, still weeding. I've found if I pull them out by hand, it keeps them away longer. I have to be careful what I pick around. "I don't want all the shit anymore. It never made me happy."

Dustin sighs as he squats near me. "I know. This is a reaction to Natalie, but you don't have to get rid of your entire life. There is nothing wrong with having ambitions and goals and working hard. You made a mistake, Sam. You don't have to give up on everything you ever did before because of it. You don't owe it to Natalie to go that far. No one, none of us, want to see you destroy the rest of your life too."

I sit back on my haunches and pull my gloves off to wipe my sweaty forehead. I'm sure I smear more dirt in with the sweat. "Don't you get it, Dustin? I already destroyed the only 'it' that mattered. The depth. The love. The care. The thing that made me a better person was Nat. I betrayed her. Therefore, I betrayed myself. I'm not losing my mind, or punishing myself. I want to be different. Better. I think this is different and better." I swipe my arm around as if encompassing the whole ramshackle lot. Okay, there is a lot of work to do. But I'm determined. And I have nothing else to do. Dustin watches me for a while. I wait for him to leave, or further comment, but instead, he slips his coat off, squats down about twenty feet from me, and begins pulling some of the weeds, as well as picking up the miscellaneous garbage. After a few hours, we stand, our knees sore and our backs groaning.

"Thank you, Dustin."

"You're welcome," he says as he slaps my back, but not too hard. "Just don't totally lose your mind, Sam. No one wants that, not even Natalie."

I don't know about that. She has yet to serve me with divorce papers, but she does not respond very often to my requests to meet. Or talk. She communicates about everyday matters since we still are legally married, but only by text or email. I saw her cruising one afternoon in her patrol car. She didn't see me. I was coming out of a hardware store when I saw her pass. She had her hair pulled back in a severe bun. Her hat over her eyes made her look so harsh and austere. There is something intimidating about her in uniform when she's in her official capacity.

I take some offense to Dustin's comment. So I am a little grubby of late. The kind of work I'm doing is dirty and makes me sweaty. I wear sweats and t–shirts there because I often get filthy. I haven't cut my hair in a while. So no, I'm not taking particularly great care of myself. But I'm obsessed and determined. This place won't be such a dangerous eyesore anymore. I work all day weekdays and weekends. I get there early and leave late. It is taking that much work to improve it.

That's fine. Because I own it now. I think growing up, I assumed the city owned the park. It was a bit of a surprise to discover it didn't. A goodhearted community leader was the first kind soul who provided the space for kids, and he did that just because. I want to do that now, too.

One afternoon, I see some kids coming by on skate-boards. They ask and nod towards the baseball diamond. It's the only part that is totally—weed, garbage and graffiti—free. Although by the second night I made it so, someone came by and tagged it overnight. I just went back to work on it again. It's happened every night since then too. And every morning, I fix it. Paint it. Scrub it. Whatever. I see it as the test now. It comes to signify a bigger test for me. A test of my morality. My ability to commit and stick through the hard stuff. So every morning, my first chore is to make sure the park is once again graffiti–free. Either whoever is doing the tagging or I will eventually tire of this routine, and move on to end this ongoing stalemate. But by God, on my life, I don't intend for it to be me.

Anyway, when the teens asked to play on the field, I nodded my permission. I restrained myself from falling on my knees and thanking them with relief for showing some interest. For giving me hope that all my hard work was not for naught. Perhaps somebody might even give a crap about this park again. After sinking my half of our savings into it, maybe someone would be interested in it long enough to justify all my effort.

NATALIE

I glance up when I hear the knock and see Dustin letting himself in. He walks over and sits on my couch where I am lounging. I look at him when he sighs heavily as if asking for my attention.

"Something up?"

"Have you spoken to Sam?"

I close the game on my tablet, tuck my legs under me and face Dustin. *Sam.* Always back to Sam. Wearily, I shake my head to the negative. "Only through texts about functional stuff, you know, coordinating the bills and adjusting our finances and such."

"Have you been by the old neighborhood recently?"

I hesitate. *What does one have to do with the other?* "It's been awhile, but last time I was there, it was a real shithole. Sad to see how drastically it declined. Why?"

"Sam's hanging out there. I mean, like he's fixing up the old field. I—I don't recognize him. He's acting like a man possessed on a mission. I was thinking maybe you could go down there and check on him."

I stare at Dustin. *Is he for real?* "What do you mean, he's 'hanging out there'?"

"I mean, you know that money he withdrew and said it was for a down payment on a place? It wasn't a house, or an apartment, or anything; it was the park. I swear to God, he's acting possessed and returning it to its former glory. For you. I think he's doing it for you, Natalie. I get you're mad. Pissed. Hurt. But maybe you could check up on him. He's literally on his hands and knees by himself, doing all the weeding, picking up trash, scrubbing out and repainting graffiti…"

I hear all those things, but I can't picture Sam out there on his hands and knees, doing physical work. I assure Dustin I will follow his advice, and the next day when I have some time, I head over to the neighborhood.

It feels good to be back on the job, especially after the odd vacation I had. It gives me a familiar high to wear my uniform and cruise the streets, patrolling citizens. After taking a couple of calls—a burglary and a minor traffic accident—I swing through the old neighborhood, and catch up on my reports.

Pulling in across from the old park, I have to agree with Dustin. Sam's lost his ever–loving mind. But the place is actually starting to look the way I remember it from a decade ago. My gaze scans the field until I find Sam, and sure enough, he's out digging post holes for a new fence. I see the material behind him. Sweat rolls down his face and washes the grime already stuck on his cheeks and neck. He's dressed in a tank and sweats, and his muscles strain as he pushes and pulls the dirt out of the hard ground. Something inside me twists with emotion. I haven't seen him since Ellensburg, about two months ago, but it's startling to see him again. I feel that deep, magnetic pull towards him also.

I wait for traffic to clear before I cross the street and

finally stop a few feet away from him. Placing my hands on my hips, I address him. "Sam?"

He straightens up. His face, so uncharacteristically dirty and sweaty, breaks into a wide smile. A big, huge, welcoming smile. He's so glad to see me, it makes something swirl in my guts. Gladness. First and foremost, a smile appears on my mouth and deepens my cheekbones. Then I squelch it. Goddamn it! Always, it's little Natalie in awe of big, popular, well-loved Sam. I grit my teeth and stop the happy feelings striving to grow in my chest.

However, this Sam doesn't look like the Sam I know. He's handsome, of course. But his sweats are ripped and hanging from his knees and his sneakers are dirty. He looks a little bit like a homeless person. I see why Dustin asked me to come there. It is sheer unreality to find Sam working at this place, of all places, and doing such physical grunt work.

"Hey, Nat," he replies casually. Like how he used to greet me when I surprised him by coming to his office. The same place where he wore designer suits that were cut to his precise measurements and made out of fabrics that cost what I could make in a whole day. His former office was huge, and his desk's massive size can only be compared in length to a car. He always had countless piles of paper and folders cluttering it. Always so busy. Always so successful.

"Uh, what are you doing?"

"Fixing it up," he answers simply, sweeping his hands around in both directions as if displaying the subject of his toil. I glance up. He isn't staring at me. Is there a double meaning in his words "fixing it"? I stare at him. Holy crap, maybe he doesn't know why he's doing that. Maybe he doesn't even know he's trying to fix that because he can't fix us. Because this once was us, and where we started. My mouth drops open, and my heart swells. This is actually better than anything else he could have done. Sending me dozens of flowers with pretty messages would have left me cold. In fact, I was kind of waiting for Sam to wage a long, drawn-out seduction. Especially after the way we left things. But this? This is it! This is definitely the way to my heart and soul. Sam knew what maybe no other man could have. Tears fill my eyes and I gulp hard to keep them from falling.

He looks so tired. His eyes are rimmed in purple rings under the dirt, grime and sweat.

"Is it working?" I ask softly.

His gaze settles back on me, and this time, his eyes clear up. They narrow on me, like he gets my meaning. He shrugs. "I don't know. I'm just trying really hard."

"Did you really buy it?"

"Uh-huh. Stupid, yeah? But it seemed so sad to let it just go to waste. So much history, and meaning and fond memories for a lot of people. I wanted it to be like that again."

What if it can't? I almost voice the obvious. I nearly let the tears that are filling my eyes fall. Somehow, observing his desperate need to fix this park... in his own way, for us, leaves my heart aching and hollow. It's terribly sweet, but he can't fix it all.

"Not stupid. But sometimes, things are too wrecked to go back to the way they used to be. Sometimes, things... and circumstances just change too much. Sometimes, it's better to level it to the ground and start all over."

He stares at me, his face frozen in abject horror. His mouth opens, then closes as he shakes his head. "I can't accept that. Not yet."

A few tears fall from my eyes and I squeeze them shut to stop myself. I glance past him. "Look at you, Sam. How long have you been at this?"

"A while. But it's nothing I can't handle. Do you remember Jim Lefsano? He ran the community center before it shut down?"

"Yes, I remember him."

"He opened another one a few miles from here. He noticed what I was doing and stopped by a few days back. I offered him the use of the place, of course, and he asked if I needed a job. Working there. It's not much. Low pay. Long hours. But the kids? They are so like us. Fierce. Competitive. I've been coaching a few of them on basketball and I really like it."

Sam working at a youth center? Coaching? Mentoring? Actually, the mentoring part completely fits. He is so good with people of all ages, so why not teens? He has a lot to offer them in athletics, so yeah, that fits. Plus, he's a natural leader. People always sense that and give him their respect. Still... Is that his job? Maybe as a volunteer, or on a weekend here and there, but full time? His permanent job? I feel like I time-traveled to an alternate planet. I don't even know what to say.

"They will be playing a few games here on Saturday. You should come sometime. They start at ten."

He's eager for me to attend. Even excited about it. I've never seen that kind of sparkle in his eyes. What he's doing here might have started out as a metaphor about us, or a gift to me, but he's actually getting something out of it. Something has stirred his soul and ignited his interest in living again. He was never this engaged about his work for Border-Line Solutions. Or if he was, he never shared it with me. Then again, maybe I never let him share it with me.

"I can't. I'm on duty." His face falls. I nod. "But I can try and swing by afterwards, for a few minutes even."

"That would be nice." He shoves the posthole digger aside and steps towards me, his dark eyes searching mine. "How are you?"

"I'm... good. Busy... Strange. I'm really strange."

"I feel that way too. Strange. Did you hear from any of the Hendrickses?"

"Yes. All of them. I text my sisters quite often. They love hearing stories about what I encounter all day long."

"I always liked those too. What about Jessie?"

"Yeah, I've talked to her a few times too. They asked me to come back for Christmas. Hard to say yet if I'll go. It's so far from now. Emily keeps asking and begging if she can come visit me before school starts for her. She wants to see San Francisco."

"Is there any chance you'd like to meet? Or go to dinner? I don't know…"

"I'm not ready yet, Sam. Look, this is amazing. You've changed a lot. I can see what happened has profoundly changed you and your outlook. It's obvious. But you've got to remember this could all be no more than a rebound. You were so shocked by what happened, you're dropping everything and going the opposite way. There is nothing wrong with your ambition, or your former job, or liking the lifestyle you used to have. The way you're shunning it all… and so fast… I don't know what to make of it, or how it fits into my life now. I sometimes wonder if it's just a strong reaction and after you get your shit worked out, you will go back to it all. Which isn't bad either. I'm just so confused and I don't know what to do right now. I just know this might not be as real as you think."

He shrugs. "Nothing I did at BorderLine Solutions gave me concrete, visible results. Not like I see here. Not like working with those kids. One kid has so many gang tats, I'm not too sure what his skin color is. But he comes in there, all bad–ass and shit, and he *listens* to me. For a few hours, he's just a fifteen–year–old kid learning about b–ball. I wish I could undo so much more. But it feels nice to do some good."

I get that. It's hard to stand there and criticize him

without falling into his arms and raving how proud of him I am. I was part of our problem before; and I didn't tell that to him enough. But this? I don't know yet. Any of it. So I simply step back and finally say, "I've got to get going. I'll see you, Sam."

He stares after me, his look longing and somehow resigned.

None of this goes the way I could have ever dreamed it would.

$\mathcal{N}$ATALIE

I WORK AT THE Tenderloin Station. It's the smallest in the city, but has the highest population of parolees. To counterbalance that there are lots of immigrant families making their homes and businesses there and trying to turn the area around. It pleases me to watch and make that happen. My day starts at seven today and I ride with my partner, Glenn Orion. We start on Market Street, the main street through our district. It's one o'clock before we get a call of any interest. Responding with our lights glaring, we speed up and down the side streets of the city before pulling up to investigate reports of a woman screaming. We park at the four–unit condo and find nothing but quiet. We get out, gently tapping our doors shut as we glance around. It's sunny, pleasant and quiet. I lightly set my fingers on top of my holstered gun for reassurance. Something pricks up the hairs on my arm. Something feels wrong. Or right. I'm not even sure why.

My partner motions that he's going around back. I nod, starting towards the unit.

"I know what you want!"

I flip around at the sudden hiss. It's a high-pitched, shrill sound before a woman steps out from behind a pillar where she was hiding. She's in her late twenties or early thirties, and as she steps out, she watches me closely. Her eyes are crossed and the pupils are dilated. She is holding a knife that's dripping something red. A quick scan reveals a series of cuts on her thighs and chest. Shallow, but they appear to be self-inflicted wounds. She's crying, but calm. She flips the knife my way, and my hand is already on my weapon. I turn my head just a fraction of a centimeter to speak into the microphone on my left epaulet. I have to call my partner. In doing so, I break eye contact for just a moment and the woman starts screaming as loud as a bullhorn. Her voice is shrill and piercing, which scares me more than normal screaming. She sounds crazy. She's either high or clearly out of her mind.

"Put your hands up! Where I can see them! You're here with them, aren't you? Wanting to take me away! I know you are. But you can't. You can't have me!" She covers her ears with her bloody hands and shakes her head back and forth as if someone is talking to her. She suddenly jerks her hands toward me. "I said, hands up!"

I immediately put my hands up where she can see them. I'm nervous, sure, but feel she's more of a danger to herself than to me. Her mental condition is what I'm worried about. I feel sympathy for her, but also apprehension. Mental health issues often lead to unpredictable behavior. Usually, it's nonviolent. But there are other times... I swallow the lump of fear in my throat and say softly, "Who is trying to get you? Can you tell me? I can help you, okay? I'm sure I can help you."

I keep my voice neutral and gentle. No shaking. No fear, although my palms are sweating and I am completely afraid. Something pits out in my stomach. *Come on, Orion! Where are you?* I chant it over and over. He must be close.

"What's your name?" I ask, keeping my eyes wide and my hands up. I am trying to make my facial expressional look calm, like we're two woman chatting in line at the grocery store.

She tilts her head as if she almost understands me. Then she says, almost in a little girl's tone, "Carmel. My name is Carmel."

"Hi, Carmel. I'm Officer Ford. I'm a cop. See? Uniform and all." I nod towards my uniform, keeping my hands high in the air. "I can help you. Is there anything I can do to help you right now? That's my job, right?" I try to sound and look nonthreatening, hands up, smiling softly, my voice warm and friendly.

She doesn't answer. Vacant eyes. Her hand flops as if she's too lazy to hold the knife up any longer to fend me off. She wears a white, fluttery gown that I'm sure is her nightdress, and a bag crossed over her chest. Her hair is matted and it sticks out in blonde strands.

"Carmel, can you tell me who is after you?"

"Them. They're everywhere. They won't leave me alone. They talk to me all the time. They tell me to kill myself. But I don't want to. I think they want to take me with them." She starts to cry. Tears pour down her face and her expression becomes that of a bewildered child.

"With them? Where?"

"Their planet, I think. Shh. They're all around you now. Everywhere... so... STOP!" She goes from whispering their presence to screaming, and again holds her arms over her face as if shielding herself from attack. I'm concerned she could hit her neck with the spastic, incautious movements of her hands and knife.

I step forward when it all happens faster than I could blink. First, she screams and her hands dig into the bag at her side. She pulls a gun out and shouts, "STOP! STOP! RIGHT NOW!" She's screaming at me. I keep my hands up and halt, trying to still my racing heart and shallow breathing. She's scared. Whatever she's hallucinating on and seeing is obviously terrorizing her. She wets herself. I can smell the acrid, stinging smell of ammonia. She fears something around here might hurt her. Drugs? Maybe. But whatever she's seeing, it's overtaken her sanity. I'm starting to get agitated, now, and I glance over my shoulder. No sign of Glenn. I hold my gaze on her, and she starts backing up. Suddenly, she points the gun lower and the gun goes off.

It's a small pistol that makes a sharp *crack*! I jump and so does she, dropping the gun to the cement. I feel something and glance down only to stare in shock and awe, as if I'm hallucinating. It's blood. It's starting to flow from my stomach, just below my bullet–resistant vest. Thankfully, below my vital organs. But still, *blood*. So much of it is spewing out of me. I glance back up in confusion and my hands naturally clasp my wound. I can see the whole inside of my flesh. My mouth opens now in complete horror. I never expected this. I didn't foresee even the possibility of this happening. Ever. But especially today. This beautiful August day! The sun is high and warm and pleasant and the woman I first encounter is small and weak, but violently crazy.

Oh, God. I don't feel right. I don't feel anything.

No.

That is all that enters my brain. That is all I can think to start shouting. Or whispering. Or crying. But I don't do any of those things. I don't even utter the word out loud. I just stare and stare. I just stand there, frozen. I stand there, destroyed. Bleeding.

No.

Blood seeps through my fingers where I clutch my stomach. Blood. So much of it goes drip–drop, drip–drop, splashing down on the ground under me. I glance down and my hand vanishes, as if it's covered in a crimson cloth. So much blood.

Still, I stand there, paralyzed.

Is this me? Is that my blood? It's so warm. That faint thought trickles from a weird spot in my brain. It's so warm, it surprises me.

I feel nothing. I don't feel my wound at all. I see it. I see it all. But I can't feel it. Is this what it feels like to die? Am I watching myself die? Is my spirit now floating above my body before going off and away? To heaven? To hell? Surely, not to hell. I was, or at least, I tried in earnest to be a good person. But now? Where will I go?

I see who shot me. She's standing right in front of me. Not even a bus length away. She stares at me, almost as shocked as I look at her. She wronged me. She destroyed my life. How could she shoot me?

I don't know.

The world starts to shift. I fall to my knees. Shit. I feel that. Through it all, I feel the severe thump when my knees crash to the concrete. The colors swirl, browns and greens and grays and blues, so much blue. Trees, leaves, concrete, buildings and sky. Sky everywhere now over me. Faces are all gone. She is gone. I am gone.

Sam.

Sam's face fills my mind's eye. Oh, Sam. What will you do now? What will you do without me? What will you do about this awful event? Oh, Sam…

No. No, Sam is gone. He's gone. He's not here.

I'm sorry, Sam. I'm sorry. I'm so sorry. I was wrong. I'm so sorry for myself most of all because it's too late for being sorry. It's too late for seeking forgiveness. It's too late for living.

I finally understand. Anything could have been fixed when I was still alive. *Anything.* But this? Death? It really is the end. It really is forever. Only now, in this last moment of my life, as the colors and sky turn gray and begin to fade to black, only now do I fully understand how much time I wasted in my life. As the black pinpricks take over my vision, and my eyes start to close, I understand. This is actually the end.

Like always, my need to be right cost me every last chance I had to be happy.

CHAPTER 19

$\mathcal{S}$AM

THE FIRST TIME I really listened to Natalie's plan to become a police officer was only days after our first kiss. The kiss that started all of this. We kept meeting in secret that summer, at my parents' apartment after everyone fell asleep. We'd make-out. And make-out. And make-out. I knew Natalie had been having sex since she was seventeen and I was too. But we waited several months before we did it with each other. It was hot. Those long nights of that summer where only we knew what was going on, we waited and stared at each other in smoldering desire all evening, trying to conceal the urges our bodies craved. We denied ourselves, and totally became entrenched with each other. All the waiting and longing made us connect even better.

She talked about the police academy and her rigorous training with the same excitement that I used to see when she beat me in a race or sport. It was the first time in years that I saw her have a real plan, and something that actually fit her. As much as my schooling and newfound friends suited me, I had to admit her idea totally suited her.

It never really occurred to me how dangerous such a career could be. It was something I only started to consider after I got older. I suppose all young people believe they're immortal, and maturity eventually proves them wrong. She faces violent people, sometimes on a daily basis who react in unpredictable and unforeseen ways. There are also drugs and violence and guns and knives to confront every day at work. As I got older, I thought more about it. But it still carries a surreal quality to me. Abstract. Yes, she could get hurt in the line of duty. But I believed it was far more likely that random violence would touch my life before she could get hurt on the job. Statistics favored her career, and I thought she wouldn't be in any real danger. I looked up the odds years ago, and from what I could find, between one and two hundred officer–related shooting deaths occur per year with a few spikes in that figure, here and there. For the close to a million people employed in law enforcement in the United States, I should worry more about heart disease or cancer before thinking Natalie could die while on duty each day. It's all a mental game. Learning the facts helped soothe my anxiety.

She is impressive. I never once denied that. She's physically superior and stronger than most men I know. She's articulate and well-spoken and she knows her opinions and speaks her mind. Not once has she backed down from any argument. To do her job, she has developed a strong sense of right and wrong and she rarely waffles on it. I admire her defined sense of order and justice. And she spends one day a week at the shooting range, making her the second best shot in her precinct. Not good enough for her, however, and she has an ongoing, private contest with the guy in the number one slot. So I know she can handle her weapons. I also know she's calm and solid in emergencies. I'm not. I know she's a far better choice for a cop than I could ever dream of being.

I really never had any cause to worry about her. She seems unstoppable to me.

Until the day she wasn't.

It was three–fourteen on a Tuesday. I spent the sunny, pleasant afternoon tackling my morning graffiti and doing some light chores around the park. I was currently working with a team of basketball players at the youth center. There is no actual "team," just some regular teens who often come there to use the facility. When my cell phone rings, I ignore it. When I finally look up and see an officer coming into the gym, he is looking around. I stop the basketball game. This isn't just a random check, or a friendly visit to the youth of the neighborhood. It is an officer named Heisson whom I've met a few times having drinks with Natalie. His face is ashen. His jaw clenches as he straightens his posture.

My stomach drops. My extremities go numb. *No! Fuck no!* I nearly fall to my knees. They are shaking. *Natalie. It's Natalie.* He's here to notify me… to let the next of kin know… because for now, legally, I'm still her next of kin.

I start shaking my head when he spots me. I don't really hear him. He suddenly grabs me by my shoulders and gives me a gentle shake. "She's alive. Okay? She's alive. She was shot, but help arrived almost immediately. It's a stomach wound. They… it won't be fatal. You'll see. But it is gravely serious. Do you hear me, Sam? She's alive. Okay?"

I nod my head in comprehension, but close my eyes at the nausea and dizziness I instantly feel. Sucking in a long breath, I open my eyes. She would never fall apart. Not now. Only afterwards. Only after she did what was expected of her, with a stoicism and efficiency that everyone else can only envy. I take a cue from her and straighten my spine. My thoughts chant over and over *She isn't dead*, and I cling to that mantra. She's alive. It's not fatal. But all my heart seems to repeat is *She was shot*.

I go, obviously, with Heisson to the hospital. There I find my wife in surgery. I pace the reception area. The hospital floor is flooded with policemen and women. Some are in uniform, some in street clothes. Some wear the more professional attire of support staff. I don't recognize three fourths of them. But I know. I get it. They are here for one of their own. Natalie is one of their best. Knowing that, my heart simply swells until it threatens to explode from my pride in her. I hang my head to hide my wimpy tears. None of these resolute people would cry. But I am. The stress of it and the shock are pretty overwhelming, but so is the profound effect she has on those around her. I see an entire community of professionals.

Heisson tells me what happened. The woman who shot Natalie was instantly subdued and arrested. She used an unregistered S&W M&P Bodyguard .38 Special. A small revolver, I'm told, and often carried by women. It happened to catch Natalie just at the edge of her ballistic vest and entered her pretty low on her belly area. They immediately apprehended the woman and were confident of a conviction if she could be proven sane. She appears to be severely mentally ill, however, so there is a good chance that could alter her trial and sentencing. I know Natalie often talks about mental illness and how she often comes into contact with it on the job. The situations can be highly unstable. But she feels a huge amount of sympathy and compassion for the victims who suffer from it. More so probably, since her dad got ill and she personally witnessed his slow deterioration, which so changed and altered him. Something over which he has no control. So I don't know how comforting that fact will be to Natalie. She doesn't see mental illness and violence as anything cut and dried anymore.

But as for the officers here? It's good news. It fairly soothes and helps many around me. They need that semblance of order. Right versus wrong and justice for all. I just want my wife to live. I just want another chance to be with her again. No, that's too selfish of me. I just want her to live and be healthy and strong. I want her to live however she wants and for her life to be happy. I'm scared. My hands are cold. My thoughts are scattered. I feel like a fraud. Most don't know we are separated or why. She is that private. It shames me to get so much feedback and consideration from people who respect and work with Natalie, when all the while, I'm the only one who betrayed her.

When she comes out of surgery, I am the first one the doctors report to. All I can concentrate on is *she's alive!* By then, my family shows up and Dustin and my dad take on all the stress of acting responsible. I wearily fall on a chair, and bury my head in my hands.

NATALIE

I wake up. There is a machine beside me. Blip... blip, it goes. Others click and clack. It's so noisy, and constant. Where am I? I remember screaming. Falling. Blood. I cringe and try to open my eyes. It must mean I'm still alive. That's my profound thought as I come to. I hear the machine monitoring my life signs so I must be alive. I hear someone's shoe scuffling across the floor. I blink and open my eyes to a light. And then... I see Sam's face over me.

"Natalie?" His eyes are red and his voice is hoarse and scratchy. He's been crying. I've only ever seen Sam cry a few times: when my mom died, when his grandfather died, when we had to put my dad in the home... and when he cheated. But that was more like just tearing up. Not this. He leans over me, so gently, holding my hand. He is sobbing against the side of me. He says my name over and over again.

It must be bad. He's worried I might die. He finally lifts his head off the bed and his liquid–filled eyes stare into my face. He's so beautiful. Like the sun breaking through the clouds after the worst storm. That's what his face does to me. Cheesy? Sentimental? Maybe. But that's where I'm at. I almost died, and I think I really appreciate the gravity of knowing that.

I shuffle around and point at my throat.

It hurts. There is a tube stuck in my throat. He notices that and suddenly disappears. He comes back with a doctor, or at least, someone in scrubs, who starts fussing over me. The tech or the doc asks me questions I can't answer as he starts to work around me. I feel exhausted and confused. I can't keep my eyes open. I fade in and out, in and out. I'm doped up. I must be. I can't think. I don't know what I feel physically... mentally... or emotionally. But every time I open my eyes, I see Sam...

～

I DON'T KNOW how much time passes before the tube is taken out of my throat. I try to talk, but it takes a few hours, or is it a day? I don't know. My sense of time is hazy as I fade in and out. But alone now with Sam, I'm desperate to talk. My throat on fire, I whisper, "S—"

He leans closer. "Shh. Don't talk." I nod, my eyes pleading. I must say what happened. I fell to the ground and was sure I was dying. I need to say that to him.

"I... tell... you... something..." Burning. Aching. I can't raise the volume.

"You forgive me? You love me? Please don't say you hate me or want me to leave. Please, Nat. Not after this."

"Love," I whisper. It's a struggle to get the words out. Tears fill his eyes and he nods his head over and over as if taking it all in. "Not forgive."

He jerks up and his eyes go round. "That's okay, I understand."

"No. I s-sorry too. For what I did. For the baby stuff."

My voice is warming up. Or I just need to get this out. He cups my jaw in his hands. "We'll talk about it all later. It only matters that you're alive." Tears gather in his eyes. He touches my chin. "You should have seen how many people came here. I think every cop within a fifty–mile radius showed up to pay their respects. And Dustin and my parents and…"

"You. I—"

"Don't worry; nothing matters right now. Just you. Just getting better."

"Matters. I don't forgive…you," I croak out. His expression falls, but he nods. He is trying to hold in his shock and hurt. I move my fingers, but can barely lift them three inches off the bed. He notices and grabs them in his hand. "But… I want to. I want to learn how to. And… I want you to learn how to forgive me."

He stills. I finally have his full attention and he quits trying to quiet me with banal platitudes. "From the ground up, Sam. We start over and rebuild this all. We figure out the baby thing and cheating and trust and we do it all together. Slowly. It will be hard. It will be exhausting."

He is gripping my hand and nearly clinging to the side of me. He whispers to me, his eyes still glazed in tears, "I'm there, Nat. Ground up. Forever."

I fall back on the pillow, too exhausted to say anymore. I look at him and he's still staring at me. We don't smile. We don't talk. There are no more words. Just staring. Only it's not awkward. It goes on for long minutes. Funny how trauma and a close scrape with death can so quickly and easily put things into perspective when all the talking in the world cannot.

He brushes his hand on my forehead and into my hair. Still staring, he says in the softest, whisper, "I love you."

I know that. I think I've always known it. But I never believed it. Not to the extent that he loves me as desperately as I do him. And of course, I don't like to desperately need or want anyone. So it probably made me resentful. But seeing him now, I feel his desperation for me to be okay, and as strong as I feel my own heart beating, I finally realize, somehow, I am the love of his life.

I am barely out of surgery. That is all I can manage to tell him as my strength begins to wane. But it is the greatest epiphany of my life. After being shot, as I was fading from consciousness, believing my mortality was over... at that very moment, I wanted nothing more than to learn to forgive the man I love.

CHAPTER 20

$\mathcal{N}$ATALIE

I STARTED TO HEAL and soon came out of the ICU. I was assigned a regular hospital room for several weeks and later went on to a rehabilitation center. Sam was my point person. He kept my sisters, his family and Jessie updated on my progress. I didn't want to talk to anyone else. I took the visits from the officers I worked with, however, which helped lift my spirits. I was amazed by how much support I received.

But I didn't want anyone close to me. Except Sam. I let him very close.

While trying to make my way a little farther around the hallway a few weeks later, I glanced up since I sensed someone watching me. I lift up my head and spot Jessie. She is standing about half the length down the hospital corridor, watching my progress. When her gaze meets mine, I notice all the fear, concern and uncertainty she must feel. She isn't sure how I feel about her being here. I close my eyes, and allow a wave of dizziness to wash over me. That's all it takes before I suddenly feel her arms and shoulder as she nearly catches me from falling. I open my eyes and we stare at each other with the same eyes. I study her face and for the first time, feel a kind of bump from my heart in my chest. I recognize something in her. Is it familiarity now that I met her? Or the way her eyes look exactly like mine? Or is it... just because she is here and I feel so vulnerable still? I feel almost like a research rat being let loose and running through a maze, when up until now, I was the damn scientist putting the rat in the maze.

"What are you doing here? I told you not to come," I whisper. It takes too much energy to utter more than a whisper. I am so weak, it scares me. I've never before felt so out of control, or so unable to buck up and overcome a physical ailment or injury.

Her gaze searches my face and her entire expression changes as something shines in her eyes. Her tears glisten and I can read her feelings on her face, and how she feels towards me. "You were shot. Bleeding. Your blood is something we share. I know you don't need me, Natalie, but I think I need to be here for myself. So I came. The girls want to come too. I'd like to stay with you, for however long you need home care. I'm pretty good at this stuff. I can take care of you for however long you need it. Let me, please? Just let me take care of you. Let me, for now, just this once, be a mother to you."

Normally, my back would stiffen in disdain at her suggestion that I need a mother. Or that I'm weak and incapable of caring for myself. *Do I need her?* I don't have it in me anymore to say no. Something has shifted, and it goes all the way down inside my very core. The fighting me, with the fierce need for independence, seems to be malfunctioning. Gratefully, I lean on her small stature. I allow more of my weight on her until finally, after all these years, and all my life, I am hugging my mother. "Okay," I whisper. My head is resting on her shoulder and I feel her lungs sighing a deep breath. She holds me so gently and with such care.

"Okay." Her tone is much stronger and snappier than mine. She seems shocked... as well as pleased by my compliance.

She carefully leads me back into my room without another mushy word. It's all business from there. I appreciate that about Jessie. She doesn't ever try to force a lot of sentiment on me. She takes care of me for several weeks, and Christina, Melissa and Emily all visit on separate occasions so as to not overwhelm me, or make my miniscule apartment too overcrowded. It's crazy to have sisters, especially in the plural. I want to feel better, and I look forward to exploring the city with them as each one discovers little pockets of interest while they stay with me. I tell them the best places to go while longing for the day when I'll feel strong enough to escort them there myself. Terms like *next time*, and *next year* and *when you come next...* all those positive and hopeful aspirations soon become a basic part of my vocabulary with these women. They once were strangers, but now they're my sisters and they are all starting to feel very special to me.

Jessie is solid to have around. She takes care of my basic needs and grooming with a no–nonsense approach that lets me spend a lot of time around her without wanting to kill her. She is surprisingly strong, too, in wheeling my injured ass around.

Sam takes me home with Jessie's help, but there is no momentous change for us. He doesn't move in and all is still not well between us. I lack the strength for several weeks to even contemplate our future together, or us, or the concept of forgiveness. It simply requires all my mental energy and physical compliance to get through the day and keep healing, while dealing with the stabbing, nagging pain.

There is no easy out for us. The first proclamation, the first decision, is perhaps the only easy part. Lying there after being shot, I felt really scared at having to face my own mortality. That made me realize I was more than willing to find a way to *try* and forgive Sam. But it was no magic elixir that could make me forget how we got here and what Sam did. Just because I chose to stick around and find a way to forgive him did not mean it could happen instantaneously.

He comes around often and sits with me. He helps me during the days, or evenings, when Jessie needs some relief. We never talk about shootings, or adultery, or broken hearts. We talk about the current TV shows, or places we'd like to go next summer, and sometimes, even the *what ifs* of future vacations. We avoid all the heavy, real discussions pertaining to our life at the time I was shot and shortly thereafter. We agree to a moratorium on all the anger, hurt, love and sadness we both feel. We are neutral for a while, which is what I need to heal more than anything. There are times when I catch Sam's dark eyes studying me as if he is confused, or trying to work out a complicated scientific theorem. Perhaps he is seeking answers to the unanswerable. But for now, being together in small, quiet, ordinary ways feels better than anything else I can imagine. I don't want to re-experience all those confusing feelings I felt leading up to the shooting. Nor am I ready to fully embrace us being together.

Sam keeps working at the youth center and improving his park. That spark I saw when he started his career after college is rekindled whenever he talks about the park.

I'm not sure when his job at BorderLine Solutions extinguished his old ambitions. I wonder, was it because of how it ended? Or because of me? Or the work? The politics? The pressure? The crazy long hours?

My heart sinks as I realize I honestly don't know the answer. Not knowing hurts me, and I strangely blush as I think about it, even though I'm currently alone in my bed. It is embarrassing to realize how little I actually know about my husband. And how these last few years have turned us into no more than two strangers. Two roommates. Roommates who have sex, yes, but can't discuss the very basics of our emotions, let alone all the deep ones.

I ask him one night, "When did we stop knowing each other?"

He clicks the remote on pause. We're watching a new release. His gaze turns to me as the tears make my throat swell and my eyesight fuzzy. "I don't know. I don't have an exact date."

"We have a lot of work to do. We're together now mostly because of our history than for the people we are now."

"Maybe. But I still feel the same love for you. What do you think we should do?"

"Start over. Maybe… maybe we should go to a counselor or something."

"Couples counseling?" His eyebrows shoot up. I get his incredulity. Before I got shot, I would never have suggested such a thing for us. It's not that I ridiculed it or thought it inappropriate for other people, I just didn't believe I could ever benefit from seeing one. Even when I got depressed over mom's death, I went to my regular doctor and he prescribed me anti-depressant. I didn't talk to anyone about it.

"Yeah… counseling," I finally say without elaborating. I'm not sure what more to say, or where else we should start. I just don't know how to do that. If there is any chance for us to move forward happily, we need help. I don't want to spend the next year, or two, or ten trying to trust Sam, but failing. Or constantly throwing his one infidelity in his face if we fight, or disagree, or if he's just ten minutes late. I know, I can already list the questions I want to ask him. That's how rocky and precarious my trust of him is now. And I think he gets that.

He rubs my leg with his hand. It's a reassuring rub. He hasn't so much as looked at me with interest in his eyes. He's worried about me. A lot. It's an odd dynamic for us. "I think... yeah. That's a good place to start. Better than anything else you or I can think of."

So with that decided, two months later, I take a list from my insurance company for our area and pick three, whom I call and make appointments with. We agree on the third one we see, a woman in her late thirties. She is attractive, and has a calm, cool, easy–going personality. The first time I meet her, I am nervous. I don't like discussing my feelings, let alone, voicing them out loud to a stranger. I don't get how this can work. Sam's more open to it than I am. I can tell by the way he sits there with his legs splayed, his arms at his sides, and his hands resting casually and at ease on his thighs.

But the woman doesn't talk like a science book. She's totally real and accessible. The first time she swears during a session while agreeing with something I say, I smile, and unfold my arms. I feel finally ready to give her a chance. Counseling is not how I thought it would be. It's good. Mainly, it's just talking. She just makes sure we don't get off track. She gives us little assignments too. We start pretty small, since we have a lot of years to wade through. There is a lot of hurt, anger, betrayal and mistrust. The biggest surprise, however, is that those feelings are coming from both of us, not just from me over Sam's cheating. I have some reconciliation to do, and now, at least, I know what I failed to do for him.

For the first time, we finally sit down and start to truly hear each other. For the first time, I allow him to talk to me, and make myself listen to him. For the first time, we begin to understand how we could love each other so much and hurt each other so deeply, without even realizing we were doing that, much less, intending to.

I sometimes wonder if I had not been shot, would I have ever taken such steps to try and learn how to forgive Sam? I can't say for sure. In all honesty, it was the worst and the best thing that ever happened to me. Kind of like his cheating. If he never cheated, I wonder if I would have ever looked inside myself deeply enough to realize what I did to him. I highly doubt it. We might not have ever even realized how unhappy we were together and how little we communicated. We might never have decided to start over one day; or see what we could build together now that we know how terrible it is to nearly lose everything and each other... twice.

EPILOGUE

$\mathcal{N}$ATALIE

WE SPEND ALMOST THREE years in weekly counseling. We don't live together the first year. We date. And it's for real. We go out to dinner on planned dates before eventually adding more casual nights where we might spend the evenings at my place or his. Sex, again, has never been a problem, but neither is it our escape this time. There isn't as much sex as there is talking. Talking, connecting and getting to know one another is not an easy process. Not when there are such massive stones we have to roll uphill still awaiting us. The biggest issues for both of us? Children and infidelity.

During those years, I go back to Ellensburg a couple of times a year and the Hendrickses visit me numerous times. Sometimes it's just one sister, and other times, more than one of them. Jessie too comes out. About a year after I was shot, she and Christina come to see me together. In that time, Christina and I slowly grow closer, until I want to tell her more about Sam and me. I finally tell her about Sam's cheating and how we're still trying to find a way to move past it. I also mention our concerns and different opinions about my infertility.

"Do you want to have kids? Someday, I mean? Do you want that to be a possibility?" Christina asks me one day.

"I don't know," I shrug. Then, in the new spirit of honesty and sharing, I add, "I think I'd like the option to decide either way, without being told what to do. Sam would like to have children. I guess, I'd like to decide together what we should do. I wish it all didn't have to be so hard."

Christina stares at me closely. We're eating lunch at a quaint, little café that overlooks the harbor. She replies in a quiet, mature, reasonable tone, "I could be a surrogate for you, if your eggs aren't viable. If that's something you'd ever consider. I'd be willing to help you if that was an option. I did some research into it…"

She goes on to explain herself as my mind kind of internally combusts. *Is she for real?* Jessie is with us, and her head whips around to study Christina too. She's been casually perusing the moving crowds outside the restaurant. She watches and listens to us. Finally, she says softly, "You don't know what you're saying, Christina."

Mother Bear Jessie is out, and doesn't like Christina's offer to me. Neither do I. It's too odd to even consider seriously.

"I know what I'm proposing. I told you already, I looked into it."

"You have no idea how hard it is to give away a baby," Jessie interjects and her tone is hard as iron.

"I don't claim to. But it wouldn't be anything like it was for you. I would know from the start it's not really mine to keep."

"It still will feel like yours."

I hold up my hand. "There's no reason to even have this conversation. I highly doubt I'm going to ask my little sister to carry my child!"

Christina snaps her mouth shut. Jessie contemplates me and sighs heavily. "No, but maybe you should remember your long-lost mother who gave you away. Take the advice of someone who knows how to have a baby and not keep it."

I stare at her. I can't speak. She can't be for real, but somehow, the solemnity in her voice tells me how serious she is. I tilt my head and shake it in refusal. "No."

Jessie nods and continues talking, "It's not an easy thing to do. But I can do it, Natalie. Like it or not, I'm capable of handling that. I'd be willing to do it. I'd consider it the first real thing I could give to you. It would actually kind of be an honor, and somehow, maybe it could seal our relationship more than anything else."

I hold her gaze. "I haven't even tried infertility treatments yet. There are a lot of things for us to try before I give up and have to take the surrogacy route."

"I get that. But if you ever need it, I'll do it. Gladly. Happily."

"What would Will say to that?"

Jessie smiles that knowing little Mom smile of hers. "He'd say, what can I do to help you?"

I reach across the table and touch her hand. "Thank you." It's all I can manage to choke out, and it's an inadequate response to the gift she's so willing and eager to suggest... for me. I wouldn't feel so emotional if I didn't clearly understand she means it. I think this gesture, her volunteering to do that for me, already changes our relationship. It's a unique gift that few women would offer another. And it only could happen between people who are deeply connected.

I don't actually take her up on it, but the option, the possibility, the "Plan B," and her willingness to help me fills me with the kind of comfort that only my own mother used to provide. I talk about it privately with my counselor, and eventually, discuss it with Sam. This is a subject we must tackle, for he is right. Previously, it was something I just decided without even consulting him. My theory that there is no compromise when it comes to having kids is no kind way to treat a spouse.

I can't just shut down, or decide that issue for Sam. I have learned how to talk to him and with him. Even if I don't change my mind, we still have to work it out together. I still have to hear him. I have to find ways to make sure our decision, whatever it is, isn't all about me.

It is another year after we move back in together that I think we start to actually share a healthy, functioning, and most of all, trusting relationship. It is only then when I seriously contemplate the question: should we try to find a way to have a child?

And when we do start to investigate the subject, it is very different from the last time. It isn't adversarial. It is about us, together, discussing all the options. It helps, of course, to only talk about it during counseling, with our buffer who keeps the subject on point and refuses to let us move outside of it. I keep the surrogate option to myself for a few conversations. When I finally express it, it's because I realize how often I keep things inside me. Sam could not live with me before because I refused to let him inside my head, or my heart, in any real or lasting way. I kept out the good stuff along with the bad. Now? I need to let him in. I need to be honest even when it isn't all that easy.

I never believed after Sam cheated on me, that I'd wind up discussing the possibility of having a child with him three years later. But I did.

And we do.

I guess, knowing me, it shouldn't have come as much of a

surprise. Once I decided to become a mother, there is no end to what I'll do to make it happen. I become fierce in my quest to have a baby. We try fertility drugs for a while. And in vitro. All the while, we also start the adoption process. Two years later, we adopt a little boy who is half Latino and half African American. I guess it comes as more of a shock to me than anyone else, when I fall in love with the then seven-year-old little boy unconditionally. Having gone through foster care and several group homes by the time he finds us, he needs a lot of love and help.

All of which I am burning to provide for him.

I was so afraid to adopt at first. It was always an issue in my life. But when I fall in love with my son, only then do I truly understand that I do not care how my children enter my life, I love them wholeheartedly as mine. Just as my mother and father always loved me. We end up with two sons, both adopted.

Once we adopt the two boys, however, we need to make a better living and Sam decides to leave the youth center and go back into the corporate world. Sam gets hired at a large firm. Although it is much like BorderLine Solutions, of course, there is no Jayden Hall, or his father reigning supreme.

Sam keeps his park open, however, and we often spend our weekends there as a family, playing sports. Both of our boys soon become avid soccer and baseball players.

With some chagrin from both of us, we move away from the city, to be nearer to his parents. We buy a house with a large yard. I still work as a patrol officer, but after moving into a far less urban area, there are subsequently fewer occurrences of violent crimes.

We are so normal and average now, doing what most people do in their thirties, but we don't forget the most important thing: each other.

There is not another time when we don't take care of each other. Falling in love was the easy part. Sustaining it is a whole different proposition and requires an entirely different set of skills. Skills, it turns out, that neither of us had initially. We had to learn them together and with professional help. Where once I may have called it a failing, now, I think it's the healthiest thing we ever did together.

I'll never say I'm glad Sam cheated, even though strangely, that was what saved us. It also led me to a strange state and a small city where I met strangers who have since become my family. *My sisters.*

But not my mother.

Jessie remains an enigma in my life. We are friends. We care for each other. We know each other. And I dare say, we love each other. Jessie gave me the gift of life. She also gave me a mother–figure who worried and wondered about me, when my own was long dead and absent from my life. In the end, we never quite became mother and daughter. She, however, became the grandmother of my two boys. And that is so from the very start. Neither she nor Will discriminates in their unconditional love for them, even later when their three daughters give them more grandkids. But my boys are their first grandchildren and naturally become a part of their lives... as well as Sam's and mine, from then on.

I finally know what to call Jessie: my boys' grandmother, and forever, one of my closest friends.

ABOUT THE AUTHOR

Leanne Davis has earned a business degree from Western Washington University. She worked for several years in the construction management field before turning full time to writing. She lives in the Seattle area with her husband and two children. When she isn't writing, she and her family enjoy camping trips to destinations all across Washington State, many of which become the settings for her novels.

Made in the USA
Coppell, TX
03 February 2023

12104893R00167